W9-CMD-969

COLD FEET

$2.50

960024

Also by Kerry Tucker

Still Waters

BROOKS

COLD FEET

A LIBBY KINCAID MYSTERY

Kerry Tucker

TEXAS STATE TECHNICAL COLLEGE
ABILENE CAMPUS - LIBRARY

HarperCollins*Publishers*

COLD FEET. Copyright © 1992 by Kerry Tucker. All rights reserved. Printed in the United States of America. No part of this book may be used or reproduced in any manner whatsoever without written permission except in the case of brief quotations embodied in critical articles and reviews. For information address HarperCollins Publishers, Inc., 10 East 53rd Street, New York, NY 10022.

HarperCollins books may be purchased for education, business, or sales promotional use. For information, please call or write: Special Markets Department, HarperCollins Publishers, Inc., 10 East 53rd Street, New York, NY 10022. Telephone: (212) 207-7528; Fax: (212) 207-7222.

FIRST EDITION

Designed by Cassandra J. Pappas

LIBRARY OF CONGRESS CATALOG CARD NUMBER 91-50480
ISBN 0-06-016530-8

92 93 94 95 96 MAC/HC 10 9 8 7 6 5 4 3 2 1

Acknowledgments

For advice on technical matters, thanks to Gail Davis, Esquire, of New York City, James David McGaughey, M.D., of Wallingford, Connecticut, and Richard Tucker, Ph.D., of the Bowman Gray School of Medicine in Winston-Salem, North Carolina.

Thanks also to Hal Morgan, Kate Mattes, Jed Mattes, Larry Ashmead, Eamon Dolan, Brenda Marsh, Lori Marsh, and Ellen Grant.

IT'S AWKWARD, isn't it, taking the shoes from someone else's feet? Something so routine, familiar—an act performed unconsciously every day, more than once a day for ourselves, but altogether another thing when the feet have no life in them, are so swollen that removing the shoes is like prying the skin from an orange. And the shoes warm, and a little damp, smelling leathery, sweaty, talcumy— like the inside of an old suitcase—and soft to touch.

And all the while the dreamy patter of the phonograph needle leaping the last groove on the record, skating across the bald center of the plastic, softly banging off the spindle, skating, and banging off the spindle again.

Pausing in the doorway to make sure that you've left nothing behind. Then turning off the light and slipping outside into the darkness, the shoes still warm, still fragrant as you drop them into your shirt, hug them against your skin, and push off into the steamy city night.

1

IT WAS NINETY-SIX DEGREES and so humid that all of New York City felt like the palm house at the Brooklyn Botanic Garden. My rubber flip-flops had gone tacky from the heat, which made them stick to my heels instead of making their usual loose-lipped thwack on the sidewalk. My camera, which I take outdoors with me as instinctively as most people carry their wallet and keys, thudded against my chest with every step while the strap chafed my neck, like an instrument of misery designed for a penitent. It was too hot to talk, too hot to wear a watch, and clearly too hot to be doing what I was doing, which was walking a dog eleven blocks through downtown Manhattan. I bought a lemonade at a deli on Prince Street, resisted the temptation to pour it over my head, drank it, and asked for a refill of water for Lucas.

By the time I got to Izu's Hairdressing Palace on Astor Place, I was putty in the stylist's hands. She was wearing a black spandex bicycle-racing suit and a crucifix, but her hair looked okay.

"Short," she said.

"Right, " I said. "Real short."

"I didn't mean *that* short," I said twenty minutes later, yanking on the inch-long stubble that I used to be able to tuck behind my ears.

It wasn't Audrey Hepburn–gamine short; it wasn't boyish Mia Farrow in *Rosemary's Baby*–short. This was serious. It was Marine recruit–short; delousing on Ellis Island–short; Hare-Krishna–short.

I touched the back of my neck. It was completely smooth.

"You shaved my neck?"

Where had I been when all this was going on? In a trance from the heat?

"It might be hard to believe," I said, "but I wanted to look nice tonight."

"Get some makeup," she said. "You'll look great with some makeup."

Lucas, who had been snoozing in a cool area under one of the sinks, ambled over, took a look at me, and made a low bleating sound.

"Thanks a lot," I said, handing her a tip. "Even my dog hates it."

"Cool dog," she said. "Three legs."

Lucas had scooted himself into a dryer chair and was sniffing the inside of the hood. I dragged him out.

"Come on, baby," I said, planting a smooch on his forehead. "We've got to go."

We walked back to Soho as slowly as we had come, this time stopping to eat popsicles in Washington Square Park and to shop at Alice Underground, a vintage clothing store on Broadway, for something I could wear to the club opening I was going to that night. I settled on a minidress, vintage 1964, kind of tight across the hips, with skinny shoulder straps and a low back. In emerald green, to set off my reddish hair. Or rather, as the dressing-room mirror reminded me, what was left of my reddish hair. It's not the kind of thing I usually wear, especially the built-in bra part, but then I don't usually go to club openings, either—or to clubs anymore at all.

By the time we arrived at Canal Street it was six o'clock, but it still felt like high noon, and the black metal loading dock at the entrance to my building was as hot as a griddle. Worried about Lucas's paws, I collected the mail from the box, stuffed it down my shirt, and lifted him up the metal steps, over the threshold, and into the elevator. When we arrived on the fifth floor, I cranked open the elevator doors, unlocked the single metal door, and stepped into Claire's and my loft, where the air was at least five degrees hotter than it was outside.

Claire had spent every day since the mercury hit ninety at a summer house she rents with friends on Long Island or at her mother's cabin in Maine, working on the catalog for some show she was curating. So the mess—piles of magazines on the floor, a nest of laundry on the sofa, an upholstered chair full of camera equipment—was all mine. With this week's heat wave I'd barely been motivated to get out of bed, let alone keep house.

I filled a bowl of water for Lucas, turned on the two window fans, and headed for the bathroom, where I sat on the edge of the tub with cold water pouring over my feet and looked through the mail. For Claire, an *Artnews,* a *Times Literary Supplement,* a catalog from Lord and Taylor, and what looked like an invitation to a political fund-raiser. My take was not so classy: a $32 check for the use of one of my photographs in a college textbook, a notice that I'd forgotten to sign my name on my student-loan check, and a plastic bag with a message from the post office attached to it that said, "Due to improper wrapping, this package received damage while in the mail. Contents may be missing or damaged. The U.S. Postal Service assumes no liability for damage or missing items." Sort of like a body bag for mail.

I snipped the plastic open with my nail scissors and lifted out the contents: a small, smashed white cardboard box, miraculously held together with a thin metallic gold ribbon, and a piece of brown wrapping paper, part of the original wrapping on the package, with my address on it.

My stomach turned slowly. The handwriting in which my address was written, tiny and precise, looked like my brother Avery's, and Avery had been dead for nearly a year.

I squinted at the paper in the light over the sink, but the postmark was unreadable.

Could the package really have been in transit since last October or before?

I untied the gold ribbon. Inside the box there was a folded-up piece of newspaper, and underneath the newspaper, a lump of white cotton batting.

I unfolded the piece of newspaper.

This has got to be a joke, I thought.

It was a picture of a fat man in a white shirt and black tie handing an envelope to a skinny man in a Hawaiian shirt unbuttoned halfway down his chest. The fat man had a pale-colored crew cut. The skinny man had slicked-back black hair. They were standing in front of a big sign that said WEST VIRGINA LOTTERY—EVERYBODY WINS, and they were grinning like a couple of fish.

The skinny man was my father, Max.

I read the caption:

> Lottery Commissioner Raymond Yarish hands BigBucks winner Max Kincaid the first quarterly payment of his $1.2 million winnings. The fifty-five-year-old salesman, who will receive checks for the next thirty years, says he has no specific plans for the money.

A handwritten message ran up the side, in the writing that, as it turned out, was my father's:

> Libby, hon, Get a load of this! Coming to NYC with another surprise. For chrissake connect your phone up again. Dad.

I stared at the picture.

Unbelievable. Max. Lucky at last. And he'd shaved three years off his age.

Maybe I was dreaming.

I lifted the cotton batting out of the box. Inside there was a necklace—a thin gold chain that held a gold ball about the size of a buckeye, engraved like the planet earth, with a little diamondlike chip roughly where New York City would be. Kind of tacky, like something you'd buy from Home Shopping Club.

Or like something I would wear.

Not that I keep track or anything, but the last time Max had sent me a present was on my sixteenth birthday. It was a toy stuffed poodle with a transistor radio inside. I'd been outwardly furious. What did he think I was? A baby? At sixteen I'd been chain-smoking for a year and had a nineteen-year-old boyfriend.

But I still keep the dog in my underwear drawer, nestled in the tissue it came in, along with a packet of letters Max wrote to me when I was twelve and he was serving time at Morgantown and feeling vaguely circumspect.

I clipped the chain around my neck. As I did, I could hear Max's voice, husky from smoking, but silky and with a practiced persuasiveness too, from off-and-on years of hawking whatever he could talk anybody into letting him sell—knife sharpeners, metal detectors, aboveground swimming pools, office supplies. Also phony rare coins by mail, the enterprise that landed him the three years in the pen.

"Libby, hon," said the voice. "You mean the world to me."

What?

The little globe thumped against my breastbone. I shook my head in disbelief.

Max a millionaire. It had to be a joke.

I showered, zipped myself into my little green dress, rummaged through Claire's makeup basket for some fancy lipstick and eye stuff, and excavated my closet floor for the gold leather sandals I'd bought two years earlier.

I looked in the mirror and put on some dangly earrings that sort of went with the new necklace. The haircutting lady was right. With a little bit of makeup I looked okay.

The color of my dress brought out the little rays of green in my irises. The shadows beneath my eyes, almost a permanent installation now that I'd developed my new bad habit of doing darkroom work at night, had disappeared. My hair didn't look as appalling as it had two hours earlier—it just looked short.

I looked happy. I looked radiant, even.

I looked—dare I say it?—like a woman in love.

But not with a guy. Not in this heat.

I was in love with my work.

I'm a photographer. For the past twelve years I've worked for a magazine called *Americans,* which its owners like to refer to as "the thinking man's *People.*" That means we do interviews with sexy-looking politicians, writers, musicians, and movie stars, but never TV stars; our articles are long enough to continue in the back of the magazine; and sometimes we print color photographs.

I started out as a photo researcher the year the magazine went on the stands, but I begged so hard to be sent on an assignment that they finally sent me just to shut me up. The art director wanted me to take pictures of a certain superstar boxer at home. I shot what I knew she expected—the celebrity walking the dog, playing with the kids, snuggling with his wife on the big white sofa. Then I surprised everybody, including me, by shooting a funny, nicely lit sequence of the champ taking a bubble bath in his Zsa Zsa Gabor–style bathroom, complete with rubber duck. They put one of the bath pictures on the cover and suddenly I was the magazine's first salaried photographer.

I like it at *Americans.* It's my family, my friends, my bread and butter. I make enough money to pay rent on half a loft in lower Manhattan with my own darkroom, a pint-size washing machine and dryer, and extremely heavy-duty locks on the door, and I can afford monthly parking in a garage that's only a twenty-minute walk from where I live.

But like lots of commercial artists, I have a hidden agenda. When I'm not taking pictures for the magazine, I'm taking them for myself, sharpening my eye, building my portfolio, hoping to do something new enough and interesting enough to get the attention of people who love photographs for photographs—not just for the people who are in them.

I think in terms of textures, light, and how far the image should push out of the frame. I go for the urban and the vernacular: signs handpainted on windows like the Raven Chanticleer School of Modelling and the Invisible Mending Company; panhandlers; prostitutes; the guy who wears a cardboard and aluminum foil camera on his head and passes out flyers for 47th Street Photo.

Last spring I decided to take a three-month leave of absence from the magazine. My brother's death had sent me into an emotional tailspin that lasted the winter: I had problems concentrating; I missed more than a couple of important appointments—maybe on purpose, maybe not; I developed an idiotic stress-related jaw disorder that meant my mouth stuck open when I yawned; I lost my appetite; and I started not wanting to get out of bed in the morning.

Claire tried to get me to see a shrink, but my health insurance would only cover 50 percent, and I'm basically too cowardly to do that much self-exploration. Besides, I was haunted by something a friend of mine had told me a long time ago about New York women—that you can tell when they hit thirty-five because they go into therapy and start wearing all black. I was thirty-four and already wearing black a lot.

I figured what I needed was time—a hunk of it—to take pictures on my own terms, for once not worrying about offending the advertisers or getting a flight out of LaGuardia by seven A.M. My Big Boss, Octavia Hewlitt, gave me the leave I asked for without flinching—it allowed her to play Lady Bountiful, her favorite role next to the role of Dragon Lady, and she managed to get in a condescending dig:

"Of course, Olivia dear," she said. "You won't be missed nearly as much as you think."

Very nice.

So while Octavia and the rest of the brass from the magazine were shuttling back and forth between New York and the Hamptons or New York and Martha's Vineyard or wherever they go in the summer, I went on a cure-all picture-taking binge that made my work at *Americans* look like fingerpainting.

All I could think about was pictures, and printing, printing, printing. And I found a subject in a group of jazz tap dancers that I responded to the way a compass needle responds to the North Pole.

They called themselves the Nonpareils. They were advanced middle-aged to elderly, and they were easily the best jazz tap dancers in the country—probably in the world.

I photographed them constantly, even in my dreams. While they were practicing, while they were at home, and while they were at the jobs they did to support their performing habits.

I was pretty sure my work was the best I'd ever done, and other people seemed to think so, too. I had my first major exhibit lined up, with Harriet Bemis at the Bemis-Snow Gallery, who had previously treated me to many, many rejections of my portfolio. And a publisher had come to see me about doing a book, a proposal that seemed like a long shot, but was encouraging nevertheless.

My jaw stopped popping out of whack, and I was eating again. Iced coffee, Fritos, and popsicles mostly, but at least three time a day.

I had six weeks to go before I returned to *Americans*, and three months before the exhibit. I was under the gun, hoping to finish taking pictures within the next ten days and to spend the balance of the time printing and framing.

Tonight the Nonpareils were performing together for the first time in over a year. I plugged a new roll of film into my Leica and crammed six more into the back of my camera bag. I got the same feeling that I get when I watch the little white needle float to "Full" on my car's fuel gauge. You know: Hot damn, I'm ready to *roll*. I planned to take some knockout pictures.

I plugged in the phone. Max was right. It was crazy to disconnect it. What if somebody died or something? Still, I got a lot of darkroom work done when it didn't ring, and I didn't have to worry about baby stockbrokers practicing cold calls on me.

I turned on the answering machine.

Lucas was asleep in the bathtub, the coolest place in the loft. How he managed to get in and out on three legs I don't know; I'd never actually seen him do it.

I dumped some dog chow into a bowl, poured him more water—two bowls this time, just in case he tipped one over by mistake—and set them on the floor next to the tub. Lucas, eyes still closed, made a low, appreciative yowl and wagged his tail. I rubbed the fur the wrong way in the space between his eyes, the way he likes it, and he pressed his heavy head against my hand.

My heart melted, and I felt a familiar dart of guilt. Poor guy, all alone, again, and in this heat. I wished they had summer camp for dogs.

I pressed for the elevator, stepped in, and bolted the loft lock behind me. As the doors ground open at the loading dock I tucked the globe on my necklace into the front of my dress. You didn't hear so much about jewelry snatchers anymore, but this little ball was begging for someone to yank it.

It felt cold against my skin.

Max, I thought, you drive me nuts.

2

ELEUTHERA WAS fired up with last-minute activity—somebody horsing with the sound system, somebody sweeping up a box of cocktail straws that had spilled on the floor, somebody placing a book of matches, an ashtray, and a bleached white seashell just so on the center of each table.

The air-conditioning system was down, or maybe it hadn't gone up yet. At any rate, the ice cubes in the drink I poured for myself shrank to the size of lima beans before my second sip.

One of the owners, Hank Monsell, was on his knees at center stage, scrubbing at a glitch in the wood floor with a piece of sandpaper. He looked up briefly when I walked by and resumed working— no smile, no wave, no acknowledgment that he'd seen me. But I knew Hank well enough to know that he didn't mean offense—he was simply focusing all his powers on the task at hand. It was the way he did everything—dancing, teaching, even eating.

I really had no business being at the club an hour before it opened, but I wanted to scope out the seating arrangements to see where I had the best chance of some unobstructed views of the stage. I found a table to the left of center stage, so I'd have a view of the dancing and easy access to the dressing room, where I hoped to take more pictures.

The condensation rolled off my glass and made a lake on the table that the cocktail napkin was too small to sop up. Swell, I thought. All this fancy furniture is going to be wrecked before the place is even open.

I panned the room with my lens. It looked beautiful, even in the heat.

Duncan Casavant, who owned the club with Hank, was also my roommate Claire's boyfriend. After launching two highly successful, noisy Tex-Mex clubs in the Village that catered to the under-thirty crowd, he had decided to make Eleuthera, as he put it, the kind of place that *he* would like to go to.

The space, in a narrow two-story building on East 13th Street, had deep wood-beamed ceilings, wide-planked dark wood floors, and a fifty-year-old wisteria tumbling around the front door.

Duncan, fresh from a Graham Greene reading binge, I figured, whitewashed the exterior brick and replaced the asphalt roof with a tin one that made pinging sounds when it rained. He imported hand-painted tiles from Jamaica and commissioned a furniture maker on Barbados to make the tables and the bar, all of them inlaid with petal-shaped chips of abalone shell. Then he lightened the place up by installing a mammoth crystal chandelier in the center of the room that held candles, not electric bulbs, and painted the back wall a pale, luminous pink, like the color inside a seashell.

His smartest idea was to bring Hank Monsell, the guy who was sanding the glitch on the floor and who was also the leader of the Nonpareils, into the venture. Monsell designed the stage area, contracted with the band, and came up with the club's name: Eleuthera, for the Bahamian island where he and his brothers had been born.

The guy in charge of putting things on the tables came by again and handed me a program for tonight's performance. He was overweight, flushed with the heat and tension, and his white tee-shirt clung to his skin like plastic wrap on a ham.

"What's the story with the air-conditioning?" I asked him.

His chin started to tremble.

"Look," I said. "Why don't you get out of here for a few minutes and get some air? I can finish putting those on the tables."

He didn't say anything, just dropped the box at my feet and walked out the back door.

Casavant was in a huddle by the kitchen door with a couple of ticked-off-looking repairmen, no doubt begging them to airlift a new HVAC system if that was what it would take to cool the place off. He looked up, flashed me a smile, threw both hands up in the air in a gesture that said "what next?" and continued talking. True to form, he was cheerful and collected, even on a night like tonight.

I worked the tables, laying a program on each one. Like most things Hank and Duncan put together, it was classy. Perfect, even. Casavant had designed it as an ivory-colored booklet, about the dimensions of a wedding invitation, tucked into a small brown slipcase. The booklet was made out of thick, lustrous rag paper and pleated like an accordion. On the front panel the single word *Eleuthera* was printed in deep brown ink in a spare, classical typeface.

When you turned the booklet over, the back panel became the front panel, and on that panel there was printed, in the same brown ink and in the same nice typeface, the single word *Nonpareils*. The remaining panels, front and back, contained photographs, printed in sepia tones.

On one side, the pictures were reproductions of vintage portraits of the dancers as they had appeared thirty or forty years ago; the other side contained individual portraits of the same dancers taken this year by me. No captions, no biographies, no text at all.

No photo credit, either. Thanks a ton, guys, I thought. Less is more might be okay when it comes to underwear on a hot day, but how was I supposed to get any business out of this?

I sighed. The program really was very pretty. Very clean, very open, very elegant. They'd make it up to me somehow.

I looked up and saw Casavant watching me from across the room, waiting for my reaction to the program. I gave him the thumbs up and he beamed back. Then he walked out the front door with the repairmen. Maybe he thought he'd have better luck with them in the fresh air.

I framed a shot of the window light as it bore through a decanter and splintered across the bar's surface, and was about to squeeze the shutter when a crashing noise erupted from the dressing room, followed by the sound of somebody yelling. The bartender and I ran into the room, expecting to see somebody who'd been bashed by a falling crate or something.

Jerome Monsell, Hank Monsell's nineteen-year-old nephew, his shirt off, stood with his back to the wall, looking scared. Hank faced him from six feet away. A wooden coat stand, broken in two pieces, lay on the floor between them.

The bartender shook his head, shrugged his shoulders, and left.

I stayed, horrified at the sight of the usually imperturbable Hank Monsell spun out of control. Hank was always the coolheaded one, the voice of reason when a disagreement broke out among the dancers, a master at helping other people save face. In fact, I'd been studying how he dealt with people—hoping to pick up some tips that would help me curb my own ready temper.

Jerome turned to me, his arms raised in entreaty.

"Hey," he said. "All I said was that I thought it might be a good idea to rearrange the order of the s-s-s-solos a little."

Hank, breathing heavily, glared at Jerome, then at the broken wood on the floor.

"You're lucky it wasn't your back," he said. Then he walked out the door.

"Rearrange them so you can go first?" I asked.

"Yeah," said Jerome. "But everybody knows th-th-that last is what they remember."

I picked up the pieces of the coat stand and pushed them under the dressing table.

"I think he's losing it," said Jerome.

"I think he's under a lot of pressure tonight," I said. "And I think you ought to be careful what you say to him."

Jerome sulked for a moment, then caught sight of his face in the mirror, ran his fingers through his hair, and brightened. He was extremely good-looking—sexy, with a trim, muscle-packed body and a knock-'em-dead grin, but also somehow cherubic, with eyelashes long enough to sweep the floor, and a soft, beautiful voice that sometimes crumbled into a stammer when he was angry or upset. I'd noticed that women who weren't immediately smitten by his looks tended to dissolve when they heard the stammer. Even I, fifteen years his senior and not easily charmed—or so I like to think—had occasionally found myself going fuzzy around the edges while talking with Jerome, like somebody on a dopey, soft-focus greeting card that says "I'd like to get to know you better . . . "

Jerome sat in a swivel chair at the dressing table and tapped out a time step on the floor in his canvas shoes. "I didn't think he was going to get that mad," he said.

Then, "You know—he's getting harder and harder to read. One minute he's telling me I dance better than he ever did, better than my daddy even, and the next he's telling me I ought to wash cars for a living. It p-p-pisses me off. I don't get it."

"I don't either," I said.

But in some ways I did. Hank Monsell was a tap-dancing legend—the mastermind behind the Nonpareils and probably the person most knowledgeable about tap dancing in the world. But at sixty-seven he wasn't exactly improving as a dancer. He was dancing well—beautifully, even—but at this point he was maintaining, not meeting new challenges. But Jerome, the son of his dead brother, was a dancing phenomenon, and getting better every day. Who could say what emotions dominated the relationship between the two? Some indescribable, highly combustible mixture of pride, protectiveness, and rivalry, I figured.

"He's afraid I'll end up like my father," he said. "In a wh-wh-wheelchair. That's why sometimes he tries to talk me out of d-d-d-dancing the way I do."

Jerome was more perceptive than I thought. Hank Monsell, Miles Monsell, and Jerome's father, the late Jerome Monsell, had danced together for years. The brothers had been famous for high-impact tap acrobatics—slamming onto the floor in splits, leaping off chandeliers onto marble staircases, that kind of thing. I'd seen film footage of one of their routines and spent most of the time wincing.

Jerome senior, the most fearless and athletic of the three, had spent the last ten years of his life unable to walk, his joints stripped of any natural lubrication, his feet a pulp of poorly healed fractures and swollen tissue.

Jerome scooted the swivel chair forward. For a horrifying moment I imagined that it was a wheelchair; then I shook the image from my brain.

"You're probably right," I said. "He doesn't want you to get hurt. You do get a little wild sometimes, don't you think?"

I was remembering a routine that Jerome had shown us the week before at a rehearsal I'd been photographing. An explosion of traditional tap combined with South American hip and arm movements and traces of rap movements. Very strenuous. Very sensual.

Jerome grinned.

Miles Monsell had entered the room while Jerome and I talked and was changing into the costume of the evening—pale yellow trousers made out of some sort of stretch fabric so the seams wouldn't rip, and a shiny white shirt unbuttoned a couple of buttons down the chest. I took a picture of him as he held a tap shoe on his knee and tested its flexibility with his thumbs.

I looked at my watch. It was only thirty-five minutes before show time, and nobody seemed interested but me.

"Where is everybody?" I said. "Where's Apollo? Where's Lacey? Where's Silver?"

Miles didn't look up.

"There's nothing to worry about," he said. "Mr. Monroe is taking a walk around the block to limber himself up."

Miles was having his usual reaction to people in a hurry. He downshifted and talked very slowly and formally, with long pauses between each thought.

He picked up the second shoe and inspected it while I waited for him to finish answering the question.

"Miss Gaines," he said, "is waiting in her car, preparing to make a grand entrance."

He took a tin of polish out of his bag and dabbed some on the toe of the shoe.

"And Silver Gaines," he said, "will get here when he gets here."

Jerome pulled on his shirt and buttoned the front.

"I think that's what she's worried about," he said.

I walked back into the club and framed some shots to shake off the tension.

I had started taking pictures of the Nonpareils after Claire showed Duncan some of my photographs. He liked them, bought two—which made me his devoted friend for life—and asked me to do some promotional pictures of the dancers for the club. After the first session, during a rehearsal at Hank Monsell's studio, I was hooked.

I'd been digging through dance histories, old recordings, boxes of old playbills—anything that could help me to understand what they were doing and could help me to do my own job better. I tape-recorded conversations during shooting sessions and took photographs of their own old photographs, thinking that maybe I could use it all in the book—if it ever happened—and planning extended captions for the pictures in my show. I was up to my elbows in work that I loved—happy as a meteorologist during a hurricane.

I stood in the front entry for a while, taking pictures of the curtains, sheer and white, as they lifted in the pathetic breeze created by a portable fan balanced on top of the coatrack. Casavant had hung the space with blown-up reproductions of old programs, photographs, and newspaper clippings—ephemera, he called it, a term I like—about the Nonpareils.

I had thought that the idea was hokey when he suggested it, but had gone through the exercise with him, collecting old scrapbooks from whoever would cooperate, and spent a solid week of evenings with Duncan selecting the most interesting images and clippings. Then Duncan arranged for a friend at a graphics firm to enlarge and tone them to make the final product look old.

As usual, Casavant was right. Shadowboxed in massive carved wood frames, the clippings and pictures looked beautiful.

The guests were arriving, and the rest of the Nonpareils, too. When Lacey Gaines entered the club on her son's arm, every head in the room turned toward them. She was a tiny, fine-boned woman— she claimed to be five feet three inches tall but was really barely five feet—with a heart-shaped face, extremely dark brown skin, and large, widely spaced brown eyes. Although from the old playbills and photographs I'd seen I calculated her age to be about sixty-five, she had the muscular, supple carriage of a much younger woman. She wore a muslin shift and a turban of the same material. Two strands of heavy coral beads swung from her neck to her waist, and she wore her trademark ivory lace gloves—the kind that cover only the back and palm of the hand and leave the fingers exposed.

She hung her cream-colored tap shoes, tied together by the laces, over her right shoulder the way a kid carries gym sneakers. Even with the shoes, she looked mystical, ageless, and otherworldly, like the carving of a woman from the prow of a pirate ship.

Lacey, not Eleuthera, and not even the Nonpareils, was attracting most of the crowd here tonight. Dancers, directors, critics, anybody who had anything to do with jazz tap was desperate to see her perform. She hadn't danced publicly for over fifteen years, and her last U.S. performance had been in 1952, the year she moved to Paris. It was like being able to see Nijinsky, or Jenny Lind, or Houdini.

Lacey disappeared into the separate dressing room Duncan and Hank had built for her, smiling and waving over her shoulder. Then Apollo Monroe, who for some reason needed a cane when he walked but could tap dance unaided, followed after and stepped into the men's dressing room.

I felt a hand on my shoulder. It was Casavant.

"So where's Silver?" he said.

"Beats me," I said. "Maybe the train got stuck."

Silver Gaines's several eccentricities included not wearing a watch but always knowing what time it was—give or take five or ten minutes—and taking public transportation at all costs.

"I should have made sure Hank was picking him up," Duncan said.

He smiled tensely, then moved into the crowd.

Claire came into the club, looking hot and exasperated. She hates summer, and told me on the phone that she planned to drive into the city only to see the show and then head straight out again. She waved at me from the doorway, found Duncan, and massaged his neck while he greeted some guests.

The lights dimmed and I returned to my table.

Hank Monsell stood at the microphone. He waited for the crowd to settle down, giving them a few extra moments to complain to their neighbors about the heat and look at their programs.

The waiters disappeared behind the double swinging doors that led to the kitchen. Duncan left Claire and sidled to a position in the shadows near the dressing room door. The voices subsided, and at last the only sound was the clanking of ice against glass and some conversation from the prematurely drunk.

"Ladies and gentlemen," Hank said, "tonight is a dream come true for me. Yes, it is."

His voice was low, raspy, and halting, like the voice of a sick man. He turned away from the microphone and coughed. I could see his hand tremble slightly as he adjusted the volume. Suddenly he looked every minute of his sixty-seven years and then some. I remembered how heavily he had breathed after his argument with Jerome in the dressing room. Despite the heat, goose bumps erupted on the backs of my arms.

"Jesusgod," I thought, "don't let him be sick. This man has to run the show tonight. This man's got to *perform*."

The audience, dead silent, leaned toward the sound. I scanned the crowd for Monsell's wife, Nicole. She was sitting three tables away, gorgeous and enormously pregnant in some sort of chemise—a "shrug" I think they're called—made of tiers of shiny purple-sequined fringe. She didn't seem concerned about Hank's performance—in fact, she didn't seem to notice it at all. She was sucking on a piece of orange rind and looking deeply into the eyes of a stunning young man with a bucket of gel in his hair.

Hank continued.

"We are fortunate to have assembled at this club tonight a tiny galaxy of stars of the first magnitude."

His voice grew a little stronger as he spoke, and I relaxed a little.

"Some of us remember a time not very long ago when a tap dancer—a fine tap dancer—couldn't get a job. Not in New York, not in Chicago, not in the City of Angels."

He paused, surveyed the crowd, and blew a kiss to someone in the front row.

"Hi, Jackie," he said. "It's been a long time."

I didn't know who Jackie was, but the audience ate it up. Monsell feigned distraction, casually inspecting his shirt cuff and adjusting the button while the crowd waited patiently for him to continue. Then he seemed to remember where he was and surveyed the audience again.   What a ham, I thought. I didn't need to worry about him. He probably faked his faltering opening lines just to get the crowd riveted to him.

"That's not true anymore," he said. "Tonight, at Eleuthera"—he caressed the word as he spoke it, supplying it with a couple of extra syllables—"we finally have a proper setting for what is—you know, I know, and finally the rest of the world knows—the highest form of dancing—jazz tap. And we are honored to donate this evening's proceeds to Home Again, which every night provides food and shelter for two hundred members of our human family."

The mention of Home Again, an organization that Duncan Casavant had founded, brought a brief round of applause.

Hank waited for the clapping to stop, then dropped his voice a shade and stepped backward.

"Of course," he said, "I only wish that my beloved brother Jerome could have lived to dance tonight. But Jerome Junior is anxious to fill his father's shoes."

The band—a piano, bass, and drums—started to deliver something slow and sweet. Monsell tapped gently to the center of the stage, motioning Miles and Jerome, waiting in the wings, to join him.

"Age before beauty, dears," he said. "Age before beauty."

The three Monsells broke into an elegant, restrained routine, a far cry from the acrobatics the brothers had displayed in their prime. Hank and Miles knew the limitations of their ages, but had surmounted them by transforming the Monsell style from flamboyant to something infinitely more subtle. The three kept their arms low and close to their bodies, raising them slightly only to punctuate the occasional turn. Sometimes they danced precisely together, as tightly attuned to each other's movements as pistons in an engine, and sometimes two of them dropped behind to perform a counterpoint to the third, who improvised in the foreground.

The stormy episode between Hank and Jerome seemed to have passed; for the moment, anyway, Hank had set aside his jealousy, or tough-love agenda, or whatever it was he was inflicting on Jerome. He even smiled during Jerome's solo moment in the middle of the act.

I photographed Hank as he glided in circles around the stage, suggesting the movements of an ice skater, through a miracle of muscle control mysteriously restraining the taps on his shoes from making any sound. Then I photographed Miles's feet and lower legs as the three men performed a step in which each brushed the inside of one shoe against the other, making a swishing sound the way drummers do with brushes.

A couple of minutes into the routine Silver Gaines, dressed in his dance clothes and carrying a crumpled—looking paper bag that I knew from experience contained his tap shoes, walked through the front door. He paused for a moment, the expression on his face, as usual, impassive, impossible to read, then walked into the dressing room.

At the end of the routine, the audience exploded into delighted applause, then broke into another wave as Hank tapped backward to the podium. He downed a glass of water and resumed his scriptless speech.

"Thank you," he said. "It's a joy to be dancing here tonight—it really is."

I was so relieved that Hank wasn't sick and that he had made it through the routine that I couldn't stop grinning.

"My joy tonight," he said, "is compounded by the fact that chasing on my heels is one of the finest dancers and dearest friends I have ever known and ever hope to know. I first saw him when he was a baby—just eleven years old, singing with Jimmy Lunceford's band at the Lafayette Theater. He had a pretty little voice like an angel—"

Here Monsell paused, folded his hands in mock prayer, looked heavenward, and crooned in a thin, babylike voice.

When the audience stopped laughing Hank continued.

"He was wearing a little silk shirt with sleeves out to here—"

Monsell held his arm out and plucked at an imaginary two-foot-wide sleeve.

"And he had a white streak in his hair that we were sure his mama had painted on for him."

I noticed that Nicole had grown bored with her companion. She was watching Hank intently and laughing a little at his descriptions.

"Then one day this little baby wandered into the Hoofers Club and started watching what was going on there. He saw John Bubbles, and he saw Eddie Rector. He saw them dance, and he said, 'Hey, I can do that!' And the miracle of it was, he could!

"Ladies and gentlemen, I've been trying to dance like that little baby all my life. He's Silver Gaines."

The lights dimmed and the small figure of Silver Gaines, maybe five feet four when he craned his neck, tapped quietly to the center of the stage. His body was slim-hipped, compact, and muscular, like the body of a gymnast. The white streak that Hank had spoken of still ran through his hair, an inch and a half wide, starting at a point in the hairline above his right eyebrow and tapering at the crown. It was dramatic-looking now, despite the fact that it competed with patches of gray at his temples; it must have looked startling on a young boy.

He began his routine slowly, to the relaxed, artless-sounding accompaniment of the bass alone. At first he confined himself to an area of the stage about three feet square, as though someone had drawn an imaginary fence around him. Superficially, at least, he danced in the cool, detached manner of classic jazz tap—arms close to his sides, feet close to the floor, an expression of serenity on his face belying the stress of the performance—like the Monsells.

One minute into the act it became clear that the small patch of floor couldn't contain the force that was Silver Gaines. Alongside the stream of traditional postures and footwork ran a second current of style that belonged to him alone—a dizzying, compressed medley of pantomime, moves borrowed from the Charleston, and jarring hip movements—all executed at breakneck speed.

He danced backward on one foot, dropped into a variation of a Russian squat, bounced back up, and then dribbled out a long, exacting series of tiny sideways steps that took him across the floor and back again with the relentless accuracy of a machine gun unloading its magazine.

I'd seen Gaines perform many times, but never with such diabolical energy. He didn't seem so much involved in engaging the spectators' interest as he was in blitzing them with his presence. It was over before I could frame my third picture.

The crowd, flabbergasted, appeared uncertain whether Gaines was finished, or whether he planned to ascend to the ceiling for his grand finale or simply evaporate. Neither feat seemed beyond him. When it became clear that the routine was over, they applauded Gaines even more vigorously than they had applauded the Monsells. He bowed quickly and disappeared into the dressing room.

Hank introduced Apollo Monroe while I edged closer to the

dressing room door, hoping to position myself at an angle where I could photograph Lacey Gaines as she emerged. As Monroe came out, I could see Lacey sitting in front of the mirror, calmly testing the screws that held the metal taps to the soles of her shoes with an amber-handled screwdriver.

Eighty-two-year-old Monroe, the only white member of the group, did a short, slow, painfully beautiful routine, specially designed to avoid shocks to his arthritic joints. I secretly thought it was unfair that Hank had placed him just before Lacey in the order of performance—the crowd was growing anxious to see her—but I underestimated Hank and the audience, which was apparently full of people able to appreciate the quality of Monroe's performance in spite of its streamlined nature. They stood and applauded until he did the dance all over again.

Finally it was time for Lacey.

The room was silent. Hank Monsell had disappeared, maybe to get another glass of water. People peered at their programs in the dim light, making out the picture of Lacey as a seventeen-year-old, dressed in a white satin sailor suit.

A few people started clapping in unison from the back of the room.

"Lacey, Lacey, Lacey," they said, and pretty soon most of the rest of the crowd joined in, chanting gently. Hank returned to the podium and the chanting subsided.

"Do you remember that galaxy of stars that I told you about earlier?" he said. "Well, if the Nonpareils are a galaxy, our next performer is the North Star. She is the dancer to whom all tap dancers look for direction, for inspiration, for a reason to keep moving. She's been away far too long. Please let's welcome her back—the inimitable, the unparalleled, the sun, the moon, and the wind combined—"

Lacey walked briskly out of the dressing room, her taps smacking richly against the wood floor, and the audience erupted into wild applause before Hank could speak her name. She had changed into a pair of man-tailored ivory silk trousers and a short-sleeved blouse of the same fabric, buttoned up the back with pearl buttons. Her gray hair was drawn back smoothly against her head and bound in a small lump against the nape of her neck.

A short, delicate tassel of diamonds dangled from one ear. On her hands were the sheer, fingerless gloves that she'd worn upon entering the club. She had laced her shoes with specially made satin ribbons that puffed into mothlike bows near her ankles.

The band was silent.

Lacey stood still a little to the left of center stage, near the baby grand piano, illuminated softly by a brass floor lamp that nestled in the curve of the instrument. Her skin, a deep, nearly black shade of brown, looked velvety, like the bark of a walnut tree after a day soaking in the rain.

She cocked her head slightly to one side and closed her eyes. It was a gesture that she always made before she began to dance, and sometimes before she began to speak. Her earring flashed with the movement.

She began to dance, slowly, without accompaniment, barely lifting her feet from the floor, her eyes still closed. Like Silver Gaines at the beginning of his routine, she stayed in a small space. Unlike Silver, she showed no signs of wanting to break its bounds, but continued her slow, liquid tattoo in the three-foot-square area as though it were all the room in the world and as though she had all the time in the world.

Compared to the refined arm movements of the dancers who preceded her, Lacye's upper body gestures seemed awkward. She held her upper arms close to her body; her hands swung loosely at the wrist; she held her shoulders stiffly.

She was doing something like an old-fashioned time step, over and over, but injecting it with such a languid beauty that it seemed like a new, miraculous invention. Then she accelerated slightly, adding a backward slide on one foot and a barely perceptible extra tap of one heel.

The band was still silent.

The taps dribbled off her feet clearly and roundly—like beads dropping off a necklace. Now she slid from side to side, her legs crossing and recrossing in front of her in a silent scissor step, her feet making no sound at all. Then she tilted back on her heels, scuttling backward and then forward on them while tapping her upraised toes together. She accompanied herself by humming vaguely under her breath, sometimes making a low "shhh" sound, sometimes a barely perceptible series of brief, hard syllables that sounded like "puh puh puh *puh*" and "ta *ta* ta ta."

The crowd sat silent and absolutely motionless—like a photograph. The man next to me had frozen at precisely the moment when he lifted a martini glass to his mouth, the rim pressed against his lips; a journalist who had scribbled frenziedly on a little yellow pad during the earlier performances stopped writing altogether. I took pictures as discreetly as I could, thankful for my Leica's quiet shutter.

Then she raised her right hand slightly toward the pianist, who picked up the beat from her and began to play. It wasn't Lacey dancing to the music; she and the pianist were making music together, each improvising, each improving on the other's last phrase, challenging each other to further complexity and more surprises.

After a while, on some imperceptible cue from Lacey, the pianist dropped out, and Lacey resumed her earlier, slower, a cappella movements. Then she began to sing, in a slow, slightly off-key, almost talking voice:

I dance because I'm happy
You know I dance because I'm free
Because His eye is on the sparrow,
And I know he's watching over me.

—dancing all the while.

It was something I'd never seen her do before.

When she was done, she dropped her head for a moment, then looked up and flashed a smile. I snapped that picture and some more as she accepted a bouquet of pink lilies from Casavant. The crowd stood up, cheered, and begged for an encore. Lacey refused to comply; instead she gave one of her lilies to a man in the front row who had gazed dreamily at her throughout the performance, and strode off to the dressing room.

People were desperate for air, and the place cleared out—faster, I'm sure, than Duncan and Hank would have liked.

Claire came over to my table and put her hand on my shoulder.

"Libby, honey," she said, "I talked Duncan into coming back out to the beach with me after they close the place up. He said he'd stay until tomorrow night. We'll have the whole day together. Can you believe it?"

"Great, Claire," I said. "Do you want me to feed his cats?"

She looked a little sheepish and handed me a set of keys.

"You've got it," she said. "I promise this is the last time. We'd take them to a kennel, but it's spur of the moment."

I wouldn't normally have minded taking care of the cats very much. The walk from my place to Casavant's near the base of the Brooklyn Bridge wasn't so bad. But now that my leave from *Americans* was fast drawing to an end, I found myself resenting any intrusion on my time.

"Come on," she said. "I'll pay for a cab to get you there."

Which also kind of ticked me off. What was I, anyway, the au pair?

"Oh, Libby," she said, "nobody's making you spend the summer in the city. You'll make yourself sick. Forget this stuff for a weekend and come out with us. We'll put the cats in a box and bring them along. The tomatoes are in, and the basil. I'll make you something good to eat and you can lay on the beach."

I must have been frowning.

"Okay," she said, "you can take pictures on the beach if you want."

I told myself to cut it out. I was hot, I was tired; I was more than a little resentful of the two of them. I mean I loved them both, and I would probably end up wearing some dumb-looking maid of honor dress at their wedding, which I figured they'd announce this fall sometime, but it bothered me that it seemed like I never got to see her for more than five minutes without him anymore.

And for some reason this summer Claire's obsession with perfect food was getting on my nerves. I mean, is it alright to worry about whether the olive oil has been made out of green or black olives when people in this city are drinking Fanta out of cans left in the trash?

I attached the keys to my camera strap.

Claire looked at me warily.

"I'll make it up to you, I promise," she said.

Her eyes glided to my necklace. She seized the little globe and held it up.

"What in the world is *this*?"

"It's a long story," I said. "I'll wait until you're back in the city."

The waiters were making up tables with white cloths and laying out food. Raw conch with lime juice, turtle fritters, and key lime pie, made with real key limes, Claire assured me, whatever they were.

Jerome Junior came out of the dressing room and headed for the food, followed by Hank and Miles. Then Lacey emerged, dressed again in her muslin shift and turban, Apollo Monroe at one elbow and Silver Gaines at the other.

I loaded a plate and sat next to Silver Gaines. He looked happier than I had ever seen him. He wasn't actually smiling, but his face looked relaxed and his eyes looked lively.

"Tell me," he said, "did you enjoy yourself? Or did you have to trap it in your camera?"

"Both," I said, which was true. "Silver," I said, "I never saw you dance like that before. You were great."

I waited for him to look at me like he usually does—as though by staring at me he could make me disappear. Instead, he lifted my camera from the table and peered through the viewfinder.

"I've been thinking," he said, "that I was wrong in telling you that I didn't want you to take any pictures of me at home, like you wanted. I've been thinking quite a bit. I don't like the idea of photography very much, but I think you're serious about what you're doing."

He took a small date book covered in Japanese paper from his pocket.

"Monday afternoon," he said, "I don't have any commitments after work. Have you been to the Bronx Zoo?"

I allowed as how I had, several times.

"Have you seen the reptile house?"

I don't like snakes much, but I tried to be cheerful. I had given up trying to take pictures of Silver early on in my project. If Silver Gaines wanted pictures in the reptile house, where he worked as a herpetologist, then the reptile house it would be.

"Fine," I said. "What time?"

"Four thirty," he said. "Or thereabouts. My office is in the back of the building, the green door just before the exit. We can eat at my apartment afterward. You can look at my old pictures, like you said you wanted to do. And don't worry—you can be back home before dark."

"What?" I said.

"You're a very worried person, aren't you?" he said.

"I don't think so."

Was I? Silver Gaines had a disturbing talent for making me feel uneasy. Maybe I didn't need to include him in the project after all.

Lacey Gaines skimmed by on her way to the buffet and tilted her head toward Silver—to whom she had been married briefly a long time ago—and me, like a dragonfly lingering briefly among the weedtops.

"I knew you two would get along eventually," she said.

And to me, "He's magic with the ladies, you know."

Silver pretended not to hear her. I was relieved to note that it wasn't a technique he'd designed especially for me. I thought about trying it myself the next time I had a meeting with Octavia Hewlitt that wasn't going my way.

A gorgeous, tall, wide-shouldered woman wearing a black dress and some sort of gigantic artsy-craftsy ceramic necklace was sliding a piece of pie onto her plate.

"Who's that?" I asked Silver Gaines.

He gave me his old blank look.

"That," he said, "is Delores Monsell."

Really? I did a double take. Delores Monsell was Hank's ex-wife, a former singer and now a weaver or textile artist, or something like that. I'd seen her briefly once before, when I'd picked up a scrapbook from her when she was teaching a class at the Art Students League. That day she'd been wearing jeans, no makeup, and some sort of poncho.

I cringed as she walked closer; I had told her weeks before that I would return the album to her right away.

I hadn't needed to worry; she wasn't interested in me. She headed straight for a table that was already too small for Lacey Gaines, Hank, and Nicole Monsell. Then she waved the pianist over with her hand and whispered something in his ear.

He headed back to his piano and began to play a blues song, something that I knew I'd heard somewhere before but I couldn't quite place. Maybe on an old Billie Holiday record, I thought. Maybe in a movie.

Roast's gone cold in the oven,

he sang, in a slightly off-key voice. After all, he was a piano player, not a singer.

Cake's gone flat in the pan,
And I'm getting all burned up
    waiting here for my man.
No more leftover lovin',

You can't reheat what's here
Cause when you do come home baby
You'll be singing the empty plate blues

The room went silent. Lacey, Miles, and Jerome stared at Hank as if they were waiting for him to say something. Silver held a forkful of salad in the air, two inches away from his mouth.

"Bitch," he hissed, so only I could hear. "What does she think she can do about that now?"

Hank broke the spell. He leaned over and kissed Delores on the cheek, then stood up and toasted her with his champagne glass.

"To Delores," he said, "for keeping the home fires burning."

She burst into laughter. Then the rest of the room did, too, although I didn't know why. In-joke, I thought. It's just as well I don't know.

Nicole poured herself another glass of champagne and started to giggle uncontrollably.

Silver looked at her with disgust, then leaned over and whispered something fiercely in her ear. Nicole's eyes glazed over with tears. Then she got up, found her bag, and walked out of the club. Hank followed her out, then came back in, rolling his eyes slightly.

Everybody else continued chatting and eating, too heady with the triumphs of the evening to be bothered by whatever little dramas had just occurred. Casavant and Hank Monsell started to toast each other, over and over, it seemed. Somebody who wrote for the *Village Voice* placed a small tape recorder at Lacey's table, and Lacey responded by intensifying her usually mild French accent.

Suddenly the heel straps of my sandals were slicing into my heels, my shoulders ached from the peculiar way I'd hunched in my seat for the performance, and my throat felt parched no matter how many glasses of water I drank.

I wasn't having a good time anymore. I decided to call it a night.

I said my goodbyes and headed for the trains at Union Square. Nicole Monsell stood at the curb in front of the club, one hand extended to hail a cab, the other dabbing at her face with a Kleenex. Now that she was standing, I could see that her usually slim ankles were swollen and sore-looking; her sequined dress strained so tightly against her pregnant belly that the hem was six inches higher in the front than in the back.

I approached her to tell her that I'd get her a cab, but she brushed me away. Fortunately, one slid up to the curb right then. I opened the door for her and she unloaded herself slowly and awkwardly into the back seat, making a point of refusing to look at me. The driver squealed into a three-point turn and took off toward Sixth Avenue.

Silver Gaines, I thought. He's magic with the ladies alright.

3

I WOKE UP at ten, furious with myself for not setting my alarm to get me up at six and in the darkroom before the heat hit. As it was, even though I was sleeping in a pair of boxer shorts and a tank top, I felt like I was wearing flannel pajamas. I turned on the radio and found out that the temperature was ninety-three degrees and climbing—before noon, no less—and that sanitation workers and the city were deadlocked on their contract negotiations. They expected to strike this week.

Swell, I thought. Maybe I should buy a deep-freeze to keep my garbage in. But then a few days into the garbage strike we'd probably have a three-day power black-out and all my frozen garbage would spoil.

Notwithstanding the impending tidal wave of refuse, I lay there happily, relishing the idea of the day spread out in front of me like an expanse of country highway. No appointments, no planes to catch, no scheduled dinner get-togethers. My closest friends all seemed to have selected August as their vacation month. Joey Dix, my movie co-dependent, was hiking in the Pyrenees, wherever they are. Dan Sikora, my long-distance on-again, off-again boyfriend, was off again until mid-September, on a photo-collecting trip out west. And even though Claire was in and out I counted her as unreachable too, the way she was completely absorbed by Duncan and her work.

I pulled a roach motel from behind the clock and looked inside.

Fourteen kills.

Not bad, I thought. But sometimes I wonder what success is when you're talking roach motels. Is a big catch what you really want? Or do you want it to be empty so you can pretend that you've licked your roach problem?

Lucas ambled over and crawled onto the mattress with me. I gave him a leisurely rubdown while the news continued on the radio. Nothing particularly unusual—just a summary of a garden-variety hot night in the big city: a domestic argument turned into a bloodbath in Queens, somebody pushed in front of a train at Times Square Station, a child killed by his father's pit bull in Brooklyn.

I shuddered and punched another button.

"All-Day Elvis," the deejay said, and dropped his needle on to "Love Me Tender."

I made some iced coffee and did a little calculating. Yep, August 16. It would be twelve, no, thirteen years ago today that Elvis died.

My friends who have children date their lives from the births of their children. "That was before Emma," they say, or "We lived in Chelsea until Mitchell." I have another friend whose life is cleanly split into the parts before and after she found her husband in bed with one of his medieval history students.

My mother's time-line was defined by the morning our family doctor told her that the pain she had in her stomach was not caused by an ulcer, as he had originally suspected, but by rapidly advancing cancer. Ever afterward, which as it turned out was about six months, her point of reference was "when I got sick," or "before I got sick."

The day Max ran out on us, the day my mother died, the afternoon I received the phone call telling me Avery was dead, too—any of those dates could have easily served to sever my life into pieces of "before" and "after." But the events that marked the evaporation of my family were so huge, and so inconceivable, or so it seemed, that I crammed them into the most unreachable part of my mental closet, to be dealt with—when?—later sometime.

Instead, my life is arranged into the parts before and after I moved to New York, and the day I did it—the same day Elvis took that extra handful of diet pills, or his arteries congealed, or whatever really happened— has a sort of mystical significance to me.

It's funny how things like that stick with you. It was the same August that Skylab was falling and the manhole covers in midtown were blowing sky-high. Son of Sam was on the prowl, and I met the description of his preferred victim to a tee: a twenty-three-year-old brunette (well, sort of) five-foot-three or under. I didn't know whether to look up, down, or over my shoulder, so I did all three. My aunt and uncle in Rochester, whom I'd lived with since my mother died, were wild with worry.

I remember my aunt shaking her head slowly from side to side when I announced that I planned to move to Manhattan as soon as I finished school.

"A moth to the flame," she said sadly. "A moth to the flame."

Thirteen years later, the hazards of the summer of Son of Sam seemed tame. The AIDS epidemic threw a foul and impenetrable pall over the city. There had been more murders in the first half of this year than in all of the year before. Last month someone stabbed a Japanese tourist to death as he waited for the IRT at Lexington and 57th Street because he didn't understand his assailant's demand to turn over his wallet and bowed in confusion instead.

But I couldn't leave. I couldn't even think about it.

It probably reveals that I am a semisociopath, but New York City is the only place that has ever felt like home to me. The Empire State Building all lit up purple for Gay Pride Week. French guys walking on tightropes at St. John the Divine. Papaya King, the Drink of the Gods. Seltzer delivery. Off Broadway. Off-off Broadway. Off-off-off Broadway. All-night everything. A *holograph* museum, for crying out loud. And everybody just as crazy as me.

I fed Lucas and dumped a tray of ice into his water bowl. Then I cleaned myself up, found a more presentable pair of boxer shorts, scuffled into my flip-flops, and made sure the keys to Casavant's apartment that Claire had given me were still attached to my camera strap.

I took Lucas along our usual morning route—down Canal to Lafayette, down Lafayette to City Hall Park—then spiked off down Fulton to Front Street.

Although it didn't seem possible, the heat was even worse than it had been the day before. The air was putrid; it felt gritty and smelled poisonous. When I looked toward the skyscrapers in the financial district it was as though I was viewing them through a lens smeared with grease. Even Lucas, who despite his disability usually bounds down Lafayette like a pup, seemed oppressed. I walked him slowly, wondering if we shouldn't be wearing gas masks or something, dutifully picking up after his business end with Baggies.

It was the first time I'd ever walked this far in Manhattan without seeing another person. There was a lump underneath a pile of blankets on a bench in the park that may have been a person, but if it was, I couldn't imagine that he or she was alive. The place where I usually got iced coffee to go was closed. No explanatory sign. Just dark and the door locked.

Casavant, I thought, you really owe me for this one.

His apartment, in a building that was once the headquarters for a tea and spice shipping company, was at the corner of Dover and Front at the base of the Brooklyn Bridge, practically tucked beneath a pylon.

I unlocked the front door, unlocked the elevator door, and unlocked the door to Casavant's place, Lucas growing more and more impatient as he smelled the cats. I cranked open a couple of living room windows and called for them.

"Shad. Shaddy, Shaddy, Shaddy!"

No cats.

"Meesh!" I said. "Here Meesh. Here, kitty, kitty, kitty."

Still no cats. I figured they'd taken a gander of Lucas out of their creepy Siamese cat eyes and headed for the closets.

I tethered Lucas to the leg of the baby grand, just in case a cat shot by and he decided to chase it, dumped some Purina into the cat bowls, replaced the old water with fresh, and sat down on the sofa for a breather before we headed back.

I usually don't get jealous of the places people live in, but Casavant's apartment was an exception. First of all, there was the view. The Brooklyn Bridge, with its lacework of cables, filled his rear picture window like some colossal animated billboard. With the windows open you could hear the sound of traffic as the vibrations thrummed through the steel—a sensational, otherworldly noise that you could get lost in—like the ocean or a storm.

Second, there was his stuff. Duncan, a boy-wonder ad man before the club-owning bug bit him, had a good eye and good stuff. He collected pictures. Not fancy oils or gallery-certified prints, but whatever struck his fancy, as long as it looked interesting. His boyhood baseball-card collection was installed in a glass-topped display table by the front door; pages from an old wallpaper sample book hung in the hallway; a five-foot-by-ten-foot poster for the 3D movie *Bwana Devil* hung in the stairwell leading to the bedroom. And in the bedroom there was a row of funhouse mirrors from a carnival—the kind that make your legs look short and fat and your head stretch out or that stretch your body so you look like Zippy the Pinhead.

The only thing he acted like a real collector about—spending serious money, getting appraisals, that kind of monkey business—was his collection of sixties rock-and-roll posters. Eight of them, blinding examples of op art silkscreened in neon colors, hung in his bedroom, and there were more in his study. He and Claire were building that collection together; they had a national network of scouts that J. Edgar Hoover would have envied.

Whatever space wasn't filled with pictures and curios was filled with books. A whole wall of them with one of those rolling ladders to take you to the top shelves like you see in Sherlock Holmes movies. And magazines. Claire said he subscribed to twenty-six of them, including the *Journal of the Royal Delphinium Society*. Part of his landed-gentry fantasy, she said.

I flipped through the pile on the coffee table. He had the summer issue of the *Journal of the Royal Delphinium Society*, along with *Harper's*, a scuba-diving magazine, *Americans*, a University of Virginia alumni magazine, a mail-order catalog of heirloom apples, the *Brooklyn Bridge Newsletter* (published in Italy, of all places), *New York* magazine, *Texas Monthly*, *Horticulture*, a catalog of beekeeping supplies, the Sotheby's Andy Warhol catalog, *Sports Illustrated*, *Grand Street*, and *Fine Woodworking*.

I pictured Duncan, Claire, and a herd of little kids happily eating apples among the delphiniums on their Long Island estate.

Would I ever see them again?

Would she let me pick out the maid-of-honor dress myself?

I closed the windows, locked up, and took Lucas back into the heat. At the corner of Lafayette and Canal I stepped into a glob of melted chewing gum; the thing, stuck to the bottom of my flip-flop, stretched clear across the street before I realized what had happened and scraped it off.

By the time we got back home I was fantasizing about trading my Rabbit for a Volkswagen bus so I could go camping. My eyes smarted, and there were flecks of sooty dirt trapped in the hair on the backs of my arms.

I showered, ate half a yogurt, and set to work.

My darkroom is long and narrow—"Pullman-style," Claire calls it—with lots of stainless steel that's easy to clean up. Sometimes it feels more like a roadside diner, with me as the cook. I even have an electric tea kettle so I can make instant coffee on the spot.

In decent weather the ventilation system is adequate, but lately I'd been toying with the idea of a major renovation with something higher power. But given that my days on Canal Street seemed numbered—of course Claire would sell the place once she and Duncan got married—I was reluctant to make the investment.

Still, it was the coolest place in the house.

The five rolls of film that I'd shot of the Monsells practicing in Hank's studio hung from clothespins on a line at one end of the room. I made some contact prints and selected what I wanted to print. As it turned out, only a few out of the batch seemed to have any potential: one of Miles sitting on the piano stool with Hank's enormous brocade scrapbook spread across his knees, pointing at a picture of himself with Ed Sullivan; a couple of Jerome Junior and Hank trying to outdo each other with variations on a step that required them to stand on the tips of their toes, like ballerinas; and one of Hank warming up, alone, by the window.

Claire had bought me a CD player for my birthday the year before. I resisted—after all, I've got an orange crate full of cassette tapes—but now I'm a blissful convert. I touched a new Emmylou Harris disk to the machine's tongue, and it lapped it up.

I pulled out a box of paper, and an old black photo album with the word *Memories* branded in loopy gold type on the cover slipped out on the counter with it.

Damn. Delores Monsell's album. I was going to have to think of a way to get it back to her.

Clippings, programs, and photographs poked out of the inside cover every which way, just as I'd left them after I'd rooted through the album with Duncan. Just once, couldn't I be more like Claire? Keep things in stacks and files and envelopes?

I took a break from printing and began to tidy the thing up, trying to slip the pictures back into the right sets of photo corners on the right pages.

Delores had written captions under nearly everything in the album, in small, rounded script that ran sideways into the margins when she ran out of room. There was a photograph of her and Hank, in bathing suits, standing on a rock at the ocean's edge. "Martha's Vineyard, August 1940," it said. "Get a load of these legs! Paula said people call this spot the 'Ink Well' because it's the only place where colored people can swim. How do you like that?"

Then there were publicity pictures of the Monsell Trio, a couple dozen of them. Hank always in the middle, Miles always at the left, Jerome Senior, who in these pictures looked eerily like Jerome Junior, always at the right, or if the pose called for it, bending on one knee in the foreground. Each photograph accompanied by Delores's text, with an emphasis on fashion, romance, and health: "At Small's Paradise, Christmas 1950," one said. "I sewed the handkerchiefs myself out of lavender satin. The shirts were baby yellow." Beautiful Delores singing in front of a microphone in a polka-dotted suit: "I just had a tooth pulled but sang anyway. Troy Tyrone was at the piano. He had just broken up with Rhea Meadows and was feeling very low."

Clippings, tickets—including one with a little tap shoe printed on it that Duncan had adapted as Eleuthera's logo. A formal head-and-shoulders portrait of Delores with a flower tucked behind one ear, and a snapshot of Miles and Jerome dancing together: "Boys a duo in Pittsburgh. Hank in bed with allergy." Delores leaning against a piano, in a dark dress with a huge corsage pinned to her chest: "January '51. Influenza epidemic. Turnouts very bad. Orchid a present from Miles to make me feel better." Or, one of my favorites, a strip of pictures of Hank and Delores from a photo booth, Hank smiling wolfishly at the camera, Delores with her mouth open and her hands over her eyes: "Waiting for a train in Chicago, 1949. I wanted these to send home to mama, but Hank kept pinching me."

Baby and school pictures of Jerome Junior; a bunch of programs from the Apollo Theater; a couple of telegrams; a small piece of lined paper with the words to "Empty Plate Blues," the song Delores had requested at the Eleuthera party, written in Delores's handwriting; a snapshot of Delores, Hank, Miles, and Silver playing cards together, Delores fanning herself with hers. "July 1954," it said. "Canasta. Silver never could catch on."

I remembered Silver hissing about Delores during that odd little episode at Eleuthera. So, I thought, it looks like bad blood between the two of them from way back.

I finished poking things back into the album, mentally kicked myself for losing—what? a half hour?—to browsing, and wrote a message to myself on a Post-It that I stuck on the door: "Return album to D. Monsell ASAP."

I started printing again, conscious of the passage of time only when the muffled click of the CD player alerted me to insert a new disk. At one I came out for a sandwich and another iced coffee, and to make sure Lucas still had plenty of water. Poor guy, I wished I could bring him into the coolness of the darkroom with me, but I couldn't risk getting dog hairs on the negatives.

Then I started the task of developing the film that I'd shot at Eleuthera. I was shaking my third tank of developer, humming along with Hank Williams, when I realized that the phone was ringing.

Damn, I thought. Why hadn't I put the machine on?

I waited for it to stop. Eleven, twelve, eighteen, nineteen rings. Who the heck doesn't give up before nineteen rings? I picked it up on the twenty-third ring and barked a hello.

I heard something like loud breathing, or panting, and then something like a woman's giggle cut short. I started to slam the receiver down when a voice stopped me.

"Libby hon. Olivia! Wait, it's me!"

No doubt about it, it was Max.

"Dad?" I call him Max when I'm being stern or disapproving or remote, and Dad when I forget to be stern or disapproving or remote. This time I was too surprised to be any of those.

"Just a minute, sweet," he said.

I couldn't tell if he was talking to me or to whoever was with him. At any rate, I never heard him call anybody "sweet" before and it gave me the creeps.

I heard some scraping sounds and then the sound of a door closing.

"Whew!" he said.

More silence.

"Where are you, Dad?"

"I'm in the john."

"Oh," I said. "The john."

A long silence. He was waiting for me to talk. When he was selling stuff, he could talk a long silvery stream. When he talked to me, he was like somebody with stage fright. I was supposed to feed him his lines, give him his cues. I obliged.

"Are you okay?"

"Yeah," he said. "I'm okay. I just needed some privacy."

That meant I was supposed to ask him who he was with.

"Who's that you've got with you?"

I was genuinely curious. Was he in a trailer with some hooker? It wouldn't have surprised me.

He made a forced-sounding chuckle, then cleared his throat. I heard a sound like someone banging on a door.

"Olivia, honey," he said, "that's your new mother."

I slumped backward against my darkroom door and slowly slid to the floor, like somebody in the movies.

I couldn't think of anything to say. I thought about hanging up.

"Libby?"

"Yeah, Dad?"

"I wanted to tell you in person, but Iris was really anxious for me to call."

Iris?

"Iris?" I said. "Her name is Iris?"

"Honey," he said, "she's beautiful."

"Dad," I said. "Are you drunk?"

Another long silence. I shouldn't have said it. It was mean.

But I sort of hoped he was drunk, and making all of this up.

"Olivia," he said, "I haven't had a drink in two days. Iris either. We're cleaning ourselves up. We have our whole lives ahead of us. Today's the first day . . . "

If he was going to say "of the rest of our lives" I didn't want to hear it.

"Dad, where are you? And I don't mean in the john."

"That's just the thing, honey," he said. "We're here. We flew in yesterday."

My heart hopped into my mouth like a toad.

"Here? In New York?"

"Almost, honey," he said. "We're in Jersey."

Jersey? Where did my father learn how to talk like that?

"We're having a little celebration," he said, "in Atlantic City."

Maybe I hadn't heard him right. Maybe he'd said "She's like your mother," not "she's your new mother."

"You're married?" I said.

"You heard it right," he said. He was warming up. He was laying on the West Virginia accent. He was relaxing.

"We flew straight here after the ceremony. I thought maybe Vegas for the honeymoon, but Iris, she's a hometown girl. Did I tell you she was from Jersey?"

"I don't think so."

"You'll love her, Lib. She's gorgeous."

Lucas pawed at the darkroom door and I reached out to pet his head. I rolled my eyes at him, like "You're never going to believe this one."

I knew what was coming, and saved Max the expense of beating around the bush.

"When do I get to meet her?"

"Now, honey," he said. "I mean, tonight. I thought we'd come in to the city, do Times Square, take you to dinner at the Playboy Club."

Times Square? The Playboy Club?

"Dad," I said. "You don't want to go to Times Square. Believe me. *Nobody* wants to go to Times Square. And the Playboy Club's been closed for ten years."

He'd probably come to New York thirty years before as a reward for selling the most phony water-softening units or something. I was getting panicky. What was I supposed to do? Invite them for dinner at my place? All I had left in the refrigerator was an egg, a half-eaten yogurt, and a box of blue popsicles.

"Libby?" he said. "I had another idea, too. I didn't want to put you to any trouble, but we thought that maybe you'd like to come out here for the night. You know, have dinner, see a show, and we'll get you a room so you can stay over."

Okay, I thought. I wouldn't have to clean the loft. I wouldn't have to cook. I wouldn't have to figure out a way to keep my father from being mugged in the big city. I could leave when I wanted to, and maybe have enough energy left to print what I'd just developed.

"Okay," I said. "That sounds great. But don't bother with the room. I'll come back into the city to sleep."

So much for the day spread before me like an expanse of country highway. He gave me the name of the casino, or hotel, or whatever it was they were staying in: a place called "Windsor's Castle" on the strip. I said I'd be there at seven.

I could hear a woman's voice in a shrill stage whisper.

"Tell her I'm dying to meet her," she said.

"Iris says she's . . . "

"I heard," I said. "Same here."

He forgot to mention the lottery. I forgot to mention the lottery. I forgot to thank him for the necklace.

Maybe I dreamed all that stuff.

It was almost four thirty. I extracted the film that I had developed from the tank and clothespinned it to the line. Then I took another shower and tried to re-create my dress-up look from the night before.

I yanked on the little green dress. It was a little sweaty smelling, but I had somehow avoided spilling anything on it. I found a straw pocketbook of Claire's that could pass for evening wear and put my sandals and some Bandaids inside. I could wear my flip-flops until I got to the casino, then do a quick change in the car.

It was too hot to wear lipstick, too hot to wear mascara, too hot to wear jewelry. I stuffed some makeup, my earrings, and the globe necklace into the bag. I could do that in the car too, in the casino parking lot. It was also too hot to wear underpants, but my better judgment took over.

Lucas was pacing around nervously, his canine antennae alert to my preparations for leaving him yet again. I took him out, once more carrying him over the metal loading dock, and walked him up to Lafayette and back. Then I made my deposit in the garbage can, carried him back over the threshold, and settled him in the bathroom with two bowls of fresh water.

I locked up, grabbed the bag, and headed to my parking garage. The usual twenty-minute walk took half an hour in the heat. The usual Sunday attendant—the guy who likes to stroke my forearm just enough so that it almost seems like accidental contact—wasn't there; his substitute also looked like somebody on a work-release program from a prison unit for sex offenders. Maybe Claire was right, I thought; maybe I ought to start shelling out the extra twenty bucks a week and park at the place run by the Chinese lady on Clinton Street.

The attendant was wearing a windbreaker zipped up to the neck, and he had the hood up. He also wore a loopy grin.

I gave him what I intended as my coldest bionic woman glare as I handed him a three, count 'em three-dollar tip, like throwing a steak to a dog to get him off your scent. "Hey!" he said. "Want to get married?"

"No thanks," I said. "Not today."

4

I'D SEEN pictures of Windsor's Castle—*Americans* ran a tongue-in-cheek interview with its owners, lawn-chemical heir Kenton Windsor and his wife Misty, a former water-skiing champion, when the casino-hotel went up—but no picture could truly convey the jaw-dropping ugliness of the place.

The building, which covered an area easily the size of a New York City block, was like the Alamo meets the Ice Capades. It was roughly loaf-shaped, with a turret at each end and a drawbridge stretching from the tinted-glass entrance to the parking lot. The exterior was coated with white stucco or polyvinyl stucco substitute, embedded with hunks of something metallic. The first four or five stories had no windows at all; slits of tinted glass perforated the top fifteen or so floors—the hotel rooms, I figured.

A gold-look crown the size of a race track revolved slowly on the roof midway between the turrets. I squinted at it as I drove into the parking lot. No, I wasn't dreaming. Those were people sitting in there. It was a bar, a revolving bar, and the patrons were drifting dreamily by, like horses on a carousel.

Laser lights, set like jewels in the spikes of the crown, rolled this way and that, throwing beams of purple, red, and orange that criss-crossed each other, evaporating into the twilit sky and drizzling down the sides of the building. At seven o'clock the effect was sub-

dued but riveting; after dark they'd be driving off the highway trying to get a second look. For the people at the revolving bar, I figured
the effect was close to hallucinogenic.

I parked at the point furthest away from the casino, next to the
trash bins, so no one would see me putting on my makeup and
shoes.

I could see the front entrance in my rearview mirror. The parking
valets were dressed like palace guards—tall fuzzy hats and muzzle
straps. One of them was goose-stepping to somebody's car to open
the door. I wondered if they made him do that or if he was just fool-
ing around.

What a place, I thought. What a picture.

I reached for my camera on the passenger seat and came up
empty. I looked on the floor. On the back seat. In Claire's bag.
Nothing.

Damn, I thought. I couldn't believe it. I forgot my camera. I
never did that. It was like a mother leaving home without her baby.
You just don't do it.

I pulled the makeup out of the bag.

I was more rattled than I thought I'd be. I'd planned on being
supercool.

"Hello, Iris. Lovely to meet you. Lovely dress. Lovely, really. Hello
Max. Lovely wife. Lovely, yes. Can only stay a minute. Thanks for the
invite. Bye."

My hands shook while I tried to stroke on the mascara, and I
smeared the lipstick out past the corner of my mouth. I hunted for a
Kleenex and tried to talk myself down.

Look, you never see him anyway. He's got a right to be happy, too. People change. They have a right to change. Stop punishing him.

I smoothed the Bandaids against my heels and yanked the sandals on. I breathed in through my mouth and out through my nose
the way Claire said they told her to do at her free trial-offer yoga
class. I tugged on my hair a little, trying to make it grow.

Then I got out of the car and headed for the drawbridge. Whatever this encounter turned out to be, it would be over in a couple of hours.

I called Max from the house phone, watching myself reflected in mirrors on the ceiling, on the counter where the phone rested, on the wall above the counter, and on the wall across from the counter. The place was freezing. I tucked Claire's bag between my feet and wedged my hands into my armpits while I waited for Max to pick up. Twenty or so assorted-sized women in short green dresses made the same gesture. I closed my eyes.

"Darling," said a woman's voice. "Come on up. We're in 64B. I thought we'd have a teeny little drink before supper. I'm so *nervous!*"

The elevator, which also had mirrors on the walls and on the ceiling, was even colder than the lobby. The lighting made my skin look mustardy.

I felt completely naked. No camera. No sweater. No stockings. There were goosebumps on my arms. My globe necklace felt icy, like a cantaloupe ball.

A hooker got in on two. Three old ladies hugging their pocketbooks to their chests got in on four and looked at the hooker and me with intense suspicion. A hotel employee wearing something that looked like a mini-milkmaid dress got in on five.

The elevator doors opened on six and I squinted at the legend on the wall that was supposed to tell me where 64B was.

I didn't need to figure anything out. Somebody beckoned me from the shadows at the end of the hall to the right.

"Livia! Livia! Hi ho! We're over here!"

Not Olivia. Livia.

As I walked toward it the figure became a tall, top-heavy woman dressed in violent red harem pants and a matching red tunic. She was wearing sunglasses, and the tunic had little gold beads sewn all over the front of it. She also had a wide load of black hair.

She walked toward me, quickly. I overcame an urge to turn and run. She seized me and wadded me in her chest, which was gigantic. The gold beads scrubbed against my cheek. I had a fleeting recollection of something somebody told me to do if I were attacked: relax and simply slump out of the attacker's grip. I tried it and it didn't work.

"Livvy, Livvy, Livvy," she said. Not even Livia anymore. "Let me *see* you."

And, "Look, Max, she's wearing the necklace. I told you she would love it."

She released me and held me at arm's length. I shrugged and stepped back a couple of feet.

"You don't know what this means to me," she said. "You're everything Max said you were,"

She sounded like she learned all her lines from TV shows. She had the fake near-British accent that women use on soap operas.

Max stepped into the doorway.

"Hey," he said. "Enough girl talk."

I stepped into the room and hugged him. He hugged back. Nothing dramatic from either of us—just the usual robotlike squeeze to the upper arms.

The woman looked scandalized.

"What's that?" she said. "No kiss?"

I clenched my lips and bussed Max on the cheek. He clenched his and bussed me back.

"You *two*," she said. "That's better."

She steered Max to the love seat in front of the TV and motioned toward me to sit in a chair next to the refrigerator mini-bar. She lay her head on his shoulder. He held his hand against her thigh.

She wasn't really wearing sunglasses. She was wearing the kind of eyeglasses that go dark in the sun and lighten up again indoors, but never light enough to look like ordinary glasses. With the glasses shading her eyes, I couldn't figure out how old she was, but she was a lot younger-looking than I expected she would be. Maybe forty-two or forty-three. Maybe forty, even.

Not old enough to be my mother, I thought. That's for sure.

The last time I'd seen Max, the day of Avery's funeral, he was wearing a hunting shirt and pants that were so long he caught his heel in them as he walked. He'd seemed small to me—small, fragile, and not well nourished. Afterward I'd wondered if that was the last time I would ever see him; he seemed far older than his fifty-eight years.

Now he was sitting on a pink satin loveseat in a two-hundred-dollar-a-night room, wearing a blue velveteen sportsjacket and a silver and turquoise belt buckle as big as a hubcap. His eyes, which my mother used to say looked like Clark Gable's, were clear.

His face was shaved. His pants fit. His shoes, blue and white patent-leather loafers with little gold anchors sewn onto the tops, gleamed like a couple of just-waxed Cadillacs.

I was speechless with awe.

Iris took his hand and held it to her cheek.

"Max? " she said. "No introduction?"

Max smiled. A big, genuine smile. I'd never seen him do that before. It was scary-looking.

"Libby," he said, "this is Iris. She's all mine."

Iris gave him a little smack on the cheek.

"Silly boy," she said. "You've got it wrong. You're all mine."

"How do you do, Iris," I said, squelching an urge to call her "mom" and see what she would do.

"This was pretty sudden," I said.

In all my dreams—and I have some pretty crazy dreams sometimes, including a repeat offender that has me riding a bus down Fifth Avenue with Eleanor Roosevelt—I never envisioned the scene unfolding here. Max—married again? He was a loner, a drifter, a two-timer, a drunk. I hadn't had an address for him in eight years. Max, with money? And a gal?

I felt like a fledgling actress just cast in a role I hadn't tried out for.

"Hey you! You with the lousy haircut! You're the stepdaughter."

And I liked my old status; I really did. I was the archetypal Motherless Child. An orphan in spite of my living father. The role was endlessly useful: When I failed at something, I could blame it on my lack of a stable family influence in my formative years; when I succeeded at something, I could wallow in exorbitant amounts of self-praise. Look at me—and I did it all myself, without any help from anyone. I must really be something.

So "stepdaughter." As in Cinderella. As in Maureen Reagan. It gave me the creeps.

"We want to do something for you, Libby," Iris said. "Buy you a present."

A present? I leapt out of my reverie. Was I supposed to bring them a wedding present?

"We want to get you something nice, from your Dad's winnings. Like a car."

Huh? A car?

I didn't want to get involved.

"No thanks," I said, "I've got a great car." Which was a lie. I'm attached to my Rabbit, but it has a hundred thirty thousand miles on it and a rust hole on the passenger side that I can fit my fist into.

Max stood up.

"We can talk about all that later," he said. "What this girl needs now is some meat and potatoes. Just look at her."

It was weird. He looked tall. I never remembered him as being tall.

Maybe it was the shoes.

Maybe it was love.

It was nine o'clock. The table was too small for three people. Iris smoked. Max smoked. I veered between feeling suffocated and wanting to smoke, too.

The service was slow. We'd finished the appetizers and were

waiting for the entrees. Steak. Max ordered steak for everybody. Forty minutes ago. At this rate I'd be lucky to be home by morning, let alone print any pictures tonight.

Iris was on her third whiskey sour, but seemed to be holding her own. We were sitting a little too near the organist, who was playing "These Boots Are Made for Walking." I already knew that Iris used to be a store detective, that she used Merle Norman cosmetics exclusively, that she loved children, that she'd had her colors done and was a winter, that her previous husband died in a sky-diving accident, and that her mother used to sing with Fred Waring and the Pennsylvanians.

I never heard anybody talk so much. She was like a human TV— just on and on, at her own pace, never really caring whether anyone responded. Max stared at her intently, nodding approvingly, adding the occasional "Isn't that something," or, turning to me and nodding toward Iris, "Isn't she something." At one point she pulled a little spiral-bound notebook out of her pocketbook and set it on the table.

"Livvy," she said. "I want to know everything about you, I really do. I want to write it down."

And then she started talking about herself again.

I swung between rapt fascination, like my father, and wanting to belt her in the chops to get her to stop.

Somewhere in the middle of Iris's recollection of the days when she used to be a glove model for a department-store chain, Max started drinking. Old Crow, straight up. Pretty serious for someone who wasn't drinking anymore. It had the same effect on him that it always had: He stopped talking and he got an unfocused look in his eyes, like he wasn't with us anymore. If he was true to his old pattern, he'd stay in this state for a couple of hours, and then he'd start getting mean. I hoped to be back in the city by then.

I tried to put some distance between myself and the situation by imagining that I was taking pictures of them. Iris was the kind of person who would look great if I put her in front of a fan and took the picture while her hair was flying around. No, I'd borrow a Harley-

Davidson and put her on it. She could wear this same harem outfit. Now Max, I thought. Max I'd put way high up on a big horse and shoot him from the ground.

Cut it out, I said to myself. You're a grown-up. Be kind.

The monologue finally ground to a halt while we were chewing on our steaks. I decided it was my turn.

"So how did you guys meet, anyway?"

For a woman with black hair, she sure blushed a lot.

"You tell, Max," she said. "I can't."

"Come on, Iris . . . " he said.

"Well, if you insist," she said. She took off her glasses and cleaned them on the edge of the tablecloth, and I finally saw her eyes. One was brown, plain old brown. The other was an intense shade of green—jade color, really. I tried not to stare, and she slipped the glasses back on. I had a friend in high school who had a dog with eyes sort of like that—one blue and the other brown. It was pretty amazing-looking. Maybe that was what had attracted Max. That and her gigantic breasts.

"I'd really had my eyes on him for quite a while," she said. "I was trying to save up for a trip to Europe with one of my girlfriends, so I was working nights at the track."

The track, I thought. Would that be the dog track or the horse track or the car-racing track?

Max cut in, anxious to defend her honor.

"In the restaurant, Lib. She was the hostess."

"Of course," she said. "I was the hostess. You know, taking people to their seats and things like that."

Knowing my father, it was probably a topless bar, but I kept quiet. It suddenly made me feel very sad, knowing that the two of them were trying to impress me—that they felt like they had to romanticize themselves for my sake. Then again, wasn't it what I always did with Max? *Sure, Dad, I live in a great place. Right in Manhattan. Of course, it's safe.*

"And," she said, "one night after the place closed up, I heard this

voice behind me, this gorgeous voice, like a movie star's or something's, and it said, 'Do you want to dance with me?' My feet were
killing me—you have to dress up to be a hostess, the other girls can
wear flats—and I told him so, and he said 'So take your shoes off,'
again, in that voice, so I did."

I looked at Max while she spoke. He was staring down into his
glass, tilting it back and forth real slow to watch the liquid stick to the
sides—a gesture I recognized as part of my own nervous repertoire.

Her voice had grown softer; she forgot the sophisticated accent.
Despite the tinted glasses, her face looked tender and full of love. I
surprised myself by almost liking her.

She moved her hands constantly while she spoke. They were big,
with long fingers and large knuckles. The fingernails, which were
long ovals painted with dark red polish, didn't look like they
belonged on them.

"He had already put the money in the jukebox. You know, it was
just one of those things. Like taking candies on the way out of the
restaurant. I just couldn't resist. We just kept dancing and dancing.
Slow dancing. I never danced with anybody like him before. I don't
usually dance at all. He said that was okay and he showed me the
steps real slow, talking in my ear with that voice of his. When we ran
out of quarters I opened the cash drawer and. . . "

Max gave her leg a nudge with his shoe. He wanted her to stop
talking; I wasn't supposed to hear about how they stole a lousy couple of dollars. I wanted her to stop talking, too, but for a different
reason. I was afraid she was going to tell me that they had sex then
and there, on the bar or something. There are some things that children don't want to know about their parents.

Iris laughed a little bit. She had some teeth missing at the side of
her mouth. I hoped Max would give her the money to have them
fixed. She seemed like the kind of person who thought it was really
important to look nice.

"Well," she said, "he about did me in. And then we kept doing
that—you know, meeting after the place closed down, and dancing.
And then after a while he moved into my place, my trailer . . . "

"A real nice place, Lib," said Max. "Real big. Like a house."

"And then the BigBucks thing happened—" She remembered her new station in life, and put the phony TV accent on again "—and here we are! Living it up! With you!"

She grabbed my hand and held it tightly between hers.

"Oh, Livvy, honey," she said. "I so much want us to be friends. Not even just friends. . . "

Sisters, I thought. I was starting to hate her again. She's going to say. . .

I was saved by the waiter, who came to ask for coffee orders.

Max's eyes were closed; I thought he was asleep and placed his order for him.

"Headache," he said. "Damn lights."

Iris took a pen from her bag and opened the little spiral notebook she had put on the table.

"Max thinks this is silly, I know," she said. "But I want to do it anyway."

She smiled at me.

"Livvy, dear," she said, "when is your birthday? I need to know."

I told her.

"And your address?"

Swell, I thought. I'm going to get Hallmark cards that say "To a darling stepdaughter."

I wrote my address in the little book.

"And your dear brother's birthday?"

"What for?" I said. "He's dead."

"Please, Livvy," she said. "I need to know."

"Why?"

"Well, Livvy," she said, "I know some people think it's un-Christian, but I'm very interested in astrology."

Yeesh, I thought. Max is really going to have his hands full.

"August 6, 1951," I said. "I think there might be something to it—astrology."

Well, sort of. At least it seemed harmless enough as a hobby. As long as you weren't deciding the fate of the free world with it or anything.

"Thank you," she said. "We'll have to work on your dad."

She excused herself and went to the ladies room.

Max's eyelashes fluttered. "Astrology," he said. "Horseshit."

I didn't want to witness any honeymoon argument.

"Dad," I said, biting my tongue. "Iris is nice. She's great. She's really in love with you, I can tell. And the lottery thing—I'm glad you won it. I think you and Iris ought to have a good time with it. And the astrology—it's okay. Let her have a little fun with it."

He pretended not to hear me, or he was unconscious.

Iris returned. Her lipstick was freshened up, and she looked happy.

"Just one more thing, Livvy," she said. "Your mother. When was your mother's birthday?"

I'd been trying not to think about my mother the whole evening. I knew that if I did I'd be in emotional quicksand. What else was a stepmother good for except to make you miss your mother?

"I forget," I said.

"Me too," said Max.

She closed her little book and smiled at us both.

"Not to worry," she said. "How about a little cordial?"

Astrology, I thought. Horseshit.

It was past ten o'clock. I thought the waiter was bringing us our coffee, but he landed at another table instead. I knew as much about Iris as I would ever want to know, and I'd seen enough of Max, too. I wanted to be in my darkroom, printing the pictures from Eleuthera. I didn't know how much longer I could be polite.

"The BigBucks thing, Max," I said for something to say, "how do you get it? I forget what the paper said. Once a year? Once a month?"

"Quarterly," he said. "I get the check quarterly."

"For how long? Five years? Ten years?"

"Thirty," he said. "Thirty years."

He pulled out his wallet and showed me the stub of a check from the West Virginia Lottery Commission. According to the breakdown of the money written at the bottom of the stub, after taxes Max was netting a little over thirty thousand dollars a year for thirty years. Enough so he could make car payments, I figured, and eat okay. Maybe even buy a little house. But not enough to live it up in Atlantic City. Not enough to keep Iris in silk harem pants for very long. Especially not enough if Max wasn't working, and he probably wasn't.

I wondered how much he'd spent already. And they were talking about buying me a car? They were even crazier than I thought.

"Iris," I said. "Max. Congratulations. This has been great, it really has. But I've got to get home. I've got to walk my dog."

Max was asleep. Iris reached over and stroked his hair.

"Maxxy, Maxxy," she said. And then to me, "I love him, Livvy, I really do."

And I figured she really did.

5

I WOKE UP early Monday morning to a call from Claire at the beach, apologizing for sending me over to feed Duncan's cats. It was inexcusable in this heat, whoever did she think she was, would I ever forgive her?—and so forth. She also said that Duncan was driving back to the city this morning and from now on would feed them himself—who did he think he was?—and so on. It was pure Claire—my old boyfriend Hugh used to call her the Emotional Outlet.

She asked what I'd done Sunday night, and I told her that I'd gone to Atlantic City to see Max and his new wife.

"You're *kidding*," she said. "How strange. How weird. Aren't you mad?"

Surprised, yes. Mystified, yes. Mad, no.

"Why would I be mad?"

"Oh, Libby, you know. Daughters are always mad when their fathers remarry. They're supposed to be. You know, no one can replace my real mother, who gets the family china—that kind of thing."

"You mean the family card table?" I said.

"Oh, come on. You know what I mean. And don't you feel jealous of her—replacing you as the woman of the family?"

"Cut it out, Claire," I said.

Why does she have to analyze everything?

I told her what she'd gotten in her mail; she told me she'd been saving bones for Lucas, and that she thought she'd be in town for a while on Friday.

I spent all morning and part of the afternoon printing pictures from the Eleuthera opening. After my disconcerting evening with Iris and Max, it was pure pleasure to be back in the company of the Nonpareils—people who were focused and sane. I printed blissfully on and on, unperturbed by the fact that the mercury was again zooming to the upper nineties.

I had a good printing session, more keepers than usual, especially the ones of Lacey Gaines in her dressing room before she knew I was taking her picture. I fixated on one image, where she was tying the laces on one of her shoes, her delicate fingers, gloveless for once, spreading the satiny bow to its fullest width, and printed it over and over. It was a beautiful picture—just her hands and the laces, but something was off. I fiddled with the contrast—making the white of the laces whiter, the dark of her skin darker—without luck. Then on an impulse I printed it in a very small format—two and a half inches by four inches—with a white border the same width as the shoelaces. It was nice—a jewel even—one of those few pictures that seem to justify a world of false starts. A hit like that can make me happy for twenty-four hours. Whistling, I printed an extra one for Lacey, and set all the prints to wash in the print washer.

At two I started to think about my appointment with Silver Gaines at the Bronx Zoo. My car was sure to overheat and die if I ran into bad traffic today, and I didn't much like the idea of dealing with a breakdown alone in the South Bronx. I looked at my subway map and plotted my route to the south entrance of the park. Then I took the prints out of the washer and laid them on my drying racks to dry, like you do when you handwash sweaters. It would probably take days in this humidity.

I walked Lucas, fed him an early dinner, refilled his water bowls, and apologized for going out two evenings in a row. He lay down on the floor and gave me the Look—an unblinking, unhappy, big-eyed stare, his tail still and flat against the floor in desolation. Maybe, I thought, I should find somebody who would come sit with him while I went out, an NYU student who'd sit on the sofa and study in exchange for four bucks an hour and all the Pop-Tarts he could eat. Thank God, I thought, Avery didn't die and leave me an actual human child. I couldn't take the guilt.

Did Gaines really say he was going to make dinner for me? It seemed too much to ask from anyone in this heat, especially someone who didn't seem to like me much anyway. I wrenched Claire's picnic cooler from its hiding place under the sink, wiped a couple of dead roaches off the handle, and threw in a plastic bag of ice. I could buy some chicken salad and beer at the deli and make myself a slightly more welcome guest.

At three-thirty I was heading toward the Bronx on the IRT, my cooler of chicken salad and beer on my knees, the part that says "Playmate" turned toward me because it was too embarrassing to have it pointing toward the public. A sewer main had busted open at 86th Street, and I saturated in the heat and stench along with a platform packed with people while a crew of maintenance workers tried to staunch the flow of swill with mops and rags. By the time I got to Fordham Road I was running a half hour late, and wondered if I smelled as bad as the station had.

The zoo was empty except for the people working the entrance

booth, a tired-looking guy sitting on the steps of the Elephant Pavil-
ion, a maintenance worker spearing litter on a pole, and a very
young mother slowly pushing a set of sleeping two-year-olds in a
double stroller by the seal island.

The woman at the entrance booth yelled to the guy with the pole
that the temperature was a hundred and three degrees. Except for the
seals, none of the animals were in the outdoor exhibit areas; they
were napping or the zookeepers kept them confined to their indoor
quarters. The air above the pavement looked wavy, and I remembered an Australian movie I once saw about a couple of children lost
in the outback. The air had looked like that in the movie.

I read a map posted on an information board and found the Reptile House—a low, Victorian-looking building with a copper roof that
had gone green. From the outside it looked like the building would
be cool inside. Cool and dim.

It turned out I was right only about the dim part. It was easily as
hot inside the building as it was outside, and certainly more humid.
The air smelled of animal smells mixed with chlorine—sort of like
the health club I used to go to.

I stopped just inside the entrance to look at a bulletin board containing photographs and newspaper clippings of people and events
having to do with the Reptile House. In one of them, a younger Silver Gaines stood with several other people, all of them holding a
snake that could have doubled as a fire hose, next to another group
of people holding a different, also revoltingly huge snake. "Which is
longer?" said the headline. "The ten-year-old reticulated python or
the thirteen-year-old anaconda?" In another a pleased-looking
woman held *Bufo marinus*, the World's Largest and Most Toxic Toad.

The snakes were in glass tanks that lined both sides of a long
hallway; their names and origins gleamed in illuminated type
beneath the tanks. It seemed to be nap-time, although I guess it's
always nap-time for snakes. I stood for a while in front of the anaconda tank, allowing my eyes to adjust to the dimness, then headed for

the office that Silver said I would find near the building's exit.

Just around the corner from the crocodile display an exquisite cream-colored snake pressed itself against the glass front of its tank. The sign said it was an Asiatic cobra. The snake's skin looked exactly as though it had been carved from whalebone or ivory; it had a waxy-looking cast and the depressions between the scales were brownish looking, the way the etched parts of scrimshaw get. Its ruff, or collar, or whatever the skin is called that extends on either side just beneath a cobra's head, rippled slightly as the snake slid from one side of the tank to the other. She was exquisite. Fantastic. I ached to take her picture, but knew I'd get nothing but flash reflections, what with the glass and the dimness.

Another cobra, identical in size and shape to the white one, but a mottled brown and tan color, moved drowsily in the back of the tank. I wondered if the first was an albino, then noticed that patches of papery brown stuff lay here and there at the side and front of the tank. The white one had just sloughed her skin. While I watched, someone opened the hinged door at the back of the tank. The white snake raised her head. The man spritzed her with what looked like water, then reached in with a metal rod, hooked the bits of skin with it, and put them in something behind the tank. He closed the panel just as the snake was coming to from the spritzing and raised her head again.

Even in the humid heat I shuddered. Not for the world, I thought, not for the world could I work in this place.

I walked quickly past more cobras, some rattlesnakes, a green lizard, and an amazing, delicate-looking, neon orange snake that seemed made of plastic.

Just past the Gila monster I found a green door that said "For Official Business. Please Ring Bell"—kind of like the door to the Emerald City in the Wizard of Oz—and banged on it. A young guy with a wispy beard—the guy who had been spritzing the white cobra, I think—opened it, then started to close it in my face. Silver

Gaines, who was sitting at a small desk facing the wall, spun around in time to catch sight of me.

"I'm expecting her, Martin," he said.

And to me, "Have a seat, Libby, I won't be long," in a way that was terse but also pleasant.

Gaines turned back to his work, making entries in something that looked like a bookkeeping ledger.

Martin scowled at Silver, then at me, then began scrubbing out a tank in a sink in the corner of the room.

I sat down in an upholstered vinyl chair and played with the arm, which had a slit in it tidily sutured shut with electrical tape.

Silver worked quickly and intently, making no movements with his body except with his left hand, in which he held the stub of a yellow pencil and made entries in the book. He was wearing khaki pants and a white tee-shirt. Even in this close, sedentary setting, there was no mistaking that he was a dancer or some other kind of athlete. Although his head was bent forward, his shoulders were erect and even; his tee-shirt, taut against his back, revealed strong, highly delineated muscles. Even his neck looked strong and supple. Although he appeared relaxed, he also seemed ready to spring into sudden movement.

Like a snake, I thought—even down to the special markings in his hair.

The thought surprised me. Like a friendly snake, I corrected myself. Was there such a thing? Maybe zoologists grow to look like their specialties the way some people grow to look like their dogs. Still, snakelike or not, he was good-looking.

I examined the books on the utility shelving to the right of Gaines. Serious business, I thought. Nothing here to reveal that Silver had anything going on in his life except reptiles. I pulled down *The Herpetologist's Guide* and opened to a description of snake sex life. As it turns out, the reproductive organs in male snakes are, as the author put it, "extraordinary." Boy snakes have two penises, which are "often arrayed with spines." By way of contrast, "The female reproductive organs have yet to be studied in depth."

I was just getting to the part where during courtship the male seizes the female in his jaws when Gaines sprang up and reached for a button-up, short-sleeved shirt that hung from a hook next to the bookcase. He put it on over the tee-shirt, turning his back to me as he buttoned it up and tucked the tail into his pants.

"Excuse me," he said, "I should have thought of this before you came in."

"It's not a problem," I said.

"Fascinating reading, isn't it?" he said.

"Fascinating," I said, placing the book back on the shelf.

"Shall we get down to business? Do you want to take pictures in here first, or with the snakes first?"

Was this the same Silver Gaines who two weeks ago walked out of Hank Monsell's studio when I started to photograph a rehearsal? What could account for the new compliancy?

The compliancy was not to be confused with enthusiasm, however. I couldn't stop feeling that Gaines was participating in this exercise not of his own accord but because someone else insisted on it.

I put the book back on the shelf. Then I asked Silver a little about his work, hoping the answers would prompt me to think of some interesting shots of Gaines. They didn't. Although he seemed to have developed a new interest in being polite with me, he was not interested in waxing lyrical about snake-keeping.

"Are you fond of any snake in particular?" I asked, hoping the question would lead to a photograph of Gaines caressing his favorite black snake, or whatever.

"No," he said. "Not really. I've written a monograph on cobras, but fond? No. Not really. I'm interested more in their habits than in the snakes themselves."

Or, "What got you interested in snakes in the first place?" hoping that his face might come alive with the recollection of a teacher who had given him a book about snakes or something like that.

"I took a course," he said.

My eyes roamed to a white metal box marked with a red cross mounted on the wall. On top of it there was a smaller cardboard box with the word *tourniquet* handwritten on it in red Magic Marker.

"Have you ever been bitten?" I asked, expecting a dramatic tale.

"Not enough," he said.

"What do you mean?"

"Some people who work with snakes are bitten enough that they acquire a certain immunity. I haven't."

I took a couple of probably boring pictures of him sitting at his desk. He didn't look uncomfortable; he just looked like he wasn't enjoying himself. I can sympathize. I don't like having my picture taken, either.

I decided to make both sessions—the one here and the one at his apartment, which I suspected would be as unrewarding as this one— as short as possible and avoid torturing him unnecessarily.

Then I asked him if I could take some shots of him holding a snake. He said nothing, but motioned me to follow him through a door that led to the backs of the display tanks.

He passed by the cobras and the rattlesnakes and opened the back of a tank containing the orange snake that I had met earlier on my way to his office.

"Don't worry," he said. "This one's not poisonous."

He extracted the snake and placed it loosely over his forearms. It raised its head and six inches of its neck straight into the air and moved it back and forth in a way that was lively—almost appealing. I photographed it as it worked its way up Silver's forearms and to his shoulders, where it again lifted its head up and wafted to and fro. Although Silver never looked half as animated as the snake, he relaxed, and I shot a roll of the two of them together.

It was ten after six—well past closing time. Martin walked in carrying a cardboard box with holes punched in the lid. Something was scratching around in it—scratching around and making squealing sounds. He lifted the lid partway up, reached in, and pulled out four or five white mice—or were they small white rats?—that he held by their tails in his hand, sort of like a bouquet. I photographed him and he didn't seem to mind; in fact he seemed to like it.

Silver was putting the orange snake back in its tank. He glanced over his shoulder at Martin and the mice.

"It's feeding time," he said to me. "We do it before and after hours when the public's not here." He said this in such a way that I understood that this was the policy of the zoo's public relations and membership departments and not Silver's own.

"Would you rather that Martin wait until after we're gone?"

Of course I would, but of course I told him to go ahead and feed them.

"I didn't realize that they ate them alive," I said, "but I suppose they would have to, in the wild, I mean."

Martin smiled a little bit at my ignorance, which he seemed to enjoy as much as he did having his picture taken.

"Yeah," he said. "Imagine—eating a live animal with your legs tied together and your arms tied behind your back."

"Imagine," I said.

GAINES AND I walked to his apartment from the zoo, cutting through the southeastern part of the park.

"What's with Martin?" I said. "Are you two on bad terms or something?"

He was silent for a while. Then he said, "Let's just say he's trying to make me fire him and I won't do it. He's a skillful worker and I need him. We'll resolve things eventually.

"Did you think I was too harsh with him?" he asked.

"No," I said. "I just thought he was strange."

As in Norman Bates, I said to myself.

"He's an unhappy man," he said, "but he loves the snakes."

Just before we emerged on the street, we walked down a steep embankment, passing a topless teenager and her boyfriend lying on their sides on a large flat rock, smoking dope, then cut to a path running out of the park. Suddenly Gaines stopped and dropped to his knees, then stood again, just as quickly, holding a long brown shoelace in his hand. Smiling, he held it out to me.

"Decayed snake," he said.

"Decayed snake?" I asked.

"No," he said. "DeKay's snake." He spelled it for me. "A city snake. I'll bet you never noticed one before."

He was right. I hadn't. Rats, yes. Mice, yes. Snakes, no.

He laid it down gently at the base of a bush.

"That's how I first found out about snakes. Here. In Bronx Park. Under my own feet."

Gaines's apartment was in a bland ten- or eleven-story concrete building on Rhinelander Avenue in a part of the Bronx that I'd been in a few times before, on an *Americans* assignment to photograph a subway graffiti artist at his home. Some kids were playing in the spray from a hydrant on the corner. A convertible drove by and the woman on the passenger side shrieked obscenities at the driver for steering so close to the water.

Gaines fell silent as we entered the building. It was clean and quiet inside—a sharp contrast to the clatter and congestion of the street. The walls, freshly painted, or freshly washed, were soft, pale green; the wood-look walls inside the elevator smelled like Lemon Pledge. Not bad, I thought. I wonder how you get on the list for this place?

We rose to the eighth floor, and opened the three sets of locks on his door—two deadbolts and a police lock that worked by spreading two shafts of steel horizontally across the door frame as you locked it and retracted them as you unlocked it. Just like the lock on my place.

He lived in three rooms—a living area separated from the kitchen by a counter with stools, and a bedroom that abutted the living area. The apartment was stark. It's hard to explain the difference, but it was an ascetic-seeming starkness, not a contrived, fashionable starkness.

In the center of the living room he had a small brown couch facing the window, which had a steel-railed balcony and looked out on a courtyard. In front of the couch there was a low wooden table with nothing on it. In the corner of the room there was a drawerless desk made of a piece of wood laid across two sawhorses. On top of the desk was a manual typewriter and a smooth black rock the size of a fist. In another corner there was a waist-high wooden chest with a stereo on top of it and speakers on either side on the floor.

The floor was a rugless expanse of gleaming wood, except for a scuffed, dull-looking circular area that extended from the front of the couch to the balcony window—his dancing area, I guessed.

A jasmine plant hung in a pot from a rod in front of the window. I recognized it because Claire gave me one for Christmas one year. Mine never bloomed, which might have had something to do with how I forgot to make arrangements for someone to water it when I went away for ten days. Silver's wasn't blooming either, but it was healthy-looking, the delicate leaves frothing up from the pot like the head on a beer.

The plant and the rock were the only ornaments in view. There were no pictures on the walls, no curtains, no rugs, no mirrors. Through the bedroom door I saw only a futon and a shelf of books.

I put my camera and the cooler on the kitchen counter while Silver poured me a glass of ice water. He watched me scan the living room.

"Were you expecting snakes?" he asked. "I had one here for a long time, but it got loose and Hank decided I couldn't keep it anymore."

"Hank?"

"Hank. Hank Monsell. He owns the building."

I don't know why it surprised me so much. I knew that Hank was involved in real estate—in fact, he'd told me about it a million times, as part of his general self-promotion scheme, the same way he went on about his beautiful wife and his successful students and the famous people he knew. It just didn't occur to me that I'd ever be in one of his buildings, or that he and Silver were landlord and tenant. In my experience landlords—except for Claire—weren't generally people you'd be friends with.

"It's his biggest building," he said. "And he is an exemplary landlord. You'll notice that the plumbing is intact, the floors are in good condition, and the locks work. Throughout the building. I help him keep it that way."

I had noticed. The building I'd photographed the graffiti artist in, on the same block, was a hellhole—lightbulbs dangling from exposed wires, floors warped and walls crumbling from frequent flooding, dismantled radiators lying in the halls. By comparison, Monsell's building was One Fifth Avenue.

"You and Hank go a long way back, don't you?" I said.

"A long way back," he said. "Our whole lives."

He walked to the kitchen; I moved to one of the stools on the living room side of the counter. He took some things out of the refrigerator and spoke while he washed and chopped.

"You know," he said, "I have a feeling that you might not understand what a great man Hank Monsell is."

He was speaking in a placid, neutral way, but I felt myself flush with offense.

"I think you might see him only as a—what would the journalists call it—a photo opportunity. I don't know if a woman like you is capable of seeing him any other way."

I winced at his words. I have a bad tendency to fly off the handle, and I've consciously tried to curb it.

I counted to five. I can never make it to the suggested ten.

"Silver," I said—calmly, I hoped, although I could feel my earlobes heating up—"I'm afraid you're giving me the same treatment you've accused me of giving Hank. You're presuming to know me when you don't really know me at all."

"Maybe," he said, "and maybe not."

He poured some oil into a pan and heated it up.

"Hey," I said, "don't do that. It's too hot to cook. I brought chicken salad."

"I appreciate that," he said. "I do. But I don't eat meat."

"Beer?" I said.

"No thanks. But don't let me stop you."

I opened the cooler and ripped a can from the plastic loops that held the six-pack together.

"As I was saying," he said, "about Hank. He is like a brother to me. And I am more a brother to him than his own brothers. He is like a parent to me and I am like a parent to him. He has purposes in his life that run far deeper than a magazine photographer could imagine."

He said "magazine photographer" with just the slightest tone of derision. He left out the adjective "white," but I knew it was understood.

I decided to avoid argument and remained silent.

"For one example," he said, "one small example. Did you know that Hank Monsell owns the building that houses the Coleman Community Center? And that he loans it for that purpose at no cost to the center?"

He didn't wait to see if I responded.

"No, of course you didn't."

"Did you know that he rents the apartments in this building at below market value, but maintains the building the way it should be maintained?"

Again, "No, of course not."

He was chopping tofu into perfect little cubes as he spoke. Quickly. Exactly. Chop, chop, chop, chop.

I thought he had finished his catechism, but he continued.

"Did you know," he said, "that the only reason Hank Monsell joined forces with your friend Mr. Casavant is that he hopes that the proceeds will allow him to start a theater in Harlem that will incubate young black talent? The only reason?"

"No," I said. "I didn't. But I think it sounds like a great idea. I hope it works."

"It will work," he said. "Anything Hank does works."

Was this why Silver had invited me to photograph him? So he could lecture me?

"That's the only reason I'm dancing at Eleuthera. And Lacey, too. You don't think she'd emerge from sixteen years of retirement without a good reason, do you? It will all go to Hank's new theater."

What did he expect me to do? Be startled? Be mad? There was nothing particularly provocative about the fact that Hank wanted to start his own place. Duncan would probably think it was a good idea too.

Silver put the food on two plates and set them on the counter. He poured my beer into a glass, and more ice water for himself.

We ate in silence. He looked preoccupied. For a while I thought he had forgotten that I was there at all. The phone on the desk rang. He picked it up, said hello, and hung up.

"Marketing survey?" I asked.

"It was a crank call," he said. "I changed my number but I still get them."

I ate the tofu. I never have liked it very much.

I tried to make small talk and fished for a subject that wouldn't be contentious.

I asked Gaines if he knew when Hank and Nicole's baby was due.

"A week," he said. "Maybe two weeks. Too short a time."

"Too short a time for what?"

"For Nicole to grow up in."

"Aren't you a little hard on her?"

"No one's ever been hard on her. That's what went wrong. A child having a child."

"She's no child, Silver," I said. "She must be thirty years old. You sound like you're her father or something."

"Or something," he said. "I guess I do."

He was drumming his fingers tensely on the countertop.

"I'm her godfather," he said. "Not that she would ever acknowledge it. Her father is dead, and I have a duty toward her. Just as she has a duty toward herself. And toward her child. She wants things—sometimes she wants to be a singer, sometimes a dancer. But she won't pay the costs. I've tried to teach her, but she won't listen."

He sounded like a letter to Ann Landers.

"Surely," I said, "now that she's a married woman you don't feel like you need to—" I searched for the word. Interfere? Oversee?—"be so involved in her life, do you? It's a pretty big burden on you, let alone her."

He looked glum. I suspected that he felt he had already stepped too far beyond his self-imposed bounds of privacy by telling me as much as he had about his relationship with Nicole, so I shut up.

He spooned more stir-fry onto my plate and we ate for a while in silence. I decided that tofu didn't taste so bad if you held some beer in your mouth while you chewed it.

Silver poured himself yet another glass of ice water.

"I was hoping," he said, "that you would think of this yourself, but you haven't."

"What?"

"That part of the money you make from these photographs belongs to us, the dancers. I think you should give it to Hank to put toward the theater."

Should I tell him how little, if any, money I would make even if I did sell some pictures at the gallery? After Harriet Bemis exacted her fifty—count it, fifty—percent? After the costs of film, paper, and frames? My pride wouldn't let me.

Then again, what if I got lucky?

"Maybe you're right," I said. "And maybe not. I'll think about it."

We washed the dishes together without speaking. As we stood there, the sun began to sink, casting its light across the courtyard and into Gaines's kitchen, illuminating the white cabinets and appliances with a pinkish glow. Had Gaines been anyone else I would have asked him to stand in that light and photographed him there. Gaines being Gaines, I knew that I'd end up with a beautifully lit portrait of a man who looked like he had a rock in his shoe.

I took a couple pictures of the stove instead.

While I dried the knives Silver opened the closet next to the front door and lifted down a large, rectangular cardboard box with a lid—the kind people used to bring clothes home from department stores in.

He put it on the coffee table and took the top off. The box was full of newspaper clippings, photographs, ticket stubs, and theater programs. I joined him on the couch and looked inside.

"I know," he said, "it's disorganized. I would like to throw all this away, and have actually been on the verge of doing it, but then a question comes up about a date, or a name, or my mother wants to see them. So this is how it is."

His mother?

Somehow I couldn't imagine Silver Gaines with a mother. He seemed like someone who sprang out of the sea foam, like Aphrodite or somebody.

I opened an album. There were a few pictures on the first three or four pages—studio portraits of Silver as a child, wearing the wide-sleeved Little Lord Fauntleroy shirt that Hank had mentioned when he'd introduced him at Eleuthera. His legs were as skinny as broomsticks, and his face was dead serious. He held his head coquettishly to one side.

"They always made me hold my head like that for pictures," he said, "to show off the streak."

It was true. In each of the studio portraits Silver posed in the same way, his head tilted as though he were listening to a faraway sound. They were kind of funny.

The rest of the album was blank. He leafed through the pages.

"It's the kind of thing a mother would do," he said. "Keep up a picture album. I was eight when I went on the road, without my mother, so the album stops there."

I placed it on the table and sifted through the rest of the pictures and paper. It was really fairly slim pickings. Many of the photographs were of Silver's family, none of them dancers. Others were duplicates of photographs I'd seen at Hank's or Miles's. I suspected he'd thrown out any pictures of himself with Lacey after they'd broken up.

Silver sensed my disappointment, which I tried to hide.

"That's all I have," he said. "Maybe Lacey can show you more. I seem to have been born without the sentimental portion of my brain."

The headline of a clipping from the *New York Times* caught my eye:

MAYOR APPOINTS COMMITTEE TO INVESTIGATE
SHOOTING DEATH OF PAUL MALONE; WITNESS ALLEGES
YOUTH WAS UNARMED WHEN FATAL SHOTS WERE FIRED.

Attached to the article, which was dated seven years earlier, was a picture of Silver, unmistakable because of his hair, standing in the doorway of his apartment—the building we were in now—with a caption that said:

Silver Gaines, who says that police interviewed him only after mounting pressure from the press and community, claims that Paul Malone had no gun and that the youth's arms were raised over his head when he was killed by a police bullet.

Silver watched me look at the clipping.

"That has nothing to do with dancing," he said. "That only has to do with being black."

There were other clippings in the same wad, from the *Times*, from the *Daily News*, from the *Amsterdam News*, and from the *Post*, having to do with the same event, some describing Gaines's allegations, others describing the investigation made by the committee. One showed head and shoulder portraits of three police officers under the headline: "COVER-UP CLEAR: HARROD, SILBER, AND CHILDRESS DISMISSED FROM FORCE." A *Daily News* article dated the same day showed the same three men, heads bowed, being escorted to a car. "DAY OF SHAME," it said. "HARROD PLACED GUN IN DEAD BOY'S HAND AT MORGUE FOR PRINTS."

I had a hazy recollection of the scandal: the idea of a cop plugging a defenseless kid—the wrong kid, as it turned out; the boy had sort of met the description of another boy who was reported to have robbed a drugstore—then taking an old gun from the police evidence vault and putting the corpse's prints on it, was harrowing enough that it stuck in my mind, although the details hadn't. I certainly hadn't made the Gaines connection.

"The boy was crying," said Silver. "He ran down an alley and he was crying. I was walking home from the center and saw everything. Harrod chased him into the alley, shot him, and covered him up with a blanket so nobody else could tell he didn't have a gun. Childress was in the squad car with him and they planned their scheme on the way to the precinct. Silber got them the gun from the evidence vault and Harrod brought it to the morgue. Others had to have been in on it as well. It was a highly choreographed conspiracy."

"Was it your testimony—" I began—

"My testimony was nothing," he said. "They refused to take even a statement from me until I went to the papers myself. Even the mayor's committee was a sham. Nothing really happened until Harrod's wife, who was planning to divorce him, decided to make life difficult for him. She tape-recorded Harrod talking with Childress about the gun, and Childress talking about destroying the original evidence records that went with the gun they had stolen from the police vault."

"These cops," I said, "—are they still around?"

He gave me a look that I was sure Nicole was familiar with. Contempt mingled with disbelief.

"Of course they're around. They should have gone to prison for life. A jury convicted all three, but the judge decided dismissal from the force and suspended sentences were enough. 'After what they've been through,' he said."

He shook his head and said it again, softly. "After what *they've* been through."

On that note I decided to call it a day. Or an evening; it was almost nine. I had a couple of good pictures of Silver with the snake at the zoo; that was enough. Both of us were tired from the heat and from trying to be polite to each other.

Gaines told me that I ought to put my Leica in the cooler for the ride home so I wouldn't look so "conspicuous," as he put it. In case he was baiting me I ignored the suggestion, slung the camera over my shoulder, and told him I'd be fine.

A block away from the building I hailed the first cab I saw and rode it home.

I was in bed, had just turned out the light, and was trying to decide whether it was too hot to pull the sheet up when the phone rang.

At first I couldn't make out the voice. It was kind of whispery.

"Hello," I said. "Who's calling, please?"

The voice was whispery again.

"Iris," she said. "Livvy, sweet, it's Iris."

"Can you speak up? I can't hear you."

"I'm in the bathroom," she said. "I don't want to wake up your father."

I laughed out loud. These two were nuts. Hiding from each other in a bathroom in an Atlantic City hotel. Like something out of a John Waters movie. Come to think of it, Divine would have made a very nice Iris.

"Iris," I said. "What do you want?"

"I want to get another chance to see you before we go back," she said. "I was so nervous yesterday—you know, the nervous bride!—that all I did was talk about myself. And what I really wanted to do was talk about *you!* I want to know all about you. Every little thing. Your boyfriends, your clothes—you know—what *you* think about things!"

I winced.

"Please don't say no," she said. "Please, please don't say no. I really want to spend a day shopping in New York. You know—Saks Fifth Avenue, Tiffany's—lunch at Rockefeller Center watching the ice skaters—"

I didn't have the heart to remind her that it wasn't mid-December. She went on.

"And all my life I've wanted a little girl. A daughter. I almost did once, Libby. A little girl. She was born dead. A 'stone baby,' my mother called her. Think of that. A 'stone baby.'"

She wasn't drunk. She was desperate.

"Sure, Iris," I said. "Sure, I'll go shopping with you." I would have promised to have mother-daughter dresses sewn for both of us if it would have made her stop talking about this "stone baby" business.

I tried to recollect what I had in the works for the next day. Meeting Hank in the morning for some final pictures—that was it, as far as I remembered. If I manufactured an appointment in the late afternoon I could keep the date with Iris down to about three or four hours.

"Iris," I said, "I've got something in the morning and something at five. I could meet you at one at—where do you want to go? Saks or someplace? Just inside the front entrance?"

"Wonderful!" she said.

"Does Dad want to come?" I sort of hoped so. Maybe he would put a chill on this cozy mother-daughter stuff.

"He said no, hon. He's beat. And besides, he wants us to have some time alone together. You know how he hates girl talk."

He can't hate it more than I do, I thought.

"See you," I said, and hung up.

7

IT WAS so hot that the water inside my snow-globe of the Seattle Space Needle had evaporated and the rubber bands that I keep on the darkroom doorknob had fused together in a doughnut.

I started the day at six A.M. by eating the bottom half of yesterday's yogurt—the part with the fruit in it—and trying to cancel the seven-thirty appointment I'd made with Hank Monsell at his studio. Like me, Hank had lately been trying to concentrate his work in the early morning to avoid the heat. But today, with the air-quality warning, I figured he'd cancel classes altogether, and I didn't want him to come downtown just on my account. It was the kind of thing he'd do, too. No matter how much he had to do—teaching, keeping the Nonpareils organized, fussing over the details of Eleuthera—he always made time for other people—even hangers-on like me.

Nicole answered the phone, and I apologized for waking her up.

"Don't you worry," she said, "it's all I do. Sleep. Sleep and sleep. The doctor says I've got to stay off my feet. Stay off my feet and sleep on my left side. I look like somebody pumped me up with a tire pump."

"Is Hank there?" I said. And spare me the details, I thought. I have a very low tolerance for pregnancy details.

"Hank?" she said, as though she'd never heard of him. "Hank? Let me go look."

She came back.

"I guess he's up and gone already," she said. "He's out of the bed and out of the house. I've been sleeping alone on the sofa bed in the living room. I can't fit in the bed with Hank anymore."

"Did he go to the studio?" I asked.

"I suppose," she said. "Do you want me to try and find him? I haven't seen him much in the past couple days; I guess I was already asleep when he got in last night. I'm sort of out of touch with what he's doing."

"No," I said. "Don't worry, it wasn't important."

"Honey?" she said.

"Yes?"

"Don't ever do this," she said. "I feel like I'll pop if somebody touches me. When I poke my leg with my finger, it leaves a dent. Really, don't ever do this."

"Nicole," I said, "please stop."

I gave Lucas a cold bath, which he hated, but which I figured would give him a few minutes of relief, then took him outside. Canal Street was already showing the effects of the strikers' refusal to make the early-morning pickup; the bags in front of the Happy Noodle factory, which I never really noticed before, stretched from the lightpost in front of the building to the corner. Some idiot runner passed us by, panting, purple in the face, ready to die, I supposed. My white tank top picked up specks of black soot as we walked, and my eyes burned as though I'd stayed up all night drinking.

On a hot day in Ohio, Lucas would have spent the day snoozing under a tree while Avery taught, or hanging out by the river while he fished. Here he pounded the steaming pavement while some lady chased after his backside with a plastic bag. Life can be full of disappointments, I thought, but what did this poor animal ever do to deserve this?

I decided to take him to Claire's at the beach for the night. Heck no, for as long as the stinking heat lasted. I could keep my date with Hank at the studio, have my rendezvous with Iris, go home and pack, and then drive out with Lucas at seven or so, after the commuter traffic thinned out. He could go for a swim. I could go for a swim. In the morning he could stay with her and I could come back.

I felt more energetic, cheerful even, as I took Lucas back to the loft and started out on my trek to Hank's studio. You know how it is—if my baby's happy, then I'm happy.

Even with two stops for iced coffee, I felt drained by the time I got to 14th Street. The short haircut was cool to a point. It also offered precious little protection from the sun; my scalp heated up like a light bulb.

Even though it seems to be caught in a perpetual downward economic spiral, 14th Street is one of my favorite streets in the city. Luchow's restaurant may have fled to midtown, but most of the stores on the blocks between Seventh Avenue and Union Square seem to have dug in their heels. The corner place that sold neon-colored Afro wigs and plastic luggage when I first came to New York still sells neon-colored Afro wigs and plastic luggage; Woolworth's is steadfast; Fayva's still offers the lowest prices on the ugliest shoes in the city. The sidewalks are wider here than on Canal Street, and there aren't as many NYU students as there are on 8th Street. Also, Bernard Goetz lives on 14th Street, or he did at the time the papers were talking about where Bernard Goetz lives, a fact that I find satisfying in an inexplicable way.

Hank's studio, which he called "The Hank Monsell Studio," was on the second floor of a turn-of-the century factory building between Sixth and Seventh avenues. A glazed terra-cotta frieze with a pattern of tools—hammers, wrenches, pliers, nails, and saws—ran across the facade between the first and second floors, dirty and chipped, but at one time beautiful, I was sure.

The building was a hive of marginal commercial activities. Monsell shared the second floor with a rubber-stamp manufacturer; the windows on the floor above the studio held signs for Painless Electrolysis, Palm Reading, and Hat Blocking.

I crossed to the north side of the street and framed a section of the building holding the frieze, three windows of the dance studio, and the electrolysis sign in my lens, then took a couple more of the palm-reading and hat-blocking windows.

I opened the front door, my spirits rising as I climbed the steps. It was the only time I'd been in the building that I hadn't been welcomed by an ever-increasing clatter of tapping feet as I approached the studio. Although I always enjoyed watching the classes, today the idea of having Hank to myself for an hour, to take pictures or just to talk, without a stream of interruptions from students asking for help fixing a shoe or cleaning up a new step, felt like a gift.

I opened the door and entered a vestibule where I would have hung my jacket if it had been a cool day.

The studio itself was an L-shape. The short side of the L was an office and small dance area; the long side was the large practice area, lined with mirrors at one end and containing an upright piano. A dressing room and bathroom filled the space between the two parts of the L.

I called out to Hank as I entered the smaller dance room, so he'd know I wasn't an intruder, but he didn't answer. Then I walked around the bend to the studio and gasped.

Hank lay on the floor, face-up, his hands clutching at the throat of his shirt. His face was puffy; his eyes were partly open.

I fell to my knees beside him.

"Hank, what's the matter? Are you all right?"

Even though I knew he wasn't.

I felt for his pulse and there wasn't one. His skin felt cool to my touch.

I felt disembodied—and strangely a little bit high. Like I'd had a drink on an empty stomach or like I had a really high fever. I heard a siren go by on the street beneath the windows, and I swatted at a fly that walked across Hank's hand.

I tilted back his head and lay my mouth on top of his, thinking briefly and stupidly that I could revive him. An odor that for some reason struck me as the odor of rotten vegetables reached my nostrils, and I drew back.

He was dead. No doubt about it.

A phrase entered my head: "Over the river." I heard someone say that about a dead person once. "Over the river."

The record player on Hank's desk, a small green plastic one, had finished playing whatever it was playing long ago; now the arm slid crazily back and forth over the grooveless center of the LP.

I kept talking out loud to Hank, describing my actions, which somehow made the situation seem more real than not talking did.

"I'll turn off the record player, Hank," I said. "I can't stand that sound."

And, "I'll call 911, Hank. They'll know what to do."

And, "Oh God, Hank, what am I going to tell Nicole?"

I heard myself talking to the 911 operator, and heard the little beep that shows they're recording the call. She asked me if he was breathing and if I felt a pulse. "No," I said, "and no." I told her he smelled bad and he was cold and he was dead.

She told me someone would be there soon.

The cops and the medics came at the same time. One of the medics tried to pry Hank's mouth open with a tongue depressor but it didn't work, and another felt for his pulse. They tilted him on his side, then let him roll again to his back. One of his shirt buttons popped open; his trousers twisted awkwardly around his shins.

I turned away.

"Cardiac arrest," he said. "He's been dead a while."

I remembered how Hank had looked on opening night at Eleuthera. How I had wondered if he were sick.

The man talked into his radio.

"Eighty-three," he said.

Another one turned to me with a clipboard.

"Relative?" he said.

"What?"

"Are you a relative?"

"No," I said. "A friend. He has a wife. And a brother. I think we should call his brother first. His wife is pregnant. This is going to be horrible."

I leafed through Hank's phone book until I found Miles's number.

"Miles," I said, "This is Libby Kincaid. I have bad news." My voice shook. I hoped I wasn't about to get hysterical.

"Hank's had a heart attack," I said. "He's dead. He's in his studio. You're going to have to tell Nicole."

There was a long silence, then a long sigh.

"I'll be there," he said. "I'll be there as soon as I can."

I told the cops that Miles was on his way.

They told me a doctor would be there in about an hour to fill out the official report. I asked if they could move Hank's body to the couch at the end of the room; somehow I thought it might keep Miles from having such a jolt.

They did. Then they put a blanket over him and left.

I thought about going out to get some fresh air. Then I remembered that the air outside wasn't fresh. I also didn't have a key to lock the door, and I didn't want one of Hank's students to show up and have the same welcome I had.

I sat at Hank's desk and looked at his blanketed body. He looked smaller dead than he had alive, but maybe he wasn't all that big in the first place. Maybe he was just one of those people who strike you as big because they're so exuberant. So alive.

I had liked him very much. Sure, he was loudmouthed, and pompous sometimes, and liked to talk about himself. But he also was generous, kindhearted, and devoted to his work. And he also got things done—lots of things—and I like people who get things done.

I wondered if I should call Silver and tell him what had happened, then decided I shouldn't. The Nonpareils's friendship was something deep and exclusive. I was what a photographer usually was. An intruder. Miles could take care of relaying the news.

To feel like I was doing something and to avoid seeing Hank I looked at the record albums stored on utility shelving behind Hank's desk. Next to them was an enormous black scrapbook full of clippings and pictures—one of the scrapbooks that we had used for lots of the graphics on the Eleuthera promotional materials.

Eleuthera. The show. What would happen now?

Poor Duncan. I supposed I should call him and I didn't want to. I wondered if Claire should be with him.

The medical examiner and Miles arrived at the same time. Jerome Junior, whom Miles must have called, followed a couple of minutes later.

Miles talked quietly with the doctor, while the doctor filled out a form. I heard them talking about undertakers.

I waited for them to finish, then approached Miles.

"I'm sorry," I said. "I'm very sorry. But I wanted you to know that when I got here the record player was on, and he was on the floor next to it. He died dancing. I thought you would want to know."

Miles walked to the record player, looked at it, then turned back to me. His voice was very quiet, like it always was.

"I'm sorry to say it," he said, "but I knew it was coming. He passed out at rehearsal a couple of weeks ago, and again when we were waiting for a bus. He wouldn't go to a doctor, but he said he'd wait until after Eleuthera opened. I tried to get him to stop—to rest—in this heat. I told Nicole he shouldn't be dancing. I told everybody. But no, they said, whatever Hank says goes."

He looked over at the blanketed body on the couch, shook his head sadly, and said it again: "Whatever Hank says goes."

Jerome sat in a folding chair by the window, his head in his hands. The doctor talked in a low voice on the phone. I stood dumbly by the wall, unable to discern whether I was wanted or unwanted, but suspecting that no one would mind if I left.

I looked at the couch again.

"Wait a minute," I said. "If he died dancing, then where are his shoes?"

Miles and Jerome followed my gaze to Hank's feet, which were wearing pale yellow socks.

I looked under the sofa, then scanned the floor of the studio.

"So where are they?" I said. "What happened to his shoes?"

I tried to remember if he'd had them on his feet when I'd found him.

No, he hadn't. I remembered watching one of Hank's socks slide down beneath his ankle bone as the medic tilted his body.

I looked behind the desk. Miles looked in the desk.

No shoes.

Jerome looked in the front vestibule. I looked in the bathroom.

No shoes.

I looked in the dressing room. Some spare shoes, but they were ladies'—not Hank's.

Miles lifted a plastic drawstring bag from the floor next to the piano and looked inside. He pulled out a pair of beige loafers.

"His street shoes," he said. "The shoes he wore to get here."

There was nowhere else to look. Except for the mess of papers and record albums on the shelves behind Hank's desk, he kept the place as streamlined as Silver Gaines's apartment. To discourage thieves, I supposed.

I walked over to Hank's body and stared at his feet. There was a dark mark on the sole of Hank's right sock, roughly where the ball of his foot was. It was a little larger than a quarter, and elongated.

I touched the mark.

The fabric felt stiff.

"What's this?" I said. "It looks like blood."

Miles and Jerome came over.

Miles plucked at the sock. It adhered to Hank's foot at the dark spot.

The doctor, who had finished with his phone call, came over to see what we were doing. Then he reached over and tugged the sock down over Hank's heel and off his foot, yanking hard when he came to the stuck part.

I shuddered. Hank's foot, a dancer's foot, was monstrous-looking. It looked like someone had slammed it repeatedly with a two-by-four, then squeezed it all back into a foot shape. But then, isn't that what tap dancing is? Slamming your feet against the wood floor, slamming a piece of wood against your feet—what's the difference?

The foot had no arch; the first joint of the big toe protruded wildly outward, sending the toe back in to meet the others at a forty-five-degree angle. The rest of his toes were recognizable as toes only because they ended in toenails; the toe bodies were distended into the shape of small plums.

In the course of my picture-taking I had seen other dancers' naked feet. It was unavoidable. Lacey took her shoes off and massaged her feet constantly while she was practicing; they were as battered and calloused as tree roots. Miles spent as much time out of his tap shoes as he did in them—letting his feet "breathe," he said—and that sight was no treat, either. But the foot that rested in this doctor's hand was something beyond the typical tap-dancer's appendage. It was horrific.

The doctor prodded and squeezed the skin on Hank's sole. Then he took a metal thing out of his bag and poked some more. Then he put Hank's sock back on him and looked at me.

"Did you see any snakes in here when you found him?"

"What?"

"We'll have to confirm this," he said, "but Mr. Monsell appears to have been bitten by a snake. Have you noticed one in the building?"

The feeling of unreality that overcame me when I'd first found Hank started to creep up on me again.

"Of course not," I said. "A fly, though. I did see a fly." Stop talking, I told myself. You sound wacky.

He turned to Miles.

"Your brother," he said, "did he keep snakes?"

"What are you talking about?" he said. "Of course he didn't keep snakes."

The doctor ripped up the form he had completed and started to fill out a new one.

"I'm afraid," he said, "that we'll have to take Mr. Monsell's body to the police morgue for an autopsy so we can be absolutely certain of the cause of death."

He started talking on the phone again.

Miles was standing still, looking out the window, shaking his head slowly from side to side. I asked him if there was anything I could do for him.

He continued shaking his head.

"No," he said. "What is he talking about? This is unbelievable."

I could hear Jerome retching in the bathroom.

"Miles," I said, "when you talk to Nicole tell her how sorry I am. Tell her I'll come see her in a little bit. I've got to be someplace."

Someplace like on the beach with Lucas. Someplace where somebody I knew wasn't lying dead on the sofa and smelling funny.

A pretty woman with a pair of red tap shoes in her hands was coming up the stairs as I went down. I grabbed her by the arm.

"You don't want to go in there," I said. "No classes today."

She pushed ahead of me anyway and I continued down the stairs. As I stepped out onto the sidewalk I heard her running down the stairs behind me. I moved to the side to let her pass.

"Oh my God, oh my God, oh my God," she was saying.

The police ambulance pulled to the curb.

My sentiments exactly.

8

I COULDN'T bear the idea of being home alone. I certainly couldn't bear the idea of printing any dancer pictures—especially pictures of Hank.

Much as I belittle office life, much as I prefer to work solo, there are times when I crave seeing familiar faces, hearing shop talk, and remembering that I have a slot in the world. This was one of those times. So I took the bus up Sixth Avenue to the building that houses *Americans* on 48th Street.

The ride took twice as long as it should have because they were ripping apart the asphalt in the right-hand lane from 26th to 28th, and there was some kind of accident in Herald Square. I sat in the back of the bus, trying to avoid being hit by a baby stroller that staggered back and forth across the aisle with the bus's movements—trying to make myself relax.

I couldn't get the smell of Hank's body or the memory of his foot—how it rested in the doctor's hand and how the doctor had held it, as though it were a curio he was thinking about adding to his collection—out of my mind. I'd seen dead bodies before—one of my cousins had been displayed in an open coffin, and I'd been involved in an accident where a man had died—but I'd never just bumped into one.

A snake bite? I wondered briefly if I had imagined that the medical examiner said that.

What was this with snakes all of a sudden? I hadn't given them a thought since elementary school, and in the last twenty-four hours I'd spent an hour in a reptile house and a friend on the other side of the city had been killed by one.

Could Silver have anything to do with it? I mean, could he have left a snake at Hank's by mistake or something? It seemed ridiculous.

A dumb image kept invading my mind's eye: a drawing in my Girl Scout handbook that showed how to make an X with a knife over a snake bite as a preliminary to sucking the poison from the wound, with the instruction not to attempt this if you had a sore in your mouth. It gave me the creeps then and it gave me the creeps now.

So maybe the doctor was just wrong. Or maybe he was nuts. Or maybe he was just trying to torment us. They'd do the autopsy and they'd find out that Hank had stepped on a nail or something.

Right. There were probably a couple of nails sticking out of the floorboard and Hank happened to step on them, or dance on them, right before he collapsed from a heart attack. Weirder things have happened.

But the shoes? Where were they?

And Nicole. What would the news do to her? She'd sounded so needy, so—exposed—on the phone this morning. What would it do to the baby?

The bus got clogged in traffic again by Bryant Park. I got out and walked the rest of the way to 48th Street, picking my way between the sidewalk garbage and the pedestrians who hugged the store side of the sidewalk as they walked, trying to avoid being too near the bags. At the corner of 45th and Fifth a huge blue plastic sack toppled off its stack and split open, sending a stream of soft drink cans and rotten fruit across the sidewalk. I tacked my way through the spill, holding my breath.

After that, walking into the *Americans* lobby—thirty-seven stories over 48th Street—was bliss. It was like walking into an immersion tank, or what I imagine an immersion tank might be like. The lights were low; the air was cool. The place vibrated with soothing, familiar electronic office sounds: the faint throb of the air-conditioning system, the soft click and whine of the photocopying machine in the alcove behind the receptionist, the muffled chirping of her computer keyboard, the beam-me-up whistle of her laser printer as she engaged its motor. There were no snakes here and no dead men.

I walked through the editorial department without seeing anyone I knew; the people who had decided they could stick out the heat wave had succumbed to the garbage wave and fled to the country, I supposed. The editorial assistants, who started and left their jobs so fast that I'd stopped trying to learn their names, looked pale and tired.

People in the art department had gotten into the habit of cramming phone messages for me on a spindle in the research library, next to the photo lab. Today, for the first time in my twelve years at the magazine, the spindle was bare. I looked in the tray that was supposed to serve as my mailbox. It had three interoffice communications about how to use the new phone system, a brochure describing what was covered on our new employee health plan, or more precisely, what wasn't covered on our new employee health plan, and a terse memo from the man who runs the supply room reminding us how expensive Post-Its are. No real mail.

LaDonna Knoblock, a researcher who had been at the magazine for as long as I had, resolutely checking facts and researching the arcane for writers and editors, watched me study my naked spindle.

"They just stopped coming," she said. "The phone messages, I mean."

"What about the magazines?"

"Octavia said to cross off your name when they came around to you because they'd just go down the black hole."

"The black hole? That's what she said?" I was getting nervous. There's nothing like coming somewhere for a little comfort and finding out you've been turned into a nonperson. Maybe I should have been checking in more often. Maybe every week.

"Libby," she said. "She just meant that because you weren't here there was no sense circulating them to you because they'd just pile up and nobody else would see them. Besides, nobody knows if you're going to be coming back."

I forced myself to smile patiently.

"LaDonna," I said. "Please, I don't need it."

Most people at the magazine, including me, thought of LaDonna as a necessary annoyance. She was abrupt, rude, and had a nasty propensity to tell people that they looked awful, or sick, or really tired, when in reality they looked just fine. She was partly antisocial and mostly asocial; she was oblivious to the world of please, thank you, instant smiles, social banter, and appropriate clothing.

When she was interested in hearing what other people were talking about, she just walked over and stood next to them, listening obviously, instead of eavesdropping, like the rest of us would. When she was done talking to you on the phone, she didn't close the conversation; she just hung up.

She had stayed at *Americans* for as long as she had for two reasons: She was a niece of one of the owners, and she had a photographic memory. If you asked her if she remembered in which issue we'd run a photograph of Frank Zappa as a child, she could tell you, right off the top of her head, not just the date of the issue but what page the picture had appeared on and its position on that page. It was kind of wonderful and kind of eerie.

Because we'd both started at the magazine at the same time, and probably because I have a soft spot for misfits, we were more or less friendly with each other. Still, there were some days when I could put up with her behavior better than others, and today wasn't one of them.

She walked over to me, stood a little bit closer than most people would consider acceptable, and peered into my face.

"God, Libby, what's wrong with you? You look terrible! Like you're really sick or something."

I instinctively put my hand up to smooth my hair that wasn't there anymore. This time she wasn't making the comment just for the momentary thrill of making me feel bad. This time she was right. I felt woozy from the image of Hank that kept floating through my mind's eye, woozy from death, woozy from the heat, woozy from how long ago I had that half a yogurt for breakfast.

I didn't want to tell her about Hank. I was afraid she'd make a crack and I'd dissolve.

"It's the air out there," I said. "It burns my eyes."

"God," she said. "Go buy some sunglasses or something."

She stared at me while I snooped at the other spindles on the counter, thinking that maybe someone had put my messages in the wrong place by mistake.

"Well," she said, "are you?"

"Am I what?"

"Coming back?"

"Of course I'm coming back. I'm not even gone. I'm just on a leave. You know, like maternity leave. Like sick leave. You know—you go, and then you come back."

I looked at the calendar push-pinned on the wall next to the coffee machine.

"In six weeks," I said. "In just six more weeks."

She smiled.

"Good," she said. "I really miss you a lot."

Her expression looked so sincere that it caught me off guard. I couldn't bring myself to tell her that I missed her, because I didn't.

"Thanks," I said. "It'll be nice to be back."

Her face took on its usual hostile cast.

"Of course," she said, "Octavia's been talking about a couple of new photographers she'd like to see here. One of them's related to Charles Lindbergh."

"Swell," I said. "I'd better go get my strength up."

"What are you doing for lunch?" she said.

Lunch. Something was tugging on my internal schedule. Wasn't I supposed to be doing something at lunchtime?

Iris! I couldn't. I just couldn't. I sat down at the desk behind LaDonna's and called Windsor's Castle. I could tell her I was sick. Heck, I could tell her the truth. I could tell her a friend just died.

"Sorry!" said the receptionist, in a British accent that I suspected was, like everything else at Windsor's Castle, phony. "Mr. and Mrs. Kincaid checked out this morning."

It was useless. She was probably on her way into the city already. And Max was probably making bad use of his spare time in the casino.

LaDonna was hanging out of her carrel.

"I can't have lunch with you," I said. "I'm meeting somebody else."

"Who's Mrs. Kincaid?" she said.

I tried the Silver Gaines technique and pretended I didn't hear her.

I called Claire at the beach to tell her I'd be coming out tonight, and to tell her about Hank so she could tell Duncan if she talked with him before I did. There was no answer.

I called Duncan's office and got his assistant, Dee, who told me that, as usual, he was in a meeting.

LaDonna started playing with my camera case.

"Please don't," I said.

"Duncan," she said. "Isn't that Claire's boyfriend?"

"Yep," I said—sharply, I guessed, because she shrank back into her carrel with a hurt look on her face.

I don't like to do things like that to people.

"I'm sorry," I said. "I didn't mean to sound that way. I'm just having a really bad day."

"Tell me about it," she said. "I have them every day."

I supposed she did.

9

IRIS WAS standing in the middle of the sidewalk in front of Saks Fifth Avenue, hip deep in a heap of shopping bags, suitcases, and garment bags. She was wearing a white silk jumpsuit with a lace heart inset on the chest and white cork-heeled sandals with clear vinyl straps over the instep. On her head she wore a yellow straw hat the size of a dish antenna, which was tied under her chin with a rose-colored ribbon. Pedestrians buffeted her from every side, assaulting her with hostile stares, but she remained steadfast, scanning the sidewalk for me.

Before I let her know I was there, I stepped back into the street and took a picture of her. I don't know why; I just had a feeling I'd want it some day. While I was taking a second shot she caught sight of me and threw me a kiss.

An elderly man in a seersucker suit kicked her biggest suitcase, snarled something, and kept on walking.

"Iris," I said, "what are you doing with all this stuff? We can't walk around with it. We've got to get rid of it."

"Livvy, honey," she said. "I don't know. I really didn't think I had all that much."

"Why didn't you leave it with Max?"

"He was mad."

"Why was he mad?"

"Because I had so much stuff! He told me to take it myself and meet him at the airport."

I figured we could take a taxi back to *Americans* and stash it there while we had lunch. I raised my hand for a cab.

"But honey," she said, "we're at Saks Fifth Avenue! I promised my girlfriend something from Saks Fifth Avenue!"

"Okay," I said. "Here's what we can do. We can drag it over here by the front door and I can watch it while you shop."

"But I wanted to shop with you!"

"It's okay, honest. I've been in there a million times. I'll go someplace else with you after lunch."

It wasn't the truth. It wasn't even near the truth. I'd been in Saks exactly once, over ten years ago, and had been so intimidated by the salesclerk that I left before she could ring up the sale. It's not my favorite place.

She disappeared into the store and I stood guard over her things. She had one of those suitcases meant only for cosmetics, two monster Samsonite suitcases with wheels attached to them, two garment bags, three paper shopping bags with pink tissue foaming out of the tops, and a hatbox, for crying out loud.

I pride myself on being able to pack for a week in one bag—one very small bag—and search obsessively for micro travel accessories: the six-inch telescoping umbrella, the alarm clock the size of a saltine, the tiny tube of Vaseline that serves as lip balm, hand cream, mascara, and shoe polish. I had the same pang of revulsion looking at Iris's baggage that an anorectic would have looking at a six-course meal.

Ten minutes went by, then twenty. I took some pictures of the traffic. Then I grabbed the shopping bags and the makeup case, took a gamble that even the most craven New Yorker wouldn't want to drag off a forty–pound suitcase in this heat, and went inside. Iris stood at a counter near the center of the store, her back to me, her hat flapping energetically as she spoke to the clerk.

"Madam," he said, "we can do no such thing. It's against store policy and against the law."

"What's going on?" I asked.

Iris turned to me. Her face was flushed.

"Livvy," she said, "I'm so embarrassed."

Another clerk, or maybe it was a manager, walked toward us.

"Do we have a problem?"

The counter clerk gestured toward Iris.

"She suggested that we mail an empty box to her home to avoid adding sales tax to her purchase. I told her that it was impossible."

"God, Iris, did you?" I said.

"I did no such thing," she said.

A couple of other customers were lurking behind us, trying to catch the drift of the situation. A security guard was walking manfully toward us from the front of the store.

"Look," I said. "My mother has decided that she doesn't want to buy the scarf after all, and we'd both be happy to walk right out of the store and never come back. Is that okay with you?"

I didn't wait for an answer. I grabbed Iris by the arm and steered her out of the store without looking back. Then I hauled her luggage to the curb and hailed a cab.

I didn't know what to say. She didn't know what to say. I decided to pretend the incident never happened.

"Look, Iris," I said. "Everybody makes mistakes. Let's forget about it."

She was sniffling. She tried to lay her head on my shoulder, but the hat wouldn't let her.

"I'm so embarrassed," she said. "The scarf was for you. I wanted so much to impress you."

She dabbed her cheeks with a Kleenex.

"And you called me 'mother.'"

I decided not to point out that I hadn't called her mother; I had merely referred to her as mother in hope that the store manager would take some pity on me as the daughter of a crazy person.

Harry Medak, the check-in security guard at the building where *Americans* is, has worked there for ten years. I knew that he had a recurring problem with kidney stones. I knew that his son was majoring in filmmaking at NYU. I knew that he would do me a favor and stash Iris's stuff in a utility closet for a couple of hours. I directed the cab driver to the building and cut a deal with Harry.

I was at a loss as to where I'd take her for lunch in midtown. I doubted that my favorite spots—Chock Full O'Nuts and Dosanko's Noodle House—would fulfill her expectations of a glamorous afternoon. So I steered her to Rockefeller Center and down the steps to the restaurant where, if it were winter, we could have watched the Christmas tree and the skaters. As it was, we got a table with a view of somebody polishing the sculpture of Prometheus, a vaguely erotic experience.

"You look tired, dear," she said.

I didn't want to tell her anything about Hank's death, or my life. I felt an overwhelming desire to erect an unperturbable wall between her life and mine. On Sunday, when I thought I'd be rid of her in three hours, I had mustered up the resources to view her with more or less detached amusement. Today I didn't have the energy. Today I wanted her gone.

"Sore throat," I said. "Maybe strep. Maybe hepatitis. The tests aren't back."

Sometimes I really surprise myself with how easily these little lies can hop off my tongue. I wonder if it's Max coming out in me.

Not that she was listening.

She plunged immediately into her monologue—a long description of a trip she'd taken to New York with her father when she was a child, including how they'd gone to a restaurant with telephones at every table, followed by a long description of a certain kind of pin she was hoping to buy for her girlfriend, followed by a long, cheerful indictment of the prevalence of illegal drugs in modern society—taking time out only to order.

By the time the burgers came I was reliving the morning at Hank's. I gagged at the sight of the meat, covered the thing with my napkin, and sawed at the tomato slice so I'd look like I was doing something.

Blessed silence fell. Then I realized that she was looking at me expectantly.

"Well," she said. "What do you think?"

"About what?"

"The family tree idea."

"I'm sorry, Iris, I sort of blanked out for a minute. What about the family tree idea?"

"For your father's birthday. I need you to help me. I thought I'd make him a pillow with his family tree embroidered on it. Well, not me, really. My girlfriend. She sort of does it on the side. Embroidery. Well, not really embroidery. *Liquid* embroidery. It comes in little tubes with ball points on them and you color it right on the cloth. Really, it's nicer than regular embroidery."

"It would be kind of small," I said.

"What?"

"The tree. It would be more like a bush. He doesn't have any brothers or sisters. His father didn't have any brothers or sisters. I don't think that even *he* knows his grandparents' names, because they died before he was born. My brother is dead, and I'm not likely to have any children."

I noticed that I was tracing the imaginary genealogy on the table-cloth with my finger.

"Heck, Iris," I said, "it wouldn't even be like a bush. It would be more like a blade of grass."

Her elbows were on the table, she was holding her hands together, and she rested her chin on them in some kind of corny high school portrait pose. She tilted her head to one side.

"Pretty please," she said. "I need the dates, I do. It would mean so much to me. That stuff about astrology I was talking about Sunday? I was just trying to keep Max from knowing I was doing this. I'm sorry. I really am. You must think I'm some kind of kook."

Pretty please, I thought. I can't bear this. I knew I was supposed to tell her that I didn't think she was a kook, but I couldn't bring myself to give her the satisfaction.

"Okay," I said. "I gave you some at dinner Sunday. What else do you need?"

"I need your grandparents' birth and death dates."

"Max's parents? I don't have any idea. Ask him."

"It's a surprise."

"And your mother's birth date."

Good grief, I thought. Not that again.

She took off her glasses. Her eyes were brimming with tears.

"Okay," I said. "Sure. It was March 17, 1928. St. Patrick's Day."

She took the little spiral-bound notebook out of her pocketbook that she had taken out in the casino restaurant and wrote down the date.

"And?" she said.

"And what?"

"When did she die?"

"You need that?"

"Of course I do. It's a family tree. They always have dates people died."

I supposed they did.

"Okay," I said. "The same day."

"The same day?"

"The same day. St. Patrick's day. Except 1969."

"How odd," she said.

Odd maybe. But I had always appreciated the symmetry of it. Like Thomas Jefferson dying on the Fourth of July.

"Got it?" I said.

She wrote it down.

"You're wonderful," she said.

I took her to Tiffany's and watched while she bought her girlfriend a pin shaped like a lopsided heart. She paid cash, and she didn't bother the clerk with the sales tax scheme.

Then we went into a drugstore and she bought herself a big

black-and-white bow attached to a hair comb that she stabbed into her ponytail then and there.

"Isn't it sweet?" she said.

She seemed very happy. Bucolic even.

By three-thirty I couldn't stand anymore. I told her that I needed to get back downtown and that we'd have to get her suitcases back from Harry Medak before his shift ended. She complied cheerfully.

We collected the suitcases and I packed them and her into a cab aimed at La Guardia.

Before she was all the way in she grabbed me and gave me a kiss on the lips.

"Darling," she said. "Daughter. This is the happiest day of my life."

The cabby snorted and rolled his eyes.

I ran like a sprung woman toward the IRT.

10

FORGET OVERNIGHT at the beach, I thought. Forget taking pictures. Forget Eleuthera. I've got to get out of this place. For a few days. For a week. For maybe longer.

Even in the loft I could smell the garbage on the street. Was it possible? Five stories up? Or was I just remembering the smell in Hank's studio?

I gagged.

I stuffed some shirts and underwear into a bag, then went to work on Lucas—his leash, brush, dog shampoo, biscuits, Purina, rubber squeaky elephant, and the special towel he sleeps with. He panted excitedly by the door, knowing we were going away.

I reached for the phone to try Claire again, but it rang just as I touched it.

It was an unfamiliar male voice.

"Mrs. Kincaid?"

"This is Libby Kincaid."

"My name is Andrew Elkind. I'm an attorney representing a man you know. Silver Gaines."

What's wrong with Silver? I thought. I figured vaguely that it must have something to do with that police business he'd spoken about on Sunday. I quickly submerged the thought that the call might have something to do with Hank's death.

"Why are you calling me?"

"I don't want to alarm you, but unfortunately Mr. Gaines has been arrested."

"Arrested? What for?"

"He's been charged with murder. Second-degree murder."

The image of Hank's foot erupted again in my mind's eye. My hands went clammy.

"From what I understand, you were also friendly with the man Mr. Gaines has been accused of killing—a man named Howard Monsell."

"Hank," I said. "Hank Monsell. He died this morning. I was there. I mean, I found him dead."

"I didn't know that," he said.

Wait a minute. Was I telling him too much? Could this be some kind of hoax? Some kind of setup? I've lived in New York so long that I think about these possibilities easily and for no reason.

"What are you talking about?" I said. "Why would Silver be arrested?"

"That's what he and I have spent the past hour trying to figure out."

"Where is he?" I asked.

"Here, of course," he said.

"Where's here?"

"One Police Plaza," he said. "He probably won't be arraigned until morning at least."

God, I thought. What if Silver really did do it?

"What do you want from me?"

"We don't know many details yet," he said. "But as I understand it, the police are suggesting the seemingly incredible scenario that my client arranged to have a poisonous snake bite Mr. Monsell. And I understand that the police claim to have a witness who says he saw a man who looked like Silver Gaines leaving Mr. Monsell's dance studio at a time that more or less coincides with the medical examiner's estimated time of death. This is all rather vague, I know."

Elkind's voice faded; then I heard the muffled sound of him speaking sharply to someone else.

"I'm sorry," he said.

He had an unusual accent. Scottish, maybe. Australian, maybe. One of those.

So where did I fit in?

I asked again, "So what do you want from me?"

What did Gaines do? Tell this guy I was his next of kin?

"And a detective I've been talking to told me that the medical examiner's preliminary report is probably going to give an estimated time of death of between six and nine o'clock last night. From stomach contents, the degree of rigor—that sort of thing."

He paused.

"Are you there?" he said.

"Sort of," I said.

I was trying to remember what the medic had said about how long he thought Hank had been dead. A while, I think he said. A while was all.

"Did Silver tell you that I was with him yesterday? Is that why you're calling me?"

I tried to replay the events of the previous afternoon in my mind.

I'd gotten to the zoo just before five—I knew that much because I'd been concerned that the gates would be closed at five and I wouldn't get in. And I'd left Silver's apartment a little before nine. It had gotten dark as I took the cab ride home.

"That is why I'm calling you," he said. "You are what we call my client's alibi witness. I'd like to have a written statement from you while the times are still fresh in your mind. People have a tendency to forget details like that with the passage of time."

"Do you want me to come there?"

"No, I don't want you to come here. Where are you, anyway?"

"Canal Street," I said.

"Good," he said. "I can stop off on my way home. I'll be there in forty minutes. I need to talk with someone else first."

I told him where he'd be most likely to find a parking space and hung up.

Lucas was stymied by the delay. He gets all excited when I get his leash out.

"Don't worry, fella," I said. "We'll be out of here in a jiff."

I added a couple of tee-shirts to my bag and washed the dishes that were in the sink. My hands shook so hard that when I lifted the glasses from the counter to the sink the spoons rattled around.

This is craziness, I thought. Of course Silver didn't have anything to do with Hank dying. Silver was with me, for crying out loud. Besides, if he were going to kill somebody, why would he do it with a snake? For Gaines, that was almost as good as leaving a business card.

But was there a reason that he'd made such a big deal out of his friendship with Hank when he was talking with me? What if the medical examiner had his times wrong? This Elkind guy called it a preliminary report, didn't he?

The doorbell rang.

There must be no traffic, I thought. The guy must have flown.

I buzzed him up and arranged my camera, suitcase, and Lucas's bag by the door. I'd talk to Elkind for five minutes and be out of here.

The elevator groaned and lurched its way up. I hollered at the door, which usually has the effect of echoing down the shaft.

"Don't worry. You're almost here."

It locked into place on five.

"Just open it up," I said.

Nobody did.

I looked into the elevator through the little glass porthole laced with chicken wire. The guy who looked back was no lawyer. He didn't have on a three-piece suit, and he wasn't carrying a briefcase.

It was a cop. No, two cops. A lady cop and a man cop. One of them banged on the elevator door.

I started to open it, but one of them held it closed.

My heart jumped like a fish. I figured they were here to tell me somebody died. Max, most likely.

The man cop started talking.

"Is this Olivia Kincaid?"

"Yes."

"You're under arrest for murder," he said. Then he let go of the handle.

I opened the door. What choice did I have?

Also, I didn't really believe he was going to arrest me. I hadn't done anything wrong. And I've always sort of liked New York cops. They have hard jobs. Lay their lives on the line.

Lucas started to bark.

They drew their guns.

I grabbed Lucas by the collar.

"Down boy," I said. "It's okay."

Lucas growled and bared his teeth.

The guy aimed at Lucas.

"God!" I screamed. "Don't shoot him!"

"Look," I said. "Let me put him in the bathroom."

Lucas dug his hind paws into the floor and I dragged him across the floor to the bathroom. The cop followed three feet behind us. I shoved Lucas inside and pulled the door shut.

When I turned around, the woman, who had a face like a

teenaged beauty queen and biceps like Hulk Hogan's, grabbed me, pulled my arms behind my back, and slammed handcuffs on me. The sound—of metal locking against metal—was like no sound I'd ever heard before. As loud as a car crash and as final as the drop of a coffin lid.

"This is crazy," I said. "Somebody's made a mistake. I'm a photographer. I work for *Americans* magazine. I didn't do anything wrong."

Nobody listened. In fact, they went about their business as though I were an inanimate object. Like an illegally parked car they were towing away.

The guy cop pulled out a little card and started reading from it.

I was entitled to an attorney. If I couldn't afford one the court would appoint one for me, and so on and so on and so on.

"An attorney?" I said. "What do I need an attorney for? I didn't do anything!"

I thought about screaming for help, then realized that the help I was likely to get would be more cops.

Maybe, I thought, if I stalled them, that Elkind guy would show and he could get me out of this.

"Hey," I said. "Do you guys want some ice water? Iced coffee?"

What kind of idiot am I?

The woman gestured toward my suitcase and Lucas's things by the front door.

"Lookit," she said. "She was all set to go."

Lucas whimpered and scratched at the bathroom door. The guy cop lifted the lid on the footlocker that I keep blankets and stuff in and use for a table. The stack of magazines that was on top slid to the floor. He looked inside and slammed the lid down.

"Hey!" I said. "That's mine! You can't just go through my stuff!"

He reached into the bag I'd packed and pulled out my white tank top. Lucas's brush, elephant, and shampoo rolled out on the floor. Then he stuffed the shirt into his pocket.

"Where's your washer?" he said.

For an absurd moment I thought he wanted to put the shirt in the washer.

"Hey," I said, "it's clean."

He walked into the kitchen part of the loft and yanked open the flimsy door that concealed the puny washer-dryer combination that I'd bought myself for a Christmas present.

He opened the washer lid.

"Roaches," he said.

Was I supposed to apologize or something?

He started opening the cabinets and looking inside. Just opening them; not closing them. The cabinet where Claire keeps spices, the cabinet where we keep the cereal, the cabinet where I throw the little leftover packets of Chinese mustard and soy sauce. Then he opened the cabinet under the sink and yanked out the picnic cooler that I'd taken to Silver Gaines's, dragging a box of detergent with it that fell on the floor, spilling a drift of white powder across the linoleum.

"Hey!" I said. "Can you cut it out? My roommate will kill me!"

Weird, isn't it? They were dragging me off to jail and I was worried about the kitchen floor. The denial mechanism is a marvelous thing.

He tipped the cooler lid open, frowned, and closed it again.

He nodded to the lady cop.

"That's it," he said.

"The cooler? You want my cooler?"

"Let's take her in."

"Wait a minute," I said. "My lawyer—he's going to be here any minute. Honest."

"Right," he said.

The lady cop shoved me toward the elevator door. My right arm, which I had broken the year before and which still hadn't resumed its full range of movement, was throbbing.

Where was this Elkind guy?

"Lucas," I said. "My dog. I don't know if he has enough water in there." I couldn't remember when I'd filled his bowl last.

I addressed this to the lady cop. I figured she might have a soft spot for babies and animals or something.

"It's a bathroom, isn't it?" she said. "There's plenty of water in bathrooms."

Then she bumped me ever so slightly behind the knee with her own knee, the way mean kids do when they want to torment somebody. I sank slightly and gasped; she yanked me back up again.

This was definitely not good-cop/bad-cop. This was bad-cop/bad-cop.

Lucas started to howl. I started to cry.

"Lucas sweetie," I said, "I'll be back in a minute!"

Right.

11

WHEN I REMEMBER being booked, three images overwhelm the rest: a yellow fluorescent lamp that hung like a broken car muffler from the ceiling over the booking desk, making a continuous buzzing sound that didn't seem to bother anybody but me; a streak of something dark brown on the countertop that looked like dried blood even though I kept telling myself it must be icing from a doughnut; and the sight of my two hands, spread wide and side by side on that same counter—the way you hold them in the handprint pictures you make for your parents in Sunday school—except this time they were held together at the wrist by metal bracelets.

I remember thinking while the woman took each of my fingers and pressed them hard against an inkpad and then onto a piece of paper that the hands looked like someone else's—that my knuckles weren't that big and my nails weren't that dirty and the veins on the backs of my hands didn't pop out like that. And I remember thinking that somehow I always knew that this was going to happen—as though it was something I'd been waiting for.

Why would that be?

The cop who took my picture told me not to smirk. Smirk? I was chewing on the inside of my cheek, trying to cause myself some pain so I could figure out whether this was reality.

They put me in an office with a woman officer and let me make a phone call. The receiver was greasy and had "CALL JESUS" written on it in felt-tip pen.

I called Claire at the beach. She answered on the twelfth ring.

"Tell me," she said. "You're fed up—you're coming out here!"

"Listen, Claire," I said. My voice was husky and weird-sounding. "Something unbelievable is going on. I'm in jail."

"What?" She choked on it.

"No, I guess I'm not in jail. I'm in a police station. I've been arrested. I didn't do anything. It has something to do with Hank Monsell. He died this morning. Did you know that? I've been calling you all day, goddammit. And Lucas. They made me leave him there locked in the bathroom and I don't know if he has any water."

The words came out of my mouth hard and fast. I sounded like an angry carnival barker. It was like my brain gave me two alternatives: either cry hysterically or talk like this.

"What? No. Hank? Dead? Libby, wait a second. I've got to pull the phone over to the chair."

I looked at the policewoman. She didn't seem to be timing me or anything. She didn't even seem very interested in what I was doing.

Claire was back on.

"Libby," she said. "First of all, I want you to know that I love you very much and no matter what."

God, I thought. She thinks I did something wrong.

"Is someone with you?" she said.

" Yes."

"A policeman?"

" Yes."

"Okay. Then I'll just ask you questions and you answer them yes or no."

She was using her work voice—the one she uses at exhibit openings and when she's talking on the phone to people at the museum. It was calm and clear.

"Libby," she said, "don't worry. Have you talked to a lawyer?"

For the past hour I had expected Andrew Elkind to burst into the police station and save me. Like he would have seen me get in the squad car and followed it. Now I realized it wasn't going to happen.

"No," I said. "I need one. I mean I need you to get me one."

"All right," she said. "I'll call Michael and tell him to send someone to you right away."

"Who?"

"Michael. My cousin. The lawyer. Remember? You dated him, Libby."

Oh yeah. Michael.

I cringed. I hadn't been particularly nice to Michael.

"Claire," I said. My voice was breaking. "Tell him I need somebody now. Right now."

"Libby," she said. "Are you wearing your watch?"

"Yes."

"What time does it say?"

I looked at my watch. It was plastic, with little pieces of pink and yellow confetti painted on the face. It usually gave me a lift, but right then it looked cheap, and kind of pathetic.

"Twelve minutes after eight."

"Michael, or someone Michael knows, will be with you by nine-thirty. I'm going to stop talking with you and call him right now. Okay?"

"Okay," I said.

"And then," she said, "I'm going to drive into the city and take care of Lucas. Alright?"

"Okay."

"Libby, honey, I love you. Everything's going to be all right."

She hung up.

Then they moved me to One Police Plaza. Handcuffed to three other women in a bus with chicken wire on the windows. It stunk like sweat and pee and vomit. For a few moments I could see parts of my neighborhood: Pearl Street, my dry-cleaners, the east side of City Hall Park.

Hey! I wanted to scream. I don't belong in here. Look! That's where I live! My dog's in there! My clothes! My camera! My life!

I was seized by an intense feeling of panic—blinding, asphyxiating panic—the kind that grabs you when you're three years old and take a wrong turn in the department store and suddenly your mother isn't there anymore.

How was Michael going to find me? How was anyone going to find me?

I was gasping for breath when they led us into the building.

A skinny kid with thick glasses and a necktie sat in an office with me. He said he was from the Criminal Justice Agency and that he needed to ask me some questions.

I told him my lawyer was on the way and I wasn't going to talk with anybody until he got there.

"Nothing about your defense," he said. "Just things to help us at the bail hearing. About your family and your job."

"My family?"

"Are you married?"

"No."

"Do your parents live around here?"

"No. My father. . . "

Is where? How much would it help me if they knew about Max?

"I don't know where my father is."

"Sisters or brothers?"

"No."

More questions.

No, no, and no.

A bad dream, I thought. That's all this is. A bad dream.

The guy left and a policewoman came in.

Nurse Ratchett, I thought.

"You're lucky," she said. "Everything's backed up. Most nights you'd be locked up by now. Keep cool and maybe you'll get to sit in here for another couple of hours. Maybe all night."

Lucky?

Nurse Ratchett was doing the Jumble in the *Daily News*. I love doing the Jumble. I usually do it at night, on a break from the darkroom. About this time of night. In fact, if I were home right now, I'd be doing the Jumble, too.

I started to cry. No big deal; no huge convulsive sobs—I was too tired for that. Just tears that filled up my eyes and dropped down my nose when I blinked.

She looked up.

"Anything wrong?"

How was I supposed to answer that?

She opened the door and hollered to somebody. A couple of minutes later a woman who looked like a whore but was probably a member of the vice squad brought us two Tabs and a KitKat bar. Nurse Ratchett handed me one of the Tabs and split up the KitKat bar.

"Honey," she said. "You look awful."

I'd been hearing this a lot lately.

"Thanks," I said.

I gulped the Tab, then slowed down. After all, it might have to last me all night.

She had a name tag. One of those little engraved plastic panels. "Tree," it said. "Lieutenant Tree."

She looked almost like a pleasant person. Black, forty-something, with a wide face, and three little gold hoops in one ear.

"First offense?" she asked.

"First offense? Me? I didn't do anything."

She leaned forward.

"Look, honey," she said. "Take it from me. First offense? Just plead and they'll go easy."

She leaned back in her chair again. She looked me up and down.

"And when you're out," she said, "stay clean. Just stay clean."

She handed me the *Daily News* and started in on a magazine called *Woman's World*. The cover said it had an article that showed how to make a jacket out of a bathmat.

I read the *News*, including the advice to teenagers, but if anybody had asked me what I'd read, I couldn't have told them.

At nine-forty I closed my eyes, tipped my head back, and started to play a game that I play when I'm at the dentist's: I pick a four-letter word. HEAT. Then I change one letter, making sure the word stays a word. HEAR. And so on. SEAR. SEAT. TEAT. TEAR. TEAM. TRAM. TRAP. CRAP.

Is this really happening?

Michael, I thought. I hoped Claire knew what she was doing.

Michael was a partner in a corporate megafirm in midtown. We'd gone out exactly once—or exactly half: I abandoned him in the middle of a meal at the Colum D'or, after he'd rejected the wine three times. The waiter was a friend of mine. I was mortified. How could I stay?

Claire was furious with me—said I hadn't given him a chance, and that he was really extremely sensitive and shy, and that he'd had some kind of nervous breakdown a couple of years ago and what was I trying to do to him, anyway? I'd felt so guilty that I'd really, really never wanted to see him again.

I was biting my nails. Not so much biting them as tearing at them with my good thumbnail and finishing off the job with my teeth.

Lieutenant Tree looked up.

"Stop that," she said. "They'll get infected."

She fixed an evil eye on me.

"Com-mu-ni-ca-ble dis-eas-es," she said, putting a spin on each syllable. "Vi-rus-es."

I sat on my hands.

The door swung open.

It was Michael. Michael and someone else. A woman about my age wearing sneakers, jeans, and an orange tee-shirt that had a picture of a cow wearing skis and the caption: "SKI TEXAS." Her hair, which was blonde, hung in a ponytail down her back. It looked wet. She looked pissed off.

Michael looked like Michael. Fancy white shirt. Silk necktie with tiny orange and pink flowers on it. Shiny shoes. A way of holding his body that said that the meter was running. A muscular tension around his nose and upper lip that said most places smell bad, but this place smells really bad.

Lieutenant Tree left.

Michael didn't sit down.

"Libby," he said. "You know this isn't the kind of work I do. I don't do criminal law."

You're telling me, I thought.

"But Claire said you needed help. So I brought Martha. Martha Grant. An excellent attorney. She seems to be doing more and more of . . . "

He gestured toward her without looking at her face. She glared back.

" . . . this sort of thing."

God, I thought. This is my lawyer? SKI TEXAS?

"I'm sorry, Libby," he said. "I'd stay, but I'm overdue somewhere. Claire got me on the car phone, and I drove right over to Martha's. I'm afraid I didn't give her much notice."

I was aware of a truly horrible taste in my mouth. Acrid, brown. The taste I used to get in my mouth during standardized tests. Plus the taste of Tab.

He left.

Martha stopped glaring and sat down in Lieutenant Tree's chair.

"I'm sorry," she said, "for being such a crank. I'd just gotten the twins to bed and me into the shower when Michael called. From the parking garage of my building. He said I had two minutes to get down to the car."

She seemed weirdly composed for someone who'd just gotten dragged out of her house to a police station. Other people in that situation—me for example—would be shaking all over and barely able to talk.

Then I remembered—she gets paid to be this way.

"Did he tell you why I'm here? That I've been arrested but I didn't do anything?"

"He said that you were a friend of his cousin's, and that he'd do anything for her. For his cousin, that is. He didn't have much to say about you, except that you're a photographer and that you were in trouble."

"Do you do this much?" I asked. "I mean, criminal things? Don't I need a criminal lawyer?"

"Look," she said, "you don't need to worry about that. We found that so many of our corporate clients were needing advice on criminal matters—you know, federal investigations, children being arrested on drug charges—whatever—that three of us are doing criminal work full-time. I like it. I think I'm one of the few people at the firm who feels like she's doing anything real."

While she was talking her eyes roved over me, taking in my raw fingernails, the sweat stains that curved like shoulder holsters from my armpits to my chest, the contorted way I crossed my left leg over my right and then wound my left foot behind my right ankle—a position I'd been frozen in since I entered the room.

Look, I wanted to say, this person sitting here isn't me. Really, you should see me usually. I'm as clean as you are. I have good posture. I run my life just fine. I do work.

But I couldn't think of a way to say it that wouldn't sound hysterical.

TEXAS STATE TECHNICAL COLLEGE
ABILENE CAMPUS - LIBRARY

She confirmed what I already knew: that Silver Gaines and I had both been charged with murdering Hank. Then she asked me to tell her everything that had happened in the past twenty-four hours, and I did: about going to the zoo and to Silver Gaines's apartment, about finding Hank in the morning—who was there and what they'd said—about the call from Gaines's lawyer, and about the cops coming to the loft and going through my things. Mostly about the cops coming to the loft. I left out the part about having lunch with Iris, which at this point seemed even more unreal than my current situation did.

She wrote everything down on a pad of yellow-lined paper and squeezed details out of me. Which subway did I take to the zoo? How did I know? When did I get there? How did I know when I left Silver's apartment? Did I talk to anyone? Did I stop anywhere? The cab—what kind was it? What did the driver look like? Anything unusual about the inside of it? The picnic cooler—the one the police had taken—what had been in it? Where did I buy the food? What time? Had I washed out the cooler? And on, and on, and on.

In a way it was soothing—almost reassuring. These are the things I did. I did them at these times, and this way, and they were all okay things to do.

No, of course I hadn't done anything wrong. But my three hours in custody had started to make me feel as though I had. Is this what happens to people? Treat them badly enough and they'll eventually feel like they deserve it?

"So what happens now?" I asked. "Do I get out of here or what?"

"Hold on," she said.

Then she opened the door and leaned out in the hall. I could see her talking with Lieutenant Tree, and then with another, older, male cop.

She came back in. She wasn't real good at meeting my eyes.

"This place is on overload tonight," she said. "But maybe you'll be lucky and your prints will be back from Albany in the morning."

I panicked.

"What do you mean?"

"You certainly won't be arraigned tonight. Let's hope first thing in the morning, though."

My right hand started to quiver uncontrollably. I'd never seen it do that before. I wondered if I got some nerve damage when I broke my arm.

"I mean, Libby," she said, "that they're going to keep you here all night. In a cell. Try to think of it as a bad motel," she said. "Although I doubt you'll get much sleep."

I didn't say anything.

"And Libby," she said. "Is there anyone you want me to call? Your parents? Someone at work?"

Max, I thought. Why would I want him to know about this?

Dan Sikora? All I knew was that he was somewhere between Ohio and San Francisco.

Joey Dix? In the Pyrenees?

Octavia? LaDonna Knoblock?

How did I ever end up so alone?

"No thanks," I said. "Claire and you can take care of me."

What I remember about the cell is this: There was a light in the hall just outside my door that stayed on all night, the toilet had no lid and no rim, and there was a metal bench to lie on.

My cellmate looked young, really young. Like she should have been in a juvenile detention center or something. Small. And pretty. In the dim light from the hall, anyway.

She was wearing thigh-high white patent-leather boots and a black miniskirt that barely covered her rear end. Her face was perfectly oval, and her blue-black hair hung straight to her shoulders.

For a little while I framed pictures of her in my mind. Her face in profile while she plucked her lower lip with her finger; the outline of her boot against the dark metal bars of the cell door; her arm and hand as she lifted a strand of hair from her head and wound it around her finger.

Pretend photographs. Another one of those games I play when I'm in danger.

Gray on black. Black on black. These will be hell to print, I remember thinking.

She passed me a cigarette and a lighter.

I lit up and passed the lighter back.

I hadn't had a cigarette in eight years, but I accepted this one as easily as if it were an appetizer that somebody passed to me at a party. No guilt. Just fear that the guard might come and take it away.

After a while they brought somebody into the next cell. She was tall and bony, and sat on the floor next to the toilet, her arms wrapped around her legs, rocking and moaning. At first I didn't think she was saying anything in particular—just that she was high and distressed or something.

After a while, though, the sounds she was making took on a form I could understand.

"Wake up, baby," she said. "Wake up, baby." Over and over.

After a while I tried to go to sleep sitting up, so I wouldn't have to lie on the mattress. I pretended Lucas was with me and imagined myself petting him—scrubbing the fur backward along the bridge of his nose and scratching him under the chin the way that makes him lift his head up for more.

I did finally fall asleep—who knows when or for how long—and dreamed a horrible dream that I was back in the loft and Lucas was howling in the bathroom. I tried to open the door but the handle was gone, and when I did finally pry it open, Lucas wasn't there.

In the morning a guard came around and gave us doughnuts— powdered sugar ones wrapped in cellophane—and coffee in paper cups. The woman in the next cell lay on her side on the floor, not rousing to the sound of the guard yelling at her to wake up, or to the sounds of the people around her. For a moment I wondered if she had died, but saw that her back rose and fell slightly as she breathed.

My roommate didn't look as young or as pretty in the daytime as she had at night. Her complexion was yellowish, and she had a patch of inflamed skin on one cheek. She set her doughnut and coffee on the floor and lit up another cigarette.

I waited until she turned her back to me and the guard passed by again; then I peed in the toilet.

I felt dirty, deadened.

My scalp itched.

I had a bloated feeling in my stomach and thighs and hoped to God I wasn't about to get my period.

I sat on the bed, opened the doughnut package with my teeth, and tried to remember what day it was.

Sunday, I thought. No. The middle of the week. Wednesday maybe. Or Thursday. It was summer all right. I knew that much.

I took a bite of the doughnut, tried to swallow, and choked. I gulped some of the coffee and choked again.

My throat had seized up. I couldn't even swallow my own spit.

Later—I don't know when—somebody came and put handcuffs on me again. On me and everybody else. They herded the load of us back out to the bus to Centre Street, to the Criminal Courts Building, to some cells in the basement.

I had that hung-over feeling that I used to get when I was young enough to party all night. My head ached; my eyes stung; even the dim light in the cell was blinding.

After a while they brought us upstairs and put us on benches in the back of the courtroom. I was craning my neck, looking for Martha Grant, when a guard took me by the upper arm and pushed me into a little room. It was more a closet, really—a dark closet with a scuffed and dirty plastic partition that separated me from a woman on the other side. She was blonde, with her hair in a bun and half-glasses on her nose, and she was wearing a black jacket. For a minute I thought she was somebody I knew from the building Hugh and I used to live in. I sat down on the stool in front of the parti-tion—it was bolted to the floor like the stools at Burger King—and stared through the plastic. The woman's face shifted into focus.

"Libby," she said. "Listen to me. We don't have a lot of time."

It was Martha Grant. Without SKI TEXAS.

"You'll stand next to me in front of the judge," she said. "Don't answer any questions. If you want to say something, tell me. I'll do all the talking. Got it?"

"Got it," I said.

"The A.D.A.'s a guy named Will Harrell," she said. "Not a very nice person, but I can deal with him okay."

She gave me a tense smile, then stood up.

"Claire's here," she said. "In the second row."

My eyes filled up with tears.

"See you in a bit," she said.

The guard brought me back to the bench.

At first I couldn't follow anything that was going on. Everybody talked too fast. Then I got the hang of it. My buddies from the holding pen were being arraigned on prostitution charges. The "victim" the cops kept talking about was the guy. The prosecutor would talk about the woman's previous record; her lawyer would talk about how she had a mother in a wheelchair and three kids and was trying to get off the street. Then the judge would set a bail amount.

I was just getting absorbed in the whole thing—in an awful way it reminded me of the old TV show "Queen for a Day" where the woman with the worst sob story won a dozen roses and a Whirlpool bath—when I heard my own name called.

"People of the state of New York versus Olivia Kincaid."

I stood up and almost passed out. A guard opened the door and led me toward the front of the courtroom and put me next to Martha Grant, like a grade-school teacher arranging her students in a school pageant.

My right hand started shaking involuntarily again, like it had the night before. I pressed it as hard as I could against my hip to stop it, but it kept shaking, even while they swore me in.

Martha said something to the judge—I couldn't tell what. It was

quiet. Martha, the judge, the guy who I figured was Will Harrell—
they were all reading something to themselves.

I focused on the industrial-strength clock that hung on the wall
above the judge's head.

The judge shoved the paper off to one side and leaned back in
his chair, one hand over his eyes. The clock's minute hand dragged
itself in spasms around the edge.

"What are you asking for, Mr. Harrell?" he said.

"I'm asking that bail be set at one hundred thousand dollars."

The judge snorted.

"Your honor," said Martha. "She has no previous record; she's
made her home in this city for thirteen years; she's been employed by
Goehring-Fells Publications for twelve of those thirteen years . . . "

"She drifts from apartment to apartment, your honor," said Harrell. "She's been out of work all summer. She has no family in the
New York area."

The judge perked up.

"She's on a summer leave from her magazine, your honor," said
Martha. "She's due back in mid-September. She's preparing for an
exhibit of her photographs that's scheduled to go up at the Bemis-
Snow gallery in November. Most of her family is dead. She has no
home but her own, your honor. And no record, your honor. No
record whatsoever."

Did I imagine it, or did the judge look skeptical?

A voice erupted from one of the front rows of spectators' seats.

"If I may, your honor," it said. "If I may!"

It couldn't be—but oh my God, it was—Octavia Hewlitt. She
was standing up in the second row, dressed in a million-dollar
butter-colored linen suit with two rows of huge gold buttons down
the front. Her hair was perfect; her chin was up in the air.

She looked like she always did—like she was running the
show. Claire was sitting next to her, yanking at her elbow.

The judge banged his hammer; a court officer rushed toward
Octavia.

The judge glared at Martha.

"Can you tell us who this is?"

Octavia spoke again.

"I'm Octavia Hewlitt, your honor," she said. "And I'll be brief. I have been Olivia Kincaid's employer for over a decade. She is timely, responsible, and hard-working. I have never for a moment had cause to doubt her integrity. She takes important matters very seriously."

The buzz of whispering that had broken out when Octavia first stood up subsided. The judge stared at Octavia and she stared back.

"Thank you," she said, and sat down.

I buried my face in my hands.

Octavia, I thought. Why are you doing this to me? I'll never see daylight again. Never take pictures anymore. Never see Lucas. I'll be an old lady before I get out of here. I'll die in here.

The judge leaned back in his chair again and locked his eyes on the ceiling.

"Thirty thousand dollars," he said. "That will be adequate. Thirty thousand dollars cash bail."

Where would I get that?

They led me back to the pen.

Ten minutes later Martha leaned in.

"Out of here," she said. "You're out of here."

Martha got her car and pulled up in front of the courthouse.

Claire and I climbed in.

"Octavia got a cab already," said Claire.

"Just what was it that went on back there?" I said. "Did you guys plan it or what? It could have backfired, you know. The judge could have hated it. I'm lucky he didn't set bail at a million dollars."

Martha was poking pens into leather loops in the lid of her brief-case.

"No, we didn't plan it," she said. "Claire called Octavia last night and asked her if she'd come sit in the courtroom—a show of support. We always try to do that, Libby. Family or friends or employers. The talking was apparently her idea. I almost died when she stood up."

"Just be grateful that it worked," said Claire. "Really."

As if my life wasn't fouled up enough already. Now I had to be grateful to Octavia.

I couldn't stand it.

Martha gave me a piece of paper.

"Complaint," it said at the top of it.

"Read this and you'll know as much as we do," she said.

It was a form, and the blanks had been filled in with tiny, dense typewriter type. A police detective had signed it under oath.

"Defendant," it said,

> acting in concert with Silver Gaines, intentionally caused the death of Hank Monsell by causing a snake to bite him. Deponent is informed by Martin Walsh, a custodian of the Reptile House of the Bronx Zoo and of an address known to the District Attorney, that on August 17 on or about six o'clock p.m. he observed Silver Gaines and a woman introduced to him as Libby Kincaid removing snakes from the tanks of the Reptile House. Deponent is further informed by Dr. Csaplar that he examined the body of Hank Monsell and that he observed a snake bite on the body's left foot, and that there was poisonous venom in the victim's bloodstream.

"Martin Walsh," I said. "The guy's a nutcase."

Martha stuffed the paper into her briefcase.

"Tell it to the judge," she said.

"And they think we took the snake out in the picnic cooler," I said. "That's why they got all excited about it and took it out of the loft."

"I guess so," said Martha.

"That's the stupidest thing I ever heard of," I said.

Martha didn't say anything. Claire didn't either.

We pulled up in front of our building.

"So what's next?" I said. "What do we do now?"

"Get ready for the Grand Jury."

"What? Are you kidding? When?"

"They'll wait until Gaines is arraigned to schedule it."

"Silver's not out yet?"

"His prints aren't back from Albany."

"But then when would the Grand Jury be?"

"A week. Maybe ten days. We'll talk about it. Get some sleep."

Some sleep? Was she crazy?

12

LUCAS KNOCKED me over when I came in the door. It wasn't so much that he was terrifically strong; it was that I was so weak and exhausted I couldn't resist.

No, said Claire, I hadn't left him without water. When she had arrived at the loft there had been half a mixing bowl of it under the bathroom sink. For some reason that fact made me inordinately happy.

Lucas yipped and licked my face. I gave him a rubdown on his belly. I was starting to realize why so many people had dogs. Who else would ever be this excited to see you when you came home?

No, Claire said, the loft wasn't really in such bad shape when she'd gotten there. I must have been dreaming about the detergent spilled all over the kitchen floor, she said; there had been just a handful of it in front of the sink.

The loft, which the morning before had seemed so close and dingy—due mostly, of course, to my housekeeping failures—suddenly looked as huge and bright as an ice skating rink.

"Claire," I said. "What did you do—bleach the kitchen counters? Repaint the ceiling? Everything looks so white!"

"Oh, Libby, come on. I was here for all of about six hours last night."

Still, after my night in lock-up, the openness of the room was almost dizzying. I leaned against Lucas and closed my eyes.

A blast of adrenaline shot me to my feet.

"Oh my God!" I yelled. "They'll come to get me again! I forgot to pay my bail!"

"Libby," said Claire, "we got that taken care of this morning. Didn't you listen to any of what was going on in the courtroom?"

"So what do I owe you?"

"Just don't skip town. That's the only thing you can't do."

"What are you talking about—skip town? You sound like somebody out of 'Dragnet.'"

"That's how it works. We didn't have to actually pay anybody any money. But if for some reason you run away before trial, they come for the money. Actually, the loft. They took the deed for collateral. But don't worry, honey. There won't be any trial. We're getting you out of this way before then."

Leave it to Claire, I thought. Give her half a chance and she becomes an expert in criminal procedure. The way she's an expert in everything else. Art. Doing her taxes. Dealing with people. Making arrangements. Getting things done.

She made me a sandwich and some soup and I ate them. Then I took a shower, changed my clothes, and lay down on the sofa.

Claire dragged over one of the kitchen folding chairs.

"Duncan," I said. "How's he taking this? Hank being dead, I mean. And Silver being arrested."

And me being arrested too, I said, but only to myself. I was still deep in my denial phase. This thing is not happening to me.

She was quiet for a while, then:

"He's shattered," she said.

"What's he going to do?" I said. "With Eleuthera, I mean."

"I don't know," she said. "He doesn't know. He hasn't talked with Jerome and Miles about it. It doesn't seem like the right—moment. He won't even talk with me about it."

I'd never seen Claire look so tired. She was under a lot of pressure from work, I knew, with a huge exhibition scheduled for December, writing the text for the catalog, dealing with the logistics of loans from other collections, insurance questions—all kinds of things.

Then there was the heat. Claire is very fair and doesn't do well in the heat. Then, of course, she'd had to spend the last eighteen hours getting me out of jail.

"I don't know, Libby," she said. "I've never seen him so low. You and I both know how much Eleuthera means to him. It seems so small, but it's been everything to him for a long time. And Hank—he adored Hank. I just don't know what's going to happen. Duncan's one of those people who thinks it's a sign of weakness to ask for help. Funny, isn't it? When he'll do anything to help somebody else?

"I suppose, though," she said, "we all have our own ways of protecting ourselves."

She got up and walked to her desk, which was heaped high with galley proofs and reference books.

I wanted to thank her for being there. Maybe Duncan couldn't turn to her for help, but Claire was the one person I knew I would come to with any need, no matter how dismal or humiliating. But for some reason I'm not any good at that big of a thank you. I tried to say something, but instead I sunk into sleep.

When I woke up I could hear Claire on the phone in the kitchen, talking in a hushed kind of way so as not to wake me up.

"Of course you're right," she said. "I've thought about it, too. But she'll feel terrible."

And

"Then I'll come by and pick you up. But I think I need to stay here tonight. I don't want her to be alone."

She hung up.

I looked at my watch. It was five-forty. I'd been asleep for almost four hours.

"Claire," I said, "I know that was Duncan. Look, I really don't need you to stay with me tonight."

Although I did, very much.

"I just have to lie here and think. I can do that without you just fine. You need a break. Go out to eat. Go out to a movie. Then stay at Duncan's. Get romantic or something."

She washed out a glass, then started to rearrange the dishes on the shelf above the sink. The saucers on top of the dessert plates. The cups behind the soup bowls. Very orderly, very pretty, very Claire-like.

"You know what we're going to do, Libby," she said, not looking at me. "Duncan and I are going to calling hours for Hank. At their place. Hank and Nicole's."

"Calling hours," I said. "Wait a minute. You didn't tell me that was going on tonight. Or did you?"

Now she was organizing the glasses. The tall ones on the left. The short ones, stacked, on the right.

"Somehow," she said, "I didn't think you'd want to go. You had such a bad night and . . . "

It took a couple of minutes to sink in. They—Claire and Duncan—were going to calling hours for Hank. But I wasn't.

"I had such a bad night," I said. "I had such a bad night, and besides, for all anybody knows Silver did kill Hank and I had something to do with it."

Lacey, Miles, Nicole. Could they really think that I was capable of such a thing?

"Something like that," she said.

I must not have looked too cheerful. Claire walked over and squeezed me by the shoulders.

"Oh, Libby," she said. "I can't stand to see you look like that. I know you didn't have anything to do with Hank dying. This is all some colossal, freakish mistake. In a few weeks it will just seem like a terrible nightmare that's over. But I think that if you showed up at Nicole's tonight, you might not feel . . . "

She scanned for a word without the wrong kind of edge.

" . . . welcome," she said. "You might not feel welcome. Because the whole situation is so . . . "

Absurd? Unreal? Terrifying?

"Ambiguous?" I said.

"That's right," she said, "ambiguous."

She shook her head gently from side to side.

"Libby," she said. "At a time like this—at calling hours when someone's just died—people generally aren't in their right minds. They'll be tired and emotional, and who knows what they'll think? Who knows what they'll say? You know, you simply ought to rest. You've been through an awful lot in the last twenty-four hours."

"You have, too," I said.

She touched my arm. And she smiled. A little.

But her eyes betrayed her. They looked very tired, and very, very worried.

Claire dressed, asked five or six more times whether I'd be okay by myself, and left.

I poked through the mail, poked through some magazines, and paid a couple of bills. I restrained myself from going to the deli, because I knew that if I went to the deli I'd buy myself a pack of cigarettes. The one I'd smoked in the cell had rekindled something inside me. I wanted another one. Bad.

When I was a teenager and I felt low or distracted or generally anxious about something I went straight for the cigarettes. A family trait. Max does it. My mother did it, too.

I went into the darkroom. Darkness, solace, productivity. Something to do with my hands. I wonder how many artists are just people trying not to smoke.

I closed the door and settled in for a work spell. Today, for the first time ever, it seemed like exactly the wrong thing to do. I looked at the prints from the Eleuthera opening that I'd left drying on the racks. They felt puckery and thick. Either they weren't yet dry or they were never going to dry at all in this humidity.

I lifted one of the prints of Lacey's hands tying her shoe ribbons—the one I'd been so pleased with Monday afternoon. Now the image looked flat. Dead. Weak.

Why had I printed it so small? What was I trying to do? Be cute? Did I really think I was going to get away with this?

I skimmed the prints off the rack and shuffled them into a pile. One sailed to the floor, under the counter where the enlarger was. I dropped to my knees, grabbed it, and slammed it on top of the rest.

My heart almost stopped. It was the picture of Hank at the opening of Eleuthera, doing the part of the trio's routine where he spun off from the group and pretended to skate, pushing soundlessly forward, his hands clasped behind his back.

In this picture his body faced away from the camera, one foot trailing coyly behind the other. He looked over his shoulder at the camera. Directly at the camera. He looked like the happiest man in the world.

Sadness overwhelmed me. I couldn't move. I couldn't cry. All I could do was stand there and stare at Hank. The way his face looked very old and very, very young at the same time. The way he bent his foot just so. The careful carelessness. The beauty in the line that arced from his shoulder, down his torso, down the inside of his leg, punctuated at last by the two taps on the bottoms of his shoes, gleaming, just so slightly, in the smoky light.

Only then did I begin to feel the real weight of the accusations that had been dropped on Silver Gaines and me.

Somebody thinks that Silver Gaines and I killed this beautiful man, I thought. They're saying Hank died because of us.

Silver Gaines, who loved Hank. "Like a brother," he'd said. "He's like a parent to me and I'm like a parent to him." Who danced only when Hank asked him to.

And me. Who until yesterday was thoroughly, happily—no, ecstatically—immersed in the lives and talents of the Nonpareils. I adored Hank. No, that wasn't the word. I revered him. His passion for dancing was contagious; just being near him had charged my own work.

Me. Who couldn't watch *Fatal Attraction* or *Deliverance*, or *Bambi* for that matter, because I was so repelled by violence and death. Who turned down the corners of certain pages in a book of Weegee's news photographs so I'd know not to look at them.

Who was doing this to us? Why did anyone believe it?

I couldn't imagine. As far as I knew, the only people who Hank and I both knew were the Nonpareils and other people involved in Eleuthera. But Hank had irons in a million other fires. Through his real estate investments. Through his teaching. Through his family. Through his decades of show business connections.

He was flamboyant, but he was gentle and generous, too. Why would anyone want to kill him?

And was there really a profound mixup as to identity, or did someone really want to make it look like Silver did it? Whatever for?

The phone rang.

"Honey," said the voice. "This is Max."

He sounded weird. Nervous. Furtive. I slid down the wall and crouched, my back against the darkroom door, my pulse racing.

Jesus, I thought. He knows. He read something about this in the paper. Was there something in the paper? I hadn't even thought to ask Claire about that.

"Hi, Max," I said. "Where are you? Are you home?"

"No, I'm back in Wheeling."

Was this the kind of thing they'd put in *USA Today*? On CNN? Was this big news?

It was my turn to say something.

"How are you doing? How's Iris?"

A long pause.

"Honey," he said, "I'm in trouble. Big trouble."

Hey, wasn't that my line?

But okay. Good. He didn't know.

Big trouble? I braced myself. Was he sick? Was a hit man after him?

"Trouble, Max? What kind of trouble?"

"With Iris. She's divorcing me."

I felt a mild sense of relief. No more Iris. Then I groped for a more appropriate response.

"Gee, Dad. I'm sorry. You guys looked so happy together. What happened? What's going on?"

"I don't know," he said.

"You don't know?"

More silence.

"She says I drink too much."

Now silence from me. He does drink too much.

"I thought you were cutting down."

"I was," he said. "Except the night before last."

The night before last. When was that? I was still disoriented from my all-nighter in jail.

The night before last. That would have been the night before I had lunch with Iris.

"Monday night," he said. "The night after we saw you. Our last night in Atlantic City. We were whooping it up. Having a hell of a time. I got a little lucky at the table—won a thousand dollars. So we did some celebrating."

The old silken deejay-like tones seeped back into his voice. A hell of a time. Whooping it up. That was Max.

"So you had some drinks."

"So I had some drinks. We had some drinks. She was drinking too, you know. She was the one who got me going."

That sounded even more like Max. It's somebody else's fault. She made me do it.

"And things got a little out of control," I said.

"I guess so," he said. "A little out of control. I don't know how much, myself."

"Because you blacked out."

"Must have."

"She's divorcing you because you blacked out?"

"She was a mistake, Libby. She wasn't like your mother. There wasn't anything there."

I hated to hear him talk about my mother. I felt like he used her to win me over. I loved your mother. So I must be okay.

I tried to ignore it.

"I think there must have been something else wrong," I said. "Not just that you blacked out."

Nothing.

Then,

"She says I swung at her."

"Swung at her?"

"That's what she says."

"Well, did you?"

"When I woke up she showed me a busted bottle. And the mirror was broken. She says I threw the bottle at her and missed. Missed and hit the mirror."

"Did you?"

"Miss? I guess so. She looked okay."

"Come off it, Max. Did you throw it at her?"

"Hell if I know," he said. "I don't think so. I never hit a woman before, if that's what you're thinking."

"So were you having a fight or something? Before you blacked out?"

"Well, I was kind of pissed off at her all day. She kept changing her clothes. Special pajamas for sleeping in. Special pajamas for not sleeping in. Dress up for dinner. Dress up for before dinner. Dress up for after dinner. Forty minutes in the john every time. You know me, babe. I like low maintenance. It was driving me nuts."

No, I don't know you, I wanted to say. But I didn't.

"So you threw a bottle at her?"

"Maybe. Maybe not. It's what she says."

I thought back to my lunch with Iris. How I had wondered why she hadn't left her luggage with Max. He was mad, she'd said. He was mad. But that was all. Nothing about him throwing something at her. Maybe she was embarrassed.

I found this new-forged intimacy with Max unnerving. "Max," I said, "I'm sorry all this happened. But you know, if a guy threw a bottle at me, I wouldn't stay around too long either."

"I guess not," he said. "I guess not."

"So Max," I said, "keep in touch, okay? Let me know how it all turns out."

Not that I was anxious to be involved in his love life. It just seemed the polite thing to say.

"Thanks, baby," he said. "I like to hear you say that."

I was about to hang up, but—

"One more thing," he said.

Shit, I thought. He does know what's going on with me. He was just trying to think of a way to get to it.

"She says she wants the lottery money. She says her lawyer says she gets half anyway."

"A lawyer?" I said. "She's already got a lawyer? She's moving kind of fast, isn't she?"

"You bet," he said. "She's serious. She says she's going through with this as fast as she can. The guy already called me. He's a horse's ass. He said they're going to wipe me out."

What was this? National Everybody-Get-a-Lawyer Week?

"Come on, Max. She can't take your lottery money. That's ridiculous. You were hardly married to her."

Could she? Divorce law was something I knew nothing about. Still, it didn't sound right.

"Then Max, you're going to have to get a lawyer, too. Somebody who can explain to you what the law is. Do you know anybody?"

"Yeah, sure, hon. I know a couple lawyers."

"From the other time?"

Meaning the mail fraud conviction.

"They weren't so good, Lib."

Meaning he served three years. Also meaning he probably still owed them a ton of money. I wondered if they had seen Max's picture in the paper, too. He might be sharing his big prize with more than Iris.

"Maybe you're right, Max. Maybe you ought to talk to somebody else."

"That's my problem, kiddo," he said.

What did he want me to do? Fly there and read the phone book with him? Like I didn't have plenty else on my mind.

"Max," I said. "You just look up lawyers in the yellow pages. Or attorneys or something. Look, I'm doing it right now."

I yanked the Manhattan yellow pages from the shelf under the counter and flipped through them.

"Here. That's how they do it. Attorneys. And then they're listed. Or Attorney Referral Service. That's it. Attorney Referral Service. You've got to have one of those around there."

"I can find a lawyer, Lib," he said. "That's not a problem. I've got a different problem."

"What, Max?"

"The problem is I can't pay one. Right now, that is. I can pay one later—when the next check comes from the lottery. And I've got a little work lined up to start in a couple of weeks. But the guy I talked to—he wants money up front. A retainer, he calls it."

"What do you mean, Max, you can't pay one? You won a million dollars. You just spent three days in Atlantic City. You won another thousand dollars Monday night. You just told me so!"

"Hold on, babe," he said. "Here's the deal. I've been going through it pretty fast. The trip and all—it was kind of a big blowout before Iris and I settled down. I spent a little more than I expected to."

"Everything?"

"From the first check, is all," he said. "I get another one later. In three months. Not too long."

"And the thousand dollars?"

"I blew it, hon. I turned around and lost it."

I was starting to get the picture. Of how the fight got started. I wondered why Iris hadn't been the one throwing bottles.

"So what happened to the money from Avery's insurance?"

I'd taken care of Avery's estate. He'd left Max five thousand dollars in life insurance.

"I paid some debts."

"Okay."

"Okay."

"So you need some cash."

"A loan, kiddo. A loan. With interest. Don't you worry. I'll pay you interest. You could make a little money on this yourself."

"Don't worry about it," I said. "What do you need? A hundred? Two hundred?"

I was trying to remember how much was in my checking account. Maybe not a lot. I hadn't written down the checks for a little while.

"Eight hundred, Lib," he said. "But it'll last for a while."

"Eight hundred dollars? The guy wants eight hundred dollars before he'll even talk to you?"

"I've got kind of a bad rep around here, hon," he said. "For money things. I made some mistakes."

My savings account. My precious little hoard of cash that Avery had left to me. My someday down payment on a place of my own if I ever figured out where I wanted to be. My don't-push-me money. I'd have to raid it. Good thing I was due back at *Americans* soon.

"Okay, Dad, who do I send it to?"

"Care of Bill," he said. "At the Cyclone."

"What?"

"The Cyclone Lounge," he said.

He spelled out an address in Wheeling.

"You're a good kid," he said. "I always said that. You're a good kid."

I found Claire's *Times* in the wastebasket under her desk and searched the front page of the metropolitan section for something about Hank's death. There'd been two gang slayings in Chinatown, one Monday and one Tuesday. The front page was devoted to them and to the garbage strike.

The article I was looking for was on an inside page, near the gutter, without any pictures. COLLEAGUE HELD IN DANCER'S DEATH, it said, then a three-paragraph account containing nothing I didn't know already. Finally, at the end, "Olivia Kincaid, a friend of Mr. Gaines, is also being held in connection with the alleged crime."

Could be worse, I thought. They could have printed my address, said who my employer was.

Then I saw some more newsprint in the trash and yanked it out. Aha! The *Daily News*. The upper half of the front page had pictures of the kids killed in Chinatown, pools of blood under their heads. The bottom half of the page had a picture of Silver, handcuffed, being pulled from a police car, scowling fiercely at the camera. SNAKE MAN NO CHARMER, it said. And, under it, GIRLFRIEND CARRIED KILLER COOLER. Then it referred to me as "Violet Kincaid," Gaines's "artist-girlfriend."

If it hadn't been about me, I would have had a good laugh. As it was, I stuffed both papers to the bottom of the basket and started to shake.

I was trying to decide whether to turn on the TV news when the phone rang.

Probably Max again, I thought, upping the ante to twelve hundred dollars or something.

"Olivia Kincaid." It was a male voice—one I didn't recognize.

"Yes?"

"Slut," he said. "I see you went bye-bye last night. Try helping out Silver Gaines and you'll be going bye-bye again. For keeps. With the dog."

Bye-bye?

With Lucas?

"Who is this?"

He hung up.

13

CLAIRE CAME BACK at about nine, alone. I was lying on the couch with Lucas, semiwatching a made-for-TV movie.

She poured herself a glass of ice water.

"So how'd it go?" I said.

"You know how those things are," she said. "It was sad. Very sad."

"Nicole. Is she doing all right?"

"I suppose so, considering they can't give her any sedatives or anything because of the baby. Her sister was there. From Philadelphia. She said she's going to move in with her for a while—to help with the baby."

I couldn't get the picture out of my mind of Nicole outside Eleuthera, huge, with her high heels in her hand, crying.

"She sang a song," said Claire. "It was very moving. She has a beautiful voice.

"And Libby," she said, "Nicole asked me to tell you something. She said she wanted you to know that she doesn't think for a moment that you had anything to do with Hank dying. She says she thinks the police are crazy. That you wouldn't have stayed there at the studio with Hank if you'd had anything to do with it."

I'd been thinking about that, too. What if I had just turned and run, out of revulsion, when I'd realized Hank was dead? What if I'd done that and someone had seen me leave the building? Then I'd be stuck even worse than I was now.

"She says she works on instinct and she knows you wouldn't have done it."

Claire shrugged.

"Tell that to the cops who dragged me out of here yesterday," I said. "But what about Silver?"

"We didn't talk about him. It hardly seemed . . . "

"The right place."

"The right place.

"Something kind of funny happened," she said.

"What?"

"Right before we left a woman came in and got into an argument with Nicole. Something about the building the woman was in. That rent was going up. And that she needed repairs done in her kitchen. She said her oven door had come off and something was wrong with the faucet. She called Nicole a bitch. It was pretty horrible. Jerome talked to her and took her out of the building."

The doorbell buzzed. The sound, which I'd last heard when the cops came to get me, gave me a chill. Great, I thought. All I need is some flashback syndrome for the rest of my life that gets triggered every time I hear a door buzzer.

"It's Duncan," she said. "He was parking the car. He wanted to come up and see you."

She took off her shoes and rubbed her feet.

"It made me think, though," she said.

"The fight between the screaming lady and Nicole? It made you think about what?"

"About the same thing you're thinking. That there's a whole

world of people out there who might have been angry with Hank over things that we know nothing about. I didn't even know he was a landlord."

I told her what Silver had told me about the place he lived in. About how he said Hank had owned it for years. About how he'd said that Hank was a good landlord and kept things up and didn't squeeze for rent money.

"I wonder how Nicole is going to deal with that," said Claire.

"With what?"

"Being a landlord. Did she help Hank with the papers and things?"

"I don't have any idea."

"If she didn't, she'll have a lot to learn."

She sighed.

"On top of having the baby and everything. It will be a lot of work for her. Maybe we can help her find a manager or something."

I thought about telling her about the phone call and decided against it. She looked too worn and worried already.

Besides, I told myself, anybody reading the paper or watching TV could have looked me up in the phone book and made the call for a thrill.

Claire let Duncan in. He kissed her, then came over to the sofa where I was sitting.

"Libby," he said. "I'm sorry about what you've been going through. I don't understand what's going on."

Claire came over and sat on the floor beside him, her head resting against his thigh.

Duncan was playing with Claire's hair. Weaving a strand of it through his fingers, lifting his hand, then releasing the strand. Over and over.

Seeing them together like that made me think of something I hadn't thought of in years. My mother used to buy castoff china at junk stores. Always pink and white, sometimes roses, sometimes butterflies—never the same pattern twice. When she'd find a cup and saucer that looked right together, even though they were different patterns, she'd be content. A "married set," she'd call it.

That's the way Claire and Duncan were—a married set. If you looked at them separately—Duncan dark and Claire fair; Duncan happiest in a world of commerce and risk, Claire most at ease in a storage room at the museum, pondering the relative merits of two lithographs; Duncan the workaholic, Claire who likes nothing better than a long afternoon nap—you'd see no future for them together. But somehow their differences interlocked perfectly.

"Duncan wanted to come to court this morning," she said, "but I told him not to. I was afraid you'd be overwhelmed if you saw too many people staring at you. Not that there weren't plenty as it was."

"They were arraigning prostitutes," I said. "Prostitutes and me. How come I keep ending up places where all the other women are dressed better than me?"

They didn't laugh.

Duncan sat still, something I'd hardly ever seen him do, and slowly traced a pattern in the condensation on the outside of Claire's water glass. He didn't seem to be listening to either of us.

"You know," he said, "I used to think I never wanted to live anywhere but New York. Even last week, when the garbage started piling up and the temperature started to climb. You've got to take the good with the bad, I told myself. It's the bad that makes the good seem good.

"And then yesterday I walked through Grand Central, and I was thinking, what's different about this place? Did they clean the ceiling? Change the lighting? And then I realized what it was. They've taken the benches out. There's nowhere for anybody to sit! There's a roped-off area for people who bought tickets. You can be an old lady with legs swelled out to here and your apartment in Queens, and there's nowhere in Grand Central for you to take a break.

"The curb, I guess," he said. "I guess they're supposed to sit on the curb."

"There's Home Again," said Claire. "You're doing something with Home Again."

She was talking about the men's shelter that Duncan had helped start, the place that benefited from the Eleuthera opening.

"You know what?" he said. "When I called the agency"—Duncan had been out of advertising for seven years, but he still talked about "the agency" as if he went there every day—"Catherine told me that they weren't 'doing' the homeless this year. She said they were 'doing' AIDS. Like she was talking about which island they were having the annual retreat at or something. What's going on? We're pitting the plagues against each other for entertainment?"

Claire came around behind the couch and rubbed his neck.

"It just seems extra bad right now," she said. "With Hank dying. With Libby and Silver. The heat. Questions about the club. Things will get better, I know they will."

"Silver," I said. "This is driving me crazy. I don't even know if he had his hearing today."

I went over to the phone and dialed the number that Martha Grant had given me, hoping she hadn't left for the day. Maybe she'd talked with Andrew Elkind. Maybe she could tell me what was going on with Silver.

"Silver Gaines," Duncan said. "I don't know what's going on with him. He scares me. He really does."

I wanted to ask him why, but Duncan seemed to have closed out the rest of the world.

"Oh, stop it, Duncan," said Claire. "Just go home and get some sleep. Everything will be different tomorrow."

The sun had gone down as we spoke.

Nobody answered at Martha Grant's office.

I stood up and turned on the light. For some reason I didn't like sitting in the dark anymore.

* * *

By morning I was so happy to be home that I couldn't bear the thought of leaving my block. I sent Lucas off with Claire, feeling like one of the World War II London mothers sending her baby across the ocean to avoid the blitz.

The garbage problem, which the health department warned would soon be compounded by a rat problem the likes of which Manhattan had never seen before, was growing monumental.

New Yorkers—me included—accept man-made disasters—blackouts, serial killers, garbage strikes—as inevitable, the way people in other parts of the country lay back and let their annual floods, tornadoes, and Santa Ana winds roll over them.

The gratifying part comes in telling the story later. I could already hear it. You think these rats are bad? You should have seen them ten years ago—the summer we had the garbage strike. The suckers were as big as pit bulls. They were playing handball on the sidewalk in front of the New York Athletic Club. They were stealing cars.

Yep, I told myself. This summer will be good for a lot of stories. The summer I got arrested by mistake. You think the cops are scary now? They arrested me in my apartment for murder! No kidding. I spent the night in jail with a woman who killed her baby. Crazy! You're telling me! The same summer as the rats—no joke.

I wrote a check to Max on the pristine yellow paper of my money-market checkbook and was surprised when the post office clerk in the express mail line didn't look at me in horror when she saw my name on the envelope's return address. You know—"Aha! Olivia Kincaid! Aren't you Mr. Gaines's friend?" or "Olivia, are you sure you've got that right? Aren't you the *Violet* Kincaid I read about in the *Daily News*?"

The same thing at the deli, where I went to refurbish my supply of yogurt and popsicles. The guy who just grunted when he gave me my change still just grunted when he gave me my change. This metropolitan anonymity that people complain about—it's really not so bad, I thought. Really not so bad at all.

I tried Martha Grant again. I wanted to know what she was doing; what she wanted me to do; if she'd found out what was going on with Silver. I wanted to tell her about the phone call I'd gotten. And I wanted to hear her tell me that everything was going to be okay.

Her secretary, a brusque, cranky woman who ignored me when I asked her what her name was, told me that Martha would be unavailable for the rest of the day and hung up.

I called Silver Gaines's number, but nobody answered. I started to get nervous. What if they hadn't let him out yet?

I tried Andrew Elkind and he answered the phone himself.

"Miss Kincaid," he said. "I'm sorry we didn't have the chance to meet the other night."

Uh oh, I thought. The statement he'd wanted from me the night I was arrested. Was he going to ask me again to do it? Wasn't that the kind of thing I was supposed to talk with Martha about?

"It's crazy, isn't it?" I said. "You know, when the cops came to arrest me, I thought they were you, and let them right in."

"A dangerous practice," he said. "Letting people into your apartment without knowing who they are."

"It's about Silver," I said. "What's going on with him? Is he out yet? Can I talk to him? Why aren't things moving?"

Silence while he talked with someone who had come into his office, read his mail, I don't know what.

"Miss Kincaid," he said. "I'm reluctant . . . that is, I can't talk with you about my client."

"What do you mean? You were the one who called me the other night."

"Things have changed since then, Miss Kincaid. If you have something you'd like to say to me, it would be more appropriate if you asked your attorney to call me."

"Are you kidding? Are you trying to tell me that I have to pay someone to talk to you? It's not like we're on opposite sides of a case or something. All I want to know is what's going on with Silver."

"In fact, Miss Kincaid," he said, "it is as though we're on opposite sides of a case or something. You and Mr. Gaines are both defendants, and the possibility exists that you will testify against each other at trial."

At trial. I wished people would stop saying "at trial." It made my heart start whirring like an automatic film advance.

"Goodbye, Miss Kincaid," he said.

I decided to clean my darkroom—not that it was all that dirty, but the ritual usually makes me feel in control of things. You know—I may be just this far away from fifteen years behind bars, but at least my enlarger is dust-free.

I dusted off the boxes, wiped down the tanks, piled everything in the center of the floor, washed the countertops, and stacked everything all over again.

Agfa-Gevaert boxes in an orange stack there. Kodak boxes in a yellow stack there. Fronts flush with the counter edge. The developing trays lined up just so. The tongs centered just so in the developing trays. Six stray slugs of Bazooka Joe bubble gum lined up nice and neat on top of my equipment cabinet. My looseleaf notebooks right side up and erect on the bookshelf.

Very nice, I thought. Just like Claire in the kitchen.

I closed the door and surveyed my domain.

I could reach everything I needed, and in the dark, no less. My own little place. Tiny. Tidy. Stocked.

Like a boat, I thought. Like an air-raid shelter.

I could stay here forever.

I scanned the flurry of yellow Post-It notes to myself that I'd stuck on the door. Some were too old to make sense anymore, like "call by six" and "6 copies by 4:30."

The rest of them made me flush with guilt. "B-Day present to Joey." Well, I'd missed that altogether. "Thank Isabella for scarf."

Isabella was Claire's mother. When had she sent me that scarf? Last Christmas? I threw the note into the trash.

"Return album to D. Monsell ASAP." I sighed. Well, at least that one I could take care of. So much for staying here forever.

I pulled the album from the top shelf. Then I called Delores Monsell at the number she'd written on the inside cover.

She sounded dreamy and sort of vague when she answered, as though I'd awakened her from a nap. I offered to call back another time.

"Oh no," she said. "Now is as good as any . . . who did you say you were again?"

"Libby Kincaid. I borrowed your album . . . "

"Oh, dear God," she said, "the album. My Hank. My dear, dear Hank."

"I'm sorry," I said. "I wasn't thinking. This probably isn't such a good time to be bringing up the subject of pictures of Hank. Really, I'm sorry."

"Who did you say you were?"

"Libby, the one who . . . "

"Oh, of course," she said. "My album. Why ever did you keep it so long? Don't you know what treasures like that mean to people?"

She must have thrown some ice water in her face. Suddenly she sounded decidedly undreamy. More like hopping mad.

"I'm sorry," I said.

"I want it," she said. "And I want it today. Not by mail. Not by bicycle courier. By you, my dear. I'm going out of town tomorrow and I want that album now."

I was shaking in my sneakers.

"Of course," I said.

She gave me directions to her house—east of Ossining, on the Hudson, up past Tarrytown—in one blast, which I copied down on a succession of Post-Its.

"That's it," she said, and hung up.

14

I WAS ON Roosevelt Drive by noon, headed for the Taconic State Parkway, up past Tarrytown and toward Ossining. I'd taken almost the same trip once before, ages ago, with Hugh. He had some fantasy about buying a farmhouse there and fixing it up. All I remembered was that there wasn't a good place in the farmhouse to put a darkroom, and that we had a fight in the car on the way back.

I stuck the Post-Its with Delores's instructions in a row on the dash. If I hadn't put two of them in the wrong order, I'd have moved along without any problems; as it was, I took a ten-minute loop backward into the Bronx before I got back on track.

The drive did me good. Racing bumper-to-bumper up FDR Drive always clears my head. It's like downhill skiing ten feet behind somebody else; sneeze and everybody's dead.

Once I got on Route 87 I felt wildly happy. I hit a radio station that was playing Bob Marley nonstop and sang along, drumming my fingers on the dashboard.

Man, I thought. If I just kept going, where would I end up by midnight? Montreal? Quebec? Wouldn't that be something? Just shoot up north like a rocket until I run out of speed. Find a crummy little motel with a saggy bed and a little kitchenette. Buy myself a couple of Cup-a-Soups and take some pictures of the town.

I wouldn't even have to tell anybody where I was going. Lucas was with Claire. Nothing in my date book. Just skip town for a lit-tle—recharge, get the mess out of my mind.

Skip town, I thought. Just skip town. It would be like old times.

Claire's voice erupted in my ear.

"Just don't skip town," she said. "That's the only thing you can't do."

My fantasy spacecraft dropped out of the sky, crashed, and burned.

I found Delores Monsell's mailbox at the end of a short dirt road, exactly where she said it would be. The lot was densely wooded and dark; the driveway was pitted and unpaved. Through the trees I could make out the remains of a small barn—charred crossbeams, one wall, and a stone foundation—and a small, beaten-looking weathered wood building surrounded by a ramshackle deck. For all its forested setting it looked like something you'd find at the beach—like a bait shop maybe. About twenty feet off to one side sat a sec-ond, smaller building, and next to it an orange Volkswagen bug, the dented back bumper held to the body with electrical tape.

As I drove closer I could hear dogs barking. Big dogs, from the sound of it. I could see that the house had a greenhouse built against it, and that the smaller building was a chicken house.

I parked, climbed the steps, and threaded my way through a col-lection of clay flowerpots, seedling trays, and huge metal vats filled with what I assumed were Delores's yarn dyes—one amber-colored, one deep purple, one an electric shade of green. Hunks of yarn steeped in the brine like stew made by the Easter Bunny.

I searched for the doorbell, couldn't find it, and pounded with my fist.

I was hot. I was thirsty.

Nobody answered.

The barking got louder.

I pounded again. The vibration set a wind chime attached to the door frame clattering.

Still no response.

I looked around the deck for a safe place to leave the album. I was about to slide it under a piece of plastic tarp when I heard footsteps. Then a voice:

"Whoever you are—I don't want any."

The dogs barked some more.

"Miss Monsell," I shouted. "I'm not selling anything. I'm here with your album."

She opened the door and nudged two dogs back with her feet. They were Dobermans—sort of muscle-bound and unpredictable-looking. Their bodies were about the same size, but one had a head that was larger than the other's.

Somewhere in the distance a kitchen timer was buzzing.

"Damn," she said—to me, not to the dogs. "Just come in the kitchen and be quiet. I'm about to burn a pan of muffins. And keep your hands up." She nodded toward the dog with the larger head. "This one likes to bite hands."

She dragged the dogs off with her to the kitchen.

"Azore. Rasheen. Bad boys. Under the table."

"You look kind of busy," I said. "Here, just take the album and I'll leave you alone."

"Five minutes," she said. "Just give me five minutes."

I followed her into the kitchen, trying to keep my distance from the animals, which was difficult since the room was about the size of a toll booth.

A haze of smoke hung at eye level. My eyes smarted. Azore and Rasheen growled somewhere near my ankles.

Baking in a heat wave? Okay, the Hudson River Valley was a little cooler than Canal Street, but it must have been over a hundred degrees in this place.

Delores opened the oven door. Her hair, which had been bound into a bun when she'd been in her dress-up mode at Eleuthera, today hung loose and swung in front of her face as she bent over. For a panicked moment I was afraid it would catch fire, but it didn't.

The air swelled with more heat, more smoke. I set the album on the table and gingerly slid a chair from the table to a space next to the door, ready to beat a hasty retreat if necessary. Rasheen or Azore growled a long growl.

"Hands," said Delores. "Remember your hands."

I squeezed my hands into fists and held them against my chest.

"Really," I said. "I think I ought to go. You seem to have a lot going on."

"Just sit still," she said.

Delores pulled a pan of blackened muffins from the oven, groaned, and started banging the pan against the countertop.

A very weird-looking chicken—tiny, with yellow and pinkish feathers that looked like they'd been backcombed, and nasty-looking little pink eyes—zigzagged through the open screen door.

"Ivana, out," Delores barked.

The chicken turned around and left.

"Good thing she doesn't have hands," I said, eyeing Rasheen and Azore.

Delores ignored me.

She was gouging the muffins out of their sockets with a steak knife. Very, very slowly.

At first glance the room appeared well attended to. Handmade bowls and mugs rested in a wooden cabinet next to the stove; dark brown baskets filled the space underneath. Mason jars of preserved fruits, rice, beans, and something that looked like dried corn lined the top shelves; bunches of dried herbs hung from the wood ceiling beams; a ceramic crock on top of the stove held a bouquet of wooden spoons.

Looking more intensely, I realized that many of the bowls and mugs were cracked and chipped, and that they were packed so crazily into the cabinet—some vertically, some diagonally, some upside down—that it would take miles of thought to figure out which ones, if any, could be taken out without triggering an avalanche.

Chicken feathers puffed out the seams of the baskets; the fruit in some of the jars looked dark and ulcerated. Traces of food—rice, a shred of tomato skin—clung to some of the wooden spoons, as though someone had forgotten to wash them before putting them back in the crock. The bunches of dried herbs were uniformly dead—brown and dusty. Hanging where they did, unreached by window light, they looked like bats.

The counter next to me was covered with clutter. Metal crochet hooks, matchbooks, bottle corks, razor blades, a tiny blue bottle labeled "Indian Rosewater," a seashell, a small ball of yarn, a single chopstick, two little lumps of yellow wax. Like she'd dumped the contents of a drawer trying to find something in a hurry.

Ten minutes went by. Maybe fifteen. The skin itched at the nape of my neck where it was starting to grow back in.

Delores seemed to have forgotten about me. That, or she had her own unique sense of time. I felt like a kid at the doctor's. Like the nurse stuck a thermometer in my mouth and didn't come back.

"Did you build this place yourself?" I asked. "Hammers and saws and stuff?"

"Uh huh," she said, nodding her head yes.

She finished one pan and was working faster on the other one. The muffins made a banging sound as they landed on the countertop.

"That room there," she said, motioning toward the living room, "used to be a chicken coop. A big one. I converted it and added the rest. That out there," she said, now motioning toward the yard and the small chicken house just beyond, "used to be a tool shed."

So these were outbuildings, I thought. Outbuildings to the burned-out barn I'd seen. I wondered what had happened to the farmhouse that must have been there once.

"I'm completely self-sufficient," she said. "I raise my own hens, chop my own wood, milk my own goats, grow my own dyeplants, brew my own beer, if you really want to know."

I didn't really, but that was okay.

I wondered how old she was. In the pictures of her when she was married to Hank, back when she'd been singing, she'd looked as though she was in her late twenties, and the pictures were mostly from the early fifties. That would make her what? Seventy? Seventy-two? Of course in those pictures she'd been wearing clothes that would have made a seventeen-year-old look middle-aged—hat, gloves, eyeliner, girdle, nylons, stiletto heels—the works.

In a way she looked younger now—without makeup, in sandals, jeans, and a tee-shirt—than she had then. I wondered what had happened to make her stop singing; to make her split up with Hank; to make her life take this swerve from jazz and nightlife into crafts and self-reliance. I wondered if she was happier now.

I wondered what I'd be doing—what I'd look like, too—when I was her age, and quickly stifled the thought.

Delores threw the muffins into a basket and lay a dish towel over the top.

"I'm not myself today," she said. "I've been thinking too much about things."

"About Hank," I said.

She was silent.

"I'm sorry," I said, "that he died."

I felt myself grow even warmer than I already was. Surely Delores read the papers; surely she'd been at Hank's calling hours. What was she thinking of me?

I let my hand drop to my side. A dog growled and I yanked it back up.

Delores was scrubbing out the pans. Once again she seemed to have forgotten I was there. Holding her attention reminded me of trying to keep a radio station clear when you're just about outside of the broadcast area. *Now I've got it. Now I don't.*

She dried the pans and put them away under the sink. She took two drinking glasses from the shelf and filled them with ice. Then she reached across the table and lifted an enormous jar filled with a murky dark red liquid. Stuff floated inside of it. Plants. Maybe sticks. I thought that maybe it was an aquarium. Or one of her home-brewed dyes.

"Iced tea?" she asked. "My own herbs. And rosehips."

She looked at me impatiently.

"It's not poison, you know."

"Okay," I said.

She poured it into the glasses. I was pretty sure she hadn't made those herself, but who knows? They were kind of bumpy and lop-sided.

She took a jar from the shelf.

"Honey?"

"Your own?"

"That's right."

Her hand trembled as she passed me my tea, setting the ice jan-gling against the glass.

"Delores," I said, "I'm suffocating in here. Can we sit somewhere else? Someplace where there's not so much heat from the oven?"

Without saying a word she walked out of the kitchen, through the living room, and into another room while I followed. Rasheen and Azore stayed in the kitchen, snoozing.

The room was her studio. Light, spacious, ventilated by a floor-to-ceiling sliding glass door at the far end that opened to a view of at least three acres of open field, fringed by the forest that filled the rest of the property. An enormous, lush piece of weaving, a pattern of large three-petaled flowers in graduated shades of purples and deep reds, hung from the ceiling to the floor of the adjacent wall.

What a contrast to my darkroom, I thought. A golden, open work space.

Her loom, large and reddish-brown, was set toward the center of the room, at a right angle to the window. She had just begun work on a new piece—something cream-colored and fine-looking. Next to the loom, within reach when Delores sat weaving, stood a freestanding shelf filled with spindles of colored yarns, arranged by color, and within the colors by intensity of shade. A circular wooden device that looked almost like a spinning wheel, but spun parallel to the floor, jutted out on an arm attached to one of the shelves.

A low hissing sound came from the far end of the room, behind the shelves holding the spindles. I walked toward it, half expecting to see a cat or some other kind of animal.

Gooseflesh erupted on my arms and back even before I was conscious of what I was looking at.

It wasn't an animal at all. It was a small record player, made out of green plastic—exactly or very much like the record player that had been in Hank's studio when I had found his body there. And like Hank's record player, this one was playing on empty—the record was finished and the arm needle scraped idly in the gutter at the center of the disk.

Delores sat in a chair by the window, sipping from her glass, her face darkened in thought.

"I'll turn this off," I said.

I pressed the power switch, just like I'd pressed the switch on Hank's machine, and watched the record exhaust itself to a stop on the turntable. The title of the song, printed in blue, circled into focus. "Empty Plate Blues," it said, and beneath that, "Lyrics and Music by Hank Monsell and Delores Monsell."

A scrap of the tune, sung in the thin voice of the piano player at Eleuthera on opening night, fluttered to my mind.

I looked at Delores.

"I didn't know you and Hank wrote this."

"Not many people do," she said. "Not many people do."

I continued to talk to her from where I was standing. For some reason the distance made it easier for me to speak.

"You know," I said, "I didn't have anything to do with him dying. Silver either. This is all some big—and I mean really big—mistake."

"And you also know," she said, "I wouldn't have let you into my house for a minute if I thought you had anything to do with Hank's death."

She looked at the ice remaining in her glass.

I wondered if she had been sitting here, weaving, listening to the record when I'd been waiting at the door. Was Hank's death shoving her into some sort of depression?

I crossed the room and looked out the window. Clothes—a few tee-shirts, underpants, two brown towels—hung from a clothesline that ran from the chicken coop to the side of the house.

The rogue chicken stepped delicately through the grass, now and then taking a fast three-hundred-sixty-degree turn. If I'd been in a picture-taking mood I would have done his portrait.

She came to.

"Hank and I did have our troubles," she said. "God knows I was tempted to kill him myself more than once when we were married. Afterward, too. Probably even before. But men and women weave a very complicated, very fragile web of understanding around themselves when they marry. A lot goes into it. A lot remains even when the marriage is over."

She studied me.

"Are you married?" she said. "Were you ever married?"

"No," I said. Two close calls, I thought. That's all.

"Hank dying," she said. "It's the end of a part of my life. Do you know what I mean?"

"Some," I said. "I do some."

And after all I did. Because of my mother. And because of my brother.

"There's a reason," she said. "A reason I wanted you to come out here. Besides the fact that I wanted the album back."

The noon sun had begun to drop as we sat there, charging the colors in the room. The reds in the flowers on her wall hanging lit up; the color of the liquid in her glass slowly intensified from plum to something oranger.

"No," she said, "I've got my own theories about who killed Hank, and they don't have anything to do with you. Or with Silver, either. Silver wouldn't kill a bug. God knows, he loved Hank. Loved him too much, I sometimes thought. Sometimes I think Silver had too hard a time keeping Hank out of his mind. But that's not the subject at hand."

She seemed to be talking more to herself than to me. And with good reason. She barely knew me. And I'm not the confidante type.

I was almost afraid to talk—afraid to break the spell. But she kept on talking.

"You know," she said, "Hank and I were together for quite some time. Inside and outside of marriage."

"I know."

Now she was talking to me, not to herself.

"But you don't know," she said, "that Hank was sexually incapable. Not always, mind you. But since shortly after the time we were married. He had a tumor in his right testicle removed a week after our honeymoon. The surgeon was not as experienced as he should have been. Or so we always suspected. At any rate, he was sterile after that.

"I was seven years older than Hank," she said, "and desperate to have a child."

This time I was the unresponsive side of the conversation.

"So I was surprised to hear that Nicole was pregnant. I think Hank must have been, too."

"Couldn't he have had corrective surgery or something?"

I don't know anything about these things, but I thought I'd give it a try.

"Please," she said. "If such a thing were possible, don't you think we'd have tried it?"

"But certainly that was a while ago. When did you and Hank break up?"

"Nineteen sixty-one," she said. "Everything was final on the Fourth of July. Can you beat that?

"But somehow," she said, "I didn't feel as much like celebrating as I thought I would."

"And now," I said, "all this time later, he's married again, and she's pregnant, just like that."

"Just like that."

"By somebody else, you suspect."

"By somebody else, I *know*."

"And you think the somebody else killed Hank?"

She looked confused.

"Now there's a thought," she said.

Then, "No, not somebody else. Nicole."

"You think Nicole killed Hank."

"Not I *think* Nicole killed Hank. I *know* Nicole killed Hank."

The weird-looking chicken staggered to the sliding screen door and stared in at us.

"I know Nicole killed Hank because I knew Hank. I know how he thought. If he knew that this baby belonged to somebody else, and of course he did, he was going to hold that fact over her head for as long as she lived. That's the way he was. He would torment her forever. Threaten to leave her. Threaten to tell the child when it was old enough to understand. Make sure Nicole dressed the way he wanted her to, talked the way he wanted her to, acted the way he wanted her to, or she'd be out on the street. Alone. With a baby.

"I know," she said, "because that's what he said he'd do to me."

"If you fooled around with somebody else."

"When I fooled around with somebody else."

"What happened?"

"I miscarried at six months," she said. "And then we got divorced."

Nicole killed Hank?

It not only seemed unlikely, it seemed impossible.

The woman was nine months pregnant and staggering around like somebody carrying a twenty-five-pound load, which of course she was.

Could Delores really believe what she was saying to me?

Or was she just making a preemptive strike to divert suspicion from herself?

I don't remember much of the drive home. Only that it was still very hot, and that after I'd parked my car and walked up Canal Street it seemed strangely quiet in the city for a weekday in the summer.

15

IT WAS TWENTY AFTER TWO in the morning and I wondered if I'd ever be able to sleep again. I lay in bed, the fan blasting across my legs, looking at a book of photographs by Helen Levitt of children's sidewalk chalk drawings from the forties—pictures of cowboys, steamships, and big-breasted ladies, and bits of whimsical, benign graffiti like "Alice Crowley is a swell gal fore my oppinion" and "Paquito is a dope and so is P.W. and tony" and "Rhoda has nice hair."

The last time I looked at the book, the pictures and messages seemed sweet and comforting; now, with insomnia chewing at my bones, they seemed eerie. Eerie and dark.

I laid the book back on its pile.

Could Delores possibly have been on target about Nicole? I thought of Nicole—her lumbering, pregnant walk when she'd left Eleuthera. Impossible, I thought. Women in that kind of shape don't kill people. They can't even if they want to. Pregnant by another man? Well, who knew? Who cared?

I turned off the light.

The melody to "Empty Plate Blues" buzzed at me like a mosquito.

I put my pillow over my head.

Why did Delores keep that handwritten version in her album? Did she really write it but Hank took all the credit? Like Colette's husband?

Of course not. I'd seen both of their names spinning on that record in Delores's studio.

So what was her real story? With her homemade this, that, and everything. Those little lumps of wax on the counter next to the phone? She was probably making a scrawny little woman out of one of those lumps right now and sticking pins in it. That was why I couldn't get to sleep.

Martha Grant still hadn't called. Claire hadn't called, either. Dan Sikora hadn't called in three weeks. Why in the world had I told him that I wanted to keep things casual for the summer? I'd probably never see him again.

Delores. *She* probably killed Hank. She kept killer dogs, didn't she? She probably had a whole reptile house in her basement. Zapped Hank and set Silver up to take the fall. Why? Who knew?

She'd practically confessed the whole thing to me while I was there. Hank hadn't had a baby with her, but he was having one with Nicole. Of course she was desperately jealous. Of course she killed him. She'd been wanting to kill him for years; she'd said so. She probably planned to do me in too, there in her studio——lock me in there with the dogs or something—but lost her nerve. And she was leaving town, no less. Tomorrow!

Maybe, I thought, I shouldn't have had that iced coffee at ten. From now on no caffeine after nine.

I rolled over, turned the light on, and wrote a note to myself on the back of a bank receipt: "Find out about Empty Plate Blues; Monsell divorce." Another one of my insomnia cures—put it on paper. The notes don't make any sense in the morning, but at night they give me the impression that I'm making things better.

I need Lucas, I thought. I'm just not used to being here without him. I shouldn't have sent him off with Claire—should have kept him here and kept him cool somehow.

If I were Max, I thought, I'd lay down with a swig of Old Crow in my mouth.

I wrestled with the sheet.

The phone rang.

I looked at my watch. Three-fifteen. Another crank call. I'd get the number changed tomorrow.

Whoever it was wouldn't quit. I picked up the receiver, planning to slam it back down.

"Libby?"

It was a woman's voice.

"Yes?"

"This is LaDonna."

"LaDonna Knoblock from work?"

"Of course."

Then nothing.

"LaDonna, are you okay?"

"Yeah, I'm okay. It's just this. I read everything in the paper. Everybody's talking about it at work. I just wanted you to know that we all—well, I just wanted you to know that everybody's worried about you and if there's anything I can do for you, tell me, okay?"

I was only semiconscious.

"Sure, LaDonna," I said. "Thanks. Thanks a lot. I'll see you later. Okay?"

"Okay," she said, and hung up.

I went into the bathroom and poured a glass of water. A roach was sitting on the head of my toothbrush. I knocked it into the sink and washed it down the drain. LaDonna Knoblock. At a quarter after three in the morning. Wide awake.

What was she? Crazy?

16

IN THE MORNING Martha Grant's secretary promised me that Martha was in the middle of a trial, promised me that closing arguments were this morning, promised me that Martha would call me back while the jury was out, and hung up.

I dialed Nicole. I wanted to tell her how sorry I was about Hank.

"It's Libby Kincaid," I said.

Nicole made a sound something like a cross between a sigh and a shriek, and then I heard a clattering sound——the sound a telephone makes when you drop it on the floor.

But the line was still alive.

"Nicole, are you okay? What's going on?"

I heard her breathing.

"Hold on," she said. "I . . . just. . . dropped . . . all of this . . . stuff . . . . "

She was crying.

"What's the matter?"

"I can't make any sense out of the papers about Hank's buildings. Things are missing, and upside down, and it says there are attachments to things when there aren't any, and I hate it . . . and . . . and . . . and . . . people keep calling and saying things don't work . . . and . . . and . . . "

She was in the hiccup stage.

"Nicole," I said. "Do you need some help? I don't know a lot about that kind of thing, but maybe if we look at the papers together we can figure them out."

More hiccups. And a couple of gasps for breath.

"Uh-huh," I thought I heard her say.

"Does that mean you want me to come?"

"Yes," she said. "This is making me . . . "—she hiccuped—"just want to die."

I tried to keep my voice steady.

"Nicole," I said, "you don't mean . . . "

"Oh, of course not," she said. "But I just hate all of this. Being so fat. The heat. The tenants calling up. One of them called Hank a . . . a . . . a . . . "

She was dissolving again.

"Hold on," I said. "I'll be right there."

I went to the darkroom and picked out a couple of pictures of Hank—the one of him doing his skating routine on opening night at Eleuthera, and one of him and Jerome Junior rehearsing together. Then I put them in an envelope to give to Nicole.

I yanked on my black skirt, which I decided was more appropriate for a visit to the bereaved than boxer shorts were, packed up my camera, and headed for the IRT.

I walked halfway down the stairs at the Canal Street station and stopped. For the first time since I moved to New York, I felt like I never wanted to ride the train again.

Too hot. Too smelly. Too small.

I thought about the sewer main that had exploded in the station when I'd been on my way to meet Silver at the zoo.

Too everything.

I turned around and walked back out.

I trekked over to the garage and bailed out my car.

It was just the weather, I told myself. Just nerves and the weather. Once this heat wave rode itself out I'd be riding the trains again. Everything would be back to normal.

Of course.

* * *

Nicole's and Hank's place was in a block of row houses on Edge-combe Avenue, between 136th and 137th streets, across from St. Nicholas Park—a dead shot up Central Park West and a twelve-block diagonal jog up St. Nicholas Avenue.

I'd been to the building once before, the previous spring, when I'd first approached Hank about taking pictures of the Nonpareils. I'd met him in his office on the first floor; then I wasn't even aware that he and Nicole lived upstairs. I'd been tense when I'd arrived, and giddily happy when I'd left with his okay to move ahead with the project.

Not this time. This time I felt tired. Tired and tense. Herb tea, I thought. I should be drinking herb tea, like Delores and Claire. Iced. I've got to stop the coffee. Really. No more caffeine.

I slid my car into a miraculously empty parking space in front of the house, and rang the bell.

Someone came down the inside stairs and unbolted the locks. A woman. At first I thought she was Nicole—she had the same delicate chin, the same bedroom eyes, the same upswept hairdo—but then I realized that she was shorter, somehow duller-looking than Nicole, and that she wasn't pregnant. She wore a navy blue skirt, stockings, bright white tennis shoes, a pressed-looking pale yellow blouse, and earrings that were little gold crosses.

She didn't smile.

"I'm Lorraine," she said, "Nicole's sister. She can't come to the door. She just about can't move."

I followed her up a massive, dim stairwell to the second floor. The building was old—Victorian probably—with high ceilings and dark, heavily varnished woodwork. I stepped into the living room.

It was filled with an unsettling combination of heavy, old, dark-looking furniture and cheap new accessories. An ancient clock in a wood frame sat on the fireplace mantel next to a cut-glass vase filled with brightly dyed feathers; worn-looking stuffed animals in neon colors—an orange buck-toothed rabbit, a pink-and-green-striped tiger with the words *Hug Me* sewn onto its stomach, an oversized version of Garfield the cat—lurked in the worn brocade sofa cushions. A pink plastic makeup mirror, the kind with strips of Ping-Pong–ball light bulbs on either side of the glass, sat on top of an old upright piano, the electrical cord dangling to the keyboard.

An elusive, peculiar smell floated in the air—something that made me think for a moment of being a kid at home. Something—I didn't know what.

Nicole sat in a front corner of the room, in a green upholstered reclining chair that had a wooden lever built into the side for cranking the foot part up and down. The sight of the chair shook me for a moment; it was exactly like one my uncle used to have—the chair that he did crossword puzzles in after work.

But the sight of Nicole shook me more. Her stomach was monstrously huge—so huge that her maternity top, a vaguely Mexican-looking blouse with red rick-rack sewn around the neck and with little puffed sleeves that made me think of porkchop frills—didn't even cover her belly button, and the waistband of her shorts was buried somewhere way down around her crotch. She lay barefoot, her legs apart. Her ankles were swollen to the size of her calves, making her legs look weirdly tubular.

An old-fashioned-looking industrial-strength electric floor fan on a tall metal stalk blew air across her legs, ruffling the papers on a tray table next to the chair, which were held down by makeshift paperweights—a man's shoe-tree, an ashtray, and a coffee mug. Another tray table, on the other side of the chair, held a telephone, a Kleenex box, a glass of water, and some magazines. She looked like somebody who didn't plan to move for a long time.

I tried to think of something nice to say, but my voice got ahead of my brain.

"Good God, Nicole," I said. "This is horrible—really horrible! Shouldn't you be in the hospital?"

"That's what I think," she said. "But they just keep making me pee and sending me home."

I looked at Lorraine for confirmation.

"She's not even dilated yet," she said. "You think this is bad? She could go another week—maybe two more weeks. When's your due date, honey?"

"Today!"

"Nobody has a first baby on time. Nobody I've ever heard of. Me—I was overdue every time."

She looked at me in a way that said: Take it from me—I know. I've had a thousand babies.

"She thinks this is bad? Just you wait, I keep telling her. This here right now—this is a piece of cake compared to what's coming around the corner. Just you wait."

She walked off down the hall, humming.

I sat down on the sofa across from Nicole and held Garfield in my lap. I was feeling a little woozy.

"Nicole," I said. "It'll be over soon. Honest."

She tugged on her shirt.

"I hate these clothes," she said. "I hate Lorraine. I hate being pregnant. I hate Hank for getting killed. I hate Silver Gaines. I hate my life."

She started to cry. The last time I'd seen her, outside Eleuthera, she'd been crying, too. And on the phone, too. Was it something about me that set her going? Or was she just a natural waterworks, like Claire?

"Look," I said, "I'm not going to pretend that I know how you feel, because I don't. I've never been pregnant and I've never had a husband who died. I'm just here to tell you that I'm sorry about Hank. And I wanted to tell you that I'm grateful to you for the message you gave to Claire—that you don't think I had anything to do with him dying. Because I didn't."

She dipped a tissue into the glass of water on the table and touched it to her forehead.

"And you're wrong about Silver," I said. "Completely wrong. I was with him all of Monday evening—starting at the zoo when I took pictures of him, and then at his apartment. Look, Nicole, I had dinner with him. I didn't leave his place until almost nine."

She closed her eyes and shook her head from side to side.

"Somebody's got it in for Silver, and is framing him for this," I said. "Somebody had it in for Hank and Silver both."

I was thinking about the argument between Nicole and Silver at Eleuthera, and about the harsh words he'd had for her the night I'd been at his apartment—the night Hank died.

"You don't know Silver like I do," she said. "You don't at all."

She was crying softly into her Kleenex.

Suddenly she clutched her belly through her shirt and winced.

"Damn!" she said.

"What's wrong?" I said. "Should I call a doctor? Call a cab? Hey, I've got my car!"

Oh my God, I thought. I've driven her into labor. What's wrong with me? I'm haranguing a widowed woman who's nine months pregnant. And I'm getting just what I deserve.

"Nicole," I said, "I'm sorry. I shouldn't have brought the subject up."

She winced again, then seemed to relax.

"Is it labor?" I said. "Are you in labor?"

"I don't think so," she said. "I think it just kicked real hard."

"Let me get you something," I said.

What? Hot water? String? I suddenly wished I'd paid more attention when Claire tried to make me watch the Nova "Miracle of Life" show on TV.

"Ice," I said. "Let me get you some ice for your water."

I walked down the hall in the direction that Lorraine had gone, assuming it would eventually take me to the kitchen, which it did.

Lorraine stood at an ironing board set up in front of the sink, slamming and sliding the iron around on a blouse with the rhythmic precision of a marine doing rifle maneuvers. Every five seconds or so she blasted the fabric with spray starch.

Ironing. That was what I'd smelled when I arrived. I hadn't

ironed anything in a long time. A really long time.

Lorraine was watching "Wheel of Fortune" on a tiny black-and-white television. Somebody had just lost some money.

She nodded her head up and down.

"Serves him right," she said. "He won five hundred dollars. But was he satisfied? No. He had to try to get more. Serves him right."

I filled Nicole's glass with ice from a bag in the freezer and water from the tap.

"I'm getting this for Nicole," I said. "She doesn't seem to be feeling so good."

Lorraine hung the blouse on a hanger, buttoned it from collar to hem, and attacked another one, barely missing a beat.

"Serves him right," she said again.

Nicole looked a little more comfortable. I gave her the water.

"Lorraine's something else, isn't she?" I said.

"I try to pretend she's not here," she said. "It's the only way I won't go crazy."

She straightened the hem of her blouse.

"I like my independence," she said. "Even Hank left me alone sometimes. Lorraine hasn't left the house since she got here except to buy groceries. She's like my warden or something."

I tried to not look at her stomach, but my eyes kept returning to it.

Independence, I thought. She likes her independence. Pretty soon she won't know what the word means.

She looked so young. And so unhappy.

"Look, Nicole," I said. "I've brought you some pictures. Of Hank. Maybe you won't want to look at them for a while, so I'll put them here, on the mantel."

The phone rang and Nicole picked up the receiver.

"Monsell residence."

Whoever it was started screaming. I could hear the voice even where I sat—a high-pitched, sustained, chipmunky sound.

Nicole was shuffling through the papers on the tray table.

"Two C?" she said. "Well, if Hank said we'll do it, of course we'll do it. I didn't know about any outlet."

She made a note on a scrap of paper with a pen that had a little teddy bear attached to the eraser end.

More chipmunky sound.

"We had to, Mrs. Meadows. It should have been raised years ago, but Hank thought it would be too hard on people. We had to. To make repairs. You know."

And then,

"We made all the correct applications. Yes. Of course we did."

And,

"Goodbye, Mrs. Meadows."

She hung up. And she was crying again.

She lifted the pile of papers from the tray table and dumped it on her stomach. They slid off and onto the floor. I pounced on them before the fan started to blow them around.

"Nicole, what's the problem? Are these the papers you were talking about on the phone?"

Lorraine appeared in the doorway.

"It's Hank's shit," she said.

I tried to shuffle them into a stack.

Lorraine folded her arms across her chest.

"He left everything in a mess," she said. "Tenants are calling every five minutes. We can't figure out who's in what buildings, let alone what Hank said he was going to fix for who. Kept it all in his head, as far as we can figure. Left her high and dry, that's what it looks like to me."

"Oh, Lorraine, please."

Nicole had shifted to her side so that she faced away from Lorraine.

"He messed with my little sister for long enough as it was—I'm not going to let him do it from the grave. As soon as this little baby is born I'm taking them away from here. Back home. And it will be like it used to be. Nicole and me, singing together. Singing together in church."

Nicole turned her head toward me.

"She doesn't believe me," she said. "She doesn't believe that I'm perfectly happy to stay right here. That I'll take care of this baby myself."

"Take care of a baby? Take care of a baby? When you're out drinking and carrying on all night in nightclubs? No ma'am. No, I don't think so."

Nicole had started humming a song, real loud, to block out Lorraine's voice, the way little kids do sometimes. And she was still crying.

The phone rang again. This time Lorraine snatched the receiver before Nicole could reach it.

"What?" she said. Then, "If you're smart enough to take it off your rent then you're smart enough to fix it yourself."

She left the room.

"Nicole," I said. "Are these the papers that have to do with Hank's buildings?"

She nodded yes and sniffed.

"It's a mess," she said. "The bank keeps sending notices about a loan that I signed for with Hank. I didn't know that it meant I'd have to pay, too."

"When did they send the first notice?"

"Oh, I don't know. A month. Six weeks ago. Two months ago. I don't know."

"And Hank knew about it?"

"Of course he did. And he kept telling me not to worry. That some other money was coming in to cover it."

"From where?"

"I don't know. I'm not interested in these things."

"So what do you do when the rent checks come in?"

"Hank took care of all that."

"Have any come in since he died?"

"A couple."

"What did you do with them?"

"They're there. With the papers."

"Isn't there somebody who's supposed to be taking care of Hank's estate? Didn't he put somebody in his will who's supposed to be the executor?"

She started crying again.

"It's me," she said.

"Look," I said. "Let's do like I said on the phone. Let me help you put these papers in some kind of order. Then maybe we can figure out what to do next. Find somebody to help you. Is Miles good with this kind of stuff?"

"I don't want Miles in my life. I'm sick of Miles and I'm sick of Jerome, and I'm sick of tap dancing. They're living in the past—all of them. Even Jerome, and he's a baby. I told Hank all this would never work out. I told him he'd die before he got his theater built. And look—I was right!"

"What theater? You mean Eleuthera?"

"Not Eleuthera. Of course not Eleuthera. The theater he wanted to build here—in Harlem."

"Silver mentioned that to me. Last week. It was the first time I'd heard anything about it."

"Well, that's a surprise. It was all Hank talked about. Ever since I met him. A little theater. For new talent. With an amateur night—like at the Apollo, he said."

She blew her nose.

"He even made drawings of how it was going to look. He was going to find the acts and be the MC. The Nonpareils would be the regular group."

She was hiccupping.

"And me," she said. "I was going to sing."

"I'm sorry," I said. "I didn't know. It sounds like it was a good idea, though."

"He bought the building already," she said. "On 124th Street.

He's renting it out—I mean he *was* renting it out—until he got the money to get the theater going. Maybe the end of next year, he thought."

"Well, that's good then, Nicole. That means money will be coming in from that. It's not like it's just sitting there empty. Is that what he got the loan for? To buy the building?"

"I don't think so. Maybe for part of it. I don't really know. I think he had some of the money for that himself. And the money from Lacey and Delores."

"Lacey and Delores?"

"He got them to put some money in, too. You know Hank—he could talk anybody into anything. He did with me—all the time."

I was sorting the papers. There were bills for repairs to the buildings. Then there were receipts for payment of bills for repairs to the buildings. And there seemed to be five or six different buildings. Maybe a couple more. It was hard to tell. One of them I recognized as the one Silver lived in on Rhinelander Avenue.

"How many buildings did he have?" I asked.

"I don't know. Four or five. Six maybe. No. Four apartment buildings—not real big ones—and then the building for the theater. And then the Coleman Center building. I don't know if the papers for that are there. So six buildings."

I divvied things up into stacks. She was right. Six properties. Six piles of paper.

Then there were applications to the Division of Housing and Community Renewal for rent increases—a wad of them—submitted by Hank early in the summer for a couple of the buildings, a couple of letters from people asking for permission to sublet, and a letter from someone saying he planned to leave his apartment.

"This isn't so bad, Nicole," I said. "Once you see what you've got."

"I hate it," she said. "I hate forms. I hate money."

One of the file folders had copies of old tax returns in it, arranged chronologically, going back six years. Three folders were full of copies of leases, arranged by property.

"These are in good shape, Nicole," I said. "Hank was really pretty organized about this stuff."

Another one had papers in it that seemed to relate to the purchase of the buildings. Copies of purchase and sale agreements. Copies of inspection reports. Copies of deeds. Tons of deeds. To eight or nine properties.

I matched the deeds to the stacks of paper that I'd organized by property: two buildings on West 152nd Street; another on 148th Street; the building that Silver lived in; the building the Coleman Center was in—also on Rhinelander Avenue; and another building on 124th Street—the place where Nicole said Hank had planned to have his theater. He'd bought most of the buildings in the late sixties, and the 124th Street building in 1981.

"It looks like the sixties were good to Hank," I said.

"What do you mean?"

"I mean he bought a lot of property just about all at once."

"Oh, that," she said. "That's because of the money from his song."

"His song?"

"You know," she said. " 'Empty Plate Blues.' They used it in a movie. I don't even know the name of it."

Because you were probably six years old, I thought.

"Then there was a record, too," she said, waving her hand toward a bookshelf filled with albums. "The soundtrack. It's around here someplace. I guess it made him a bunch of money all at once."

And he sensibly pumped it into real estate so it's still making money, I thought. Why couldn't Max think of anything like that? On the other hand, why couldn't I?

And what was Delores doing living in a chicken coop and driving a car held together with electrical tape?

"He doesn't make money on the song anymore?"

"Are you kidding? Have you ever heard it?"

I decided not to bring up the subject of the night at Eleuthera.

"That song's as corny as can be," she said. "No, nobody wants to be singing that kind of stupid junk anymore."

There were three deeds left over. The deed to Hank and Nicole's house here on Edgecombe Road, which Hank bought in 1970, and two others—bad photocopies of deeds to property on Harnett Avenue. Unlike the others, these didn't describe the property as having been deeded to Hank, but to something called "Gardner Frye, Trustee for Ubednego Realty Trust."

"What are these, Nicole? Do you know anything about buildings on Harnett Avenue?"

She looked at the papers, then shook her head no.

"Way over there? No. These aren't Hank's. It's just some old stuff. I don't know anything about it."

"How about this Ubednego Realty Trust? Do you know anything about it? Have you ever heard of it?"

She handed the papers back.

"I told you," she said, "I'm sick of this stuff. Sick to death. And I have to go to the bathroom."

She lowered the leg section of the chair, then eased herself into a standing position, shrugging off my attempt to help her up. Then she placed one hand on the small of her back, the way pregnant women for some reason do, and walked slowly down the hall.

Any suspicion I'd had that Nicole might have played a part in Hank's death fled my mind.

The woman could barely move.

I listened for the bathroom door to click shut and looked at the deeds again.

Both of them had been signed the same day in September two years ago.

For a minute I wished my Leica were a little spy camera, like the cigarette-lighter-sized Minox they used to advertise in the back of the

National Geographic. Instead I tore the cover sheet off one of the leases and used Nicole's teddy-bear pen to copy down information from the deeds—the addresses, the dates, the name of the person who sold it: "T. Thomas, trustee for Nakoe Realty Trust." And something else that looked possibly interesting: recorded at New York County Registry of Deeds, Liber 6952, page 48 and page 49. Then I scribbled the addresses of the other properties on the back.

I folded the paper up small and stuffed it into my pocket.

Somebody yelled up from the street.

"Nicole!"

A very high, sing-songy voice.

I nearly jumped out of my skirt.

I peered out the front bay window.

It was Lacey Gaines. Lacey. Smiling and holding a bunch of huge white and pink flowers up toward the window.

"Nicole!" she said. "I've brought you some treats!"

"I'm not Nicole," I said. "I'm Libby."

I looked down the hall to see if Nicole was coming yet. She wasn't.

"Hold on," I yelled. "I'll let you in."

I went down the stairs and unbolted the locks.

"Olive!" she said. "What in the world are you doing in these parts?"

Was I imagining things, or was she refusing to look at my face while she talked?

I followed her up the stairs.

"Visiting," I said. "Bringing Nicole some pictures."

"Of me?"

She was serious.

"Of course not of you," I said. "Of Hank."

Lorraine walked into the living room and scowled at Lacey. Lacey smiled back.

"Hello, gorgeous," she said. "What a pretty little outfit you've got on."

Lorraine walked back into the kitchen.

"Lovely," said Lacey. "What a lovely woman."

"Nicole's in the bathroom," I said. "She looks terrible."

"Oh come now," she said. "Every pregnant woman looks beauti-ful. All those extra hormones. Really!"

She was in her souped-up mode. The way she was after the show at Eleuthera. Lots of posturing. Big talk. She was ripping the tissue paper off the flower stems with dramatic hand gestures.

But she still wasn't looking at me while she talked.

"Aren't you supposed to be in jail somewhere?" she said.

There was an edge to her voice that surprised me."Thanks a lot, Lacey," I said. "I'd forgotten about that for a moment."

She yanked the colored feathers out of Nicole's vase and stuffed the flowers in.

"I think you're presuming quite a bit," she said, "coming to Nicole's home just now, given the circumstances."

"Lacey," I said. "Please tell me that you're not serious. Please tell me that you don't think Silver and I had anything to do with Hank dying."

She smoothed her hair in the mirror over the mantel, then turned around.

"Oh, who knows," she said. "But I do think that we're all capable of far more exotic behavior than we like to think we are. Don't you think so too?"

Nicole came back into the room, hoisted herself into the reclining chair, and cranked up the foot.

"I thought I saw some lightning," she said.

Lacey moved to Nicole's side, stuffed a pillow behind her head, and started talking to her about the importance of keeping a bottle of cologne in the refrigerator for days like these, ignoring me.

The doorbell rang.

"They're here," said Lacey.

"Who?"

"The fellas," she said.

Lorraine went downstairs to let them in.

I looked in the mirror over the mantel and caught sight of Lacey scowling at Nicole and gesturing toward me with her head.

"I forgot," Nicole said to her, in a voice louder—because of the sound of the fan—than she meant it to be. "I forgot when all of you were coming."

I felt myself flushing.

Jerome and Miles walked into the room; each gave Nicole a kiss. Jerome looked at the piles of papers I had organized on the table next to the reclining chair.

"What are you doing with all this?" he said to Nicole. "It doesn't seem to be the kind of thing you should be worrying about right now."

She motioned toward me.

"Libby," she said. "It was confusing, and Libby was helping me sort it out."

He gave me a quick, hard look.

"We thought it would be a little easier to deal with if it were organized better," I said.

He picked up the papers, brought them to the sofa, and put them on his knee, as if he thought I had plans to take them or something.

"Really," I said. "We were just getting them under control."

He just looked at me.

"Apollo couldn't make it," Miles said. "His doctor told him he ought to . . . "

Lacey held her hand toward him in a gesture that meant "stop talking."

I got the message. I decided to spare her the task of asking me to leave, picked up my camera, and headed for the door.

Over the sound of the fan there was a low rumble of thunder.

What was going on here?

"Goodbye," I said to Nicole. "It looks like you were right about the storm."

17

JUST AS I PRESSED the gas pedal there was a crash so loud that the car shook. I threw myself into the passenger seat thinking—what?—nuclear attack? A sniper?

Then the rain came down.

Blessed, blessed rain.

Really, I said to myself. I've got to take relaxation classes or something.

And maybe I was overreacting to what was going on back there at Nicole's. Maybe Jerome and Miles didn't care that I was there at all. Maybe Lacey was just feeling extra prima donnaish or something.

Still, I felt stung. A week ago I counted Jerome, Miles, and Lacey among my friends.

What was going on?

I rolled the windows up, set the wipers swinging, and pressed the buttons that were supposed to defog the windows.

The wipers couldn't keep up with the rain.

I pulled over on Eighth Avenue and waited for it to slow down.

When it didn't, I reached into the glove compartment for my street map and my red travel umbrella—the one I'd gotten for sending thirty dollars to Channel 13—opened it, and ran into a place called Ed the Chef's.

The windows were steamed over and the patrons were dripping

water on the linoleum. I placed an order for coffee and a piece of pie. Then I headed for the pay phone and called Claire. I wanted to tell her that now that the heat wave had broken I wanted Lucas back in the city with me, but she didn't answer. So I called Duncan's office to find out if he knew where Claire was, but Dee answered and said she didn't know where he was. I told her about Nicole, and asked her if she knew anybody who could help her manage Hank's buildings.

"Where are they?" she said.

"Harlem mostly. And a couple in the Bronx. And maybe something on Harnett Avenue."

"We'll figure something out," she said. "Maybe today, if he comes in."

I drank my coffee and ate my pie. The rain was still slamming down, and it felt like the temperature had dropped twenty degrees in ten minutes. I warmed my fingers on the mug and ordered a second piece of pie. I'd been eating the vending machine kind for so long I'd forgotten you could get them with real fruit inside.

I opened my map and pulled the scrap of paper with the information about Hank's deeds from my pocket.

Harnett Avenue. I connected it with the South Bronx. Maybe I took some pictures there once. Maybe somebody I hung around with ten years ago lived there.

I found it on the map—a ten-block street just south of the Bruckner Expressway in Hunts Point.

The storm had calmed down. I paid for my meal and headed across the Macomb Dam Bridge, juggling my map on my knees.

I left 163rd Street at Hunts Point Avenue and found myself at Harnett Avenue even before I'd started to look for it. I checked my addresses—numbers 1307 and 1309—took a guess, and turned right, driving slowly, searching for numbers.

Past a locksmith's, past a fortune-teller's, past a pawnshop. Past a funeral parlor with a neon sign. Past a man unloading rainwater from an awning that extended over the fruit and vegetable display in front of his store. Past a dreary white slab of a building called the Harnett Juvenile Detention Center.

Past a couple of blocks of apartment buildings growing flush against the sidewalk—the eleven-hundred block, the twelve-hundred block. Past a mailman wedging an umbrella handle between his jaw and shoulder while he sorted through the mail in his bag. Past an old woman pushing a baby stroller with a clear plastic hood over the top of it. I wondered how the baby could breathe.

Then suddenly a block with no noticeable commerce—no noticeable life. A wall of row houses with boarded-up doors; boarded-up windows; a shattered windowbox hanging to the ground from one screw; concrete stoops so corroded from age and disrepair that they could pass for piles of rocks; soggy, matted drifts of cardboard, newspapers, potato chip bags. An outline of a person in a window evaporated as I drove by—or was it my own reflection?

The street addresses were gone—pried off, scraped off, painted over.

No, I was wrong. The number 1305 was sprayed in a vapor trail of black aerosol paint on the pediment over a door, which was locked with a chain and padlock.

Next to 1305 stood two twelve- or thirteen-story buildings, made from concrete and bald of any architectural detail that might have made them look inviting even when they were new. They didn't have street numbers on them, but they had to be 1307 and 1309.

The third-floor windows on the second building were boarded up, and someone had taped what looked like part of a blue translucent plastic raincoat across a broken window on the fourth floor.

I parked in front of a sawed-off meter. The only other car on the block didn't have any tires on it.

How stupid was I to bring my camera with me here? Who would talk with me if they saw me with it? What would they think I was? A cop? A social worker documenting bad conditions so I could put a kid in custody of the state?

I stuffed it under the seat, flicked open the umbrella, locked the car, and climbed the steps to 1307. The door was propped open with a woman's shoe—or what had once been a woman's shoe—a phony snakeskin T-strap with the point of a nail where the heel used to be. The framework on the door buzzer-intercom system was gone; yellowed plastic buttons dangled from the naked wiring like tentacles.

I thought about the building Silver lived in. The freshly painted hallways, the smell of Lemon Pledge in the elevator. This can't be Hank's too, I thought.

Maybe this was a building he was thinking of buying and fixing up. Maybe that was the deal.

I grabbed a tentacle and squeezed it, wondering if I was grounded in my sneakers. I leaned my head toward the crack in the door to listen for the buzz.

Nothing.

My feet suddenly went soggy.

I glanced down. I was standing in a shallow puddle. A used syringe floated next to my right foot.

I knocked on the door.

Nothing happened.

I nudged the broken high-heel aside, opened the door, and wedged the shoe back in place. Then I walked into the front hall and pressed my ear to the first door on the left. I could hear the sound of a radio and maybe the clink of a spoon against a dish.

I banged on the door with my fist. I heard a scraping sound, then footsteps.

A woman opened the door. She was young and thin, and she was wearing a man's white undershirt and a pair of underpants. A strand of hair fell forward against her face. She pushed it back, then continued to make the same brushing motion against her forehead even though the hair was in place.

She had been extremely attractive once, maybe even very beautiful—with high cheekbones, sculpted, voluptuous lips, and slightly tilted eyes. But now the lid of one eye was swollen and infected-looking and one of her front teeth was broken. Her skin, once caramel-colored, maybe, had gone yellowish; the insides of her arms crawled with needle marks.

She hopped from one foot to the other, like a little child, unable to stand still for a moment.

"How much," she said. "How much do you want?"

It was noon, but the room was dark. Shades hung over some of the windows; a torn blanket hung over another. There was no furniture in the room—just some boxes and some sleeping places made from nests of blankets and sheets. I could make out the outline of a figure lying in one of the nests; two large whitish hands poked out from one side of the sheets.

Rainwater seeped through a crack in the molding on one of the windows and collected in a depression in the floor. The bathroom at the back of the room had no door, and even from where I stood I could tell from the smell that the toilet had backed up.

"Nothing," I said.

She looked at me suspiciously.

"Nothing right now, I mean. It's not what I'm here for."

The owner of the feet rose up from his nest. I couldn't make out his features—only that he was enormous and at least half naked. His stomach gleamed in the dim light, a grayish dead-white color—like the belly of a fish.

"Who the fuck is it?" he said, and sunk back down into the sheets.

The woman looked at the figure for a moment, then turned back to me.

"Good," she said. "Because we hardly have anything."

"Look," I said to her. "I'm from Legal Aid."

She started to shut the door.

I put my foot in it, just like I'd seen in the movies.

"Wait a minute," I said. "We think your landlord is stealing your money. We think he's charging too much rent."

Where did that come from?

Her good eye lit up for a heartbeat, then darkened again, like the light on a smoke alarm that tells you the battery is okay.

The figure rose from the sheets again.

"Whoever you are, you're staying too long," he said.

"My man," she said to me. "He used to be a hockey player."

"I only need a second," I said to her. "I just need to make sure that we're talking about the same landlord. Who do you send the rent money to?"

Would she fall for this? Would anybody?

"I don't know his name," she said. "Nobody does. We just pay it to the address we have."

"What's that?"

"Just a post office box."

"Do you know it? Do you know the post office box?"

She started wiping at her face again.

"Three hundred sixty-five," she said.

Great number, I thought. I wondered if she'd just made it up to get rid of me.

"Is that all?"

"That's all," she said.

"The zip code?" I said.

"I don't know zip codes."

I was starting to lose contact.

"One more thing," I said. "Have you ever heard of something called the Ubednego Company? No. The Ubednego Realty Trust?"

"No," she said. Then,

"Hey, wait a minute. Are you trying to sell me something?"

The hockey player rose again.

"When do we get the money back?" she said.

Good question.

"I don't know," I said. "Pretty soon. I'll let you know."

I got in my car.

I felt bad. About the woman. How she looked. How she couldn't live much longer, looking that wasted.

About lying. As if enough people hadn't taken advantage of her already.

Somebody was standing on the steps of the building kitty-corner across the street. He was wearing a yellow rain poncho with a built-in visor, and the visor was pulled down low over his face. He looked familiar.

Ridiculous. How could somebody look familiar if I couldn't even see his face?

I looked in my rearview mirror and pulled into the street. A brown car, parked across the road, started its engine and pulled out at almost the same time.

I drove down to Hunts Point Avenue and turned north toward the expressway.

The brown car did, too.

Why would someone be following me?

Idiot, I said to myself. Nine out of ten cars on Harnett would be heading for Hunts Point Avenue and the Bruckner Expressway. It's the only way to get out of here.

I turned down a side street to see what would happen.

The brown car turned down the side street too.

I hoped it wasn't a dead end.

I tried to figure out what kind of car it was—tried to imagine myself describing it to the police. Then I remembered that the police weren't my friends anymore.

It was a brown car—that was all I knew. With no front license plate, of course. Maybe a Ford. Maybe a Chevy. I couldn't tell.

A brown car with brown tires. And some guy driving it. At least from the general nature of the head and shoulders I thought it was a guy. But then again, the car's windshield was tinted, its wipers were going, and it was a rainy day.

I looped back to Hunts Point Avenue from another side street, and the car followed.

Hell.

I went through a red light and it followed.

Brilliant, I thought. What do the cops do to you when they ticket you for a traffic violation and find out there are murder charges pending against you? Pistol-whip you?

What if the guy in the car had a gun? Maybe he was going to drive right past me and shoot me through the window. They did that in the movies, too.

Was this my crank caller?

I threaded my way to the expressway entrance. I was on the ramp that feeds into traffic. The brown car was on it too, just behind me.

There was a space. I could pull out now.

No. A line of traffic was bearing down on the entrance lane. I waited for a moment, until it was almost too late, then floored the gas and pulled in front of the first car.

Honking, but no screech of brakes, no crash.

I looked in the rearview mirror. The brown car was still on the exit ramp.

The woman in the car behind me gave me the finger.

I got off at the first exit and wove my way through Mott Haven, across the river, through East Harlem, and down Park Avenue through midtown, into downtown, checking and rechecking the rearview mirror for the brown car.

It never appeared again. By the time I got to the Village, I was having second thoughts. Was it really following me? After all, it didn't try to run me off the road, did it? Maybe it was just some kid having some stupid fun.

Maybe it wasn't even brown.

I parked in a lot on Canal, bartering away twenty-three dollars and my principles for the psychological comfort of being able to make a quick getaway.

As the elevator ground upward I heard the reassuring sound of Lucas's bark.

I hugged him and looked for Claire, who wasn't there.

"So where is she?" I asked him.

He barked and banged his head against my leg.

Claire's bag was on her bed; a couple of mammoth dahlias stood in a vase on the kitchen counter; there were salad fixings and a lump of mozzarella cheese in the refrigerator. I chipped a popsicle out of the freezer with a spoon.

The phone rang.

It was Martha Grant.

"I'm sorry I haven't gotten back," she said. "I've been on trial."

"Is it over?"

"Finally," she said. "Maybe I can act like a human being again."

"Did they convict him?"

She sighed.

"Unfortunately, yes."

Now why did I have to ask that?

"But he didn't really stand much of a chance," she said. "He bragged about it to three other people, including his soon-to-be ex-girlfriend."

I decided not to ask what "it" was.

"Look," I said, "I just feel like we ought to be talking more. Like we ought to be doing something."

"Of course," she said. "In fact, I have a list right here of things we should explore. I was thinking you could come in and . . . "

"Right now," I said. "I want to do something right now."

"Libby," she said. "Are you okay? You sound upset."

I decided against telling her about the brown car. What was there to tell? A phone call from a nut and a car I could hardly describe?

"I'm just a little tired," I said. "A little tense. Wouldn't you be?"

"Of course. Let's get to work, then. We could hire an investigator to do some of these things, or send out a paralegal, but some I think you could do on your own, if you want."

A nice way of saying this will cost a million if you don't do it yourself, I suppose.

"First," she said. "Can you find out who was at the deli when you bought the chicken salad and beer? Somebody might remember seeing you, you know, and that would help."

I grabbed a hunk of Post-Its. "Deli," I wrote down. "Who at counter."

"And your camera," she said. "You said you were taking pictures of Silver at his apartment. Did you take any pictures on the staircase? Outside? On the balcony? Somewhere people would remember seeing you with a camera and the time you were there? We've already sent somebody up to ask around, but it wouldn't hurt for you to look."

She's really grasping at straws, I thought. This sounds like something out of a "Magnum" episode. I'm a goner.

"Pictures," I wrote. "Any clues?"

Fat chance, I thought.

"What else?" I asked.

"That's all for now," she said.

"That's all?"

"Don't worry," she said.

For the first time, I detected a note of real tension in her voice.

"Martha," I said. "What about Silver? Is he out?"

"No, he's not," she said. "I just talked to Elkind. They remanded him."

"What's that mean?"

"No bail. It turns out he had an old no-show on his record for resisting arrest and assaulting an officer—a civil disobedience thing from 1963, according to Elkind."

"They can just keep him there?"

"Until the Grand Jury, anyway."

Poor Silver. For some reason the image of his jasmine plant, shedding dead leaves, came to my mind.

"Martha," I said. "Seeing as how we know that Silver and I didn't kill Hank, don't you think we ought to be trying to figure out who *did* kill him?"

"We're all open to suggestions," she said.

"I looked at some papers at Nicole's," I said. "Papers that have to do with Hank's real estate holdings. Everything seemed on the up and up—you know, he was a real good landlord; you should see Silver's building——except there were a couple of deeds to property in the Bronx that Nicole had never heard of. Are you there?"

"I'm here."

"So I drove up there this morning, and it turns out that one of them is some kind of crack house or something. Not like anything you'd think Hank would be involved in, you know?"

"I don't know anything about Hank's real estate dealings," she said. "But go on."

"So I'm wondering," I said. "I'm wondering if there might be some connection. That Hank was involved in something nobody seems to know about."

"That's kind of vague, Libby."

"I know," I said.

I took the piece of paper with the Harnett Avenue deed information on it from the inside of my camera case.

"How do you find out about something called a realty trust?" I asked her.

I read her the names and the dates and the recording information.

"I'm not sure," she said. "But somebody around here does. Somebody will get back to you."

"This afternoon?"

"Of course."

There was mail for me on the table. An invitation to a gallery opening that happened two days before; a discount film-processing offer; and a postcard from Max. A yellowed appointment postcard left over from a stint years ago when he sold office supplies on commission. He'd crossed out the type that said "I'll be in town on _____ with our New Line" and written underneath in pencil:

Thanks for the cash. I'll make it up to you. Max

Then, way at the bottom, as if it were an afterthought:

Call me. New tel. 304-922-7742.

Call me.

Why? So he can ask for more money?

I squeezed the card into my fist. Then I spread it out again, flattening the creases with my thumb.

Call me.

I dialed the number.

Somebody coughed a couple of times, then said,

"Thunderbird."

Thunderbird?

"Is this a bar?" I asked. That would be like Max, I thought. To have a new phone number in a bar.

"Nope, not a bar," he said.

"A hotel?"

"Nope again," he said. "I'll save you guessing. A motel. Thunderbird Motel. What can we do for you?"

"I'm looking for someone named Max Kincaid," I said. "I'm his daughter."

He started to chuckle. Then he coughed again. Then he came to.

"Max Kincaid?" he said. "Fellow that won the lottery? My, my, my. As they say, even a blind pig is bound to find an acorn once in a while."

Nice, I thought.

"Is he there?" I asked.

"No ma'am," he said. "We haven't seen Max around here in a couple days. Checked in with his new wife, he did. Honeymooners. You know about that, don't you?" he said.

"I know it."

"Not getting along real well. Did you know that?"

"That's what he told me," I said.

"She moved out before she slept in the bed," he said. "Said the place wasn't up to her standards. Said there wasn't any ice machine or swimming pool."

He laughed again.

"Haven't seen Max either," he said. "Except for this picture in today's paper."

"What picture in the paper?"

"My, my," he said. "Where do you live, anyway?"

"Not near enough to read your paper," I said. "What was the picture about?"

He started laughing, or coughing, or choking, or whatever it was again.

"Now don't get me wrong," he said. "I like Max. He keeps things tidy and he's okay with me. But he sure did marry himself some big trouble."

"What was the picture of?"

"Why, Max and the bride, leaving the courthouse."

I heard him shuffling things around.

"I've got it around here somewhere, if you'll hold on a minute."

What did he think I was doing? Talking on a picture-phone?

"Right, here it is. There's a picture of Max, a pretty nasty look on his face. Nice necktie, though. He's got a big fat-faced fellow—his lawyer, it says—holding on to his arm. And there's the bride—the very picture of meanness, if you ask me—a-coming down after him on the stairs, holding her hat on with her hands, and her little lawyer fellow carrying her pocketbook.

"Here," he said. "It's just a short little piece underneath. 'Marital blitz,' it says. 'Max Kincaid and wife Iris Kincaid leave Family Court early today after filing simultaneous claims for divorce. Mrs. Kincaid claims she is entitled to most of the one-and-a-half-million-dollar BigBucks win claimed by her husband in early summer. Terrence Dowley, Mrs. Kincaid's attorney, says she will settle for nothing less than a trial. Guy Carpenter, the attorney for Mr. Kincaid, would not comment on the matter.

"My, my," he said. "What a mess. I've been holding on to this to give to Max. Do you want me to send it to you instead?"

"No thanks," I said. "I don't need it. When did you say you last saw Max?"

"Well, a fellow here says he saw him yesterday morning."

"Did he leave anything in his room?"

"You're worried he's left town or something?"

Careful, I thought. He'll think Max skipped without paying the bill. Which he probably has.

"I'd just like to have an idea where I could find him if I had to."

"Don't you worry. He left a pair of nice new shoes and some fancy pajamas behind. He'll be back. I'm sure of that."

Right, I thought. The shoes probably didn't fit right and the pajamas were probably Iris's idea of loungewear. When the going gets tough, Max heads for Trailways.

"What did you say Max's lawyer's name was again?" I said.

"Carpenter. Guy Carpenter. That's quite a name around here. His dad was a state rep a while back."

"Do you think you could do me a favor and look up his number in the phone book? I may need to talk with him sometime."

He found the number for me.

I thanked him and was about to hang up.

"Hold on," he said. "Are you Max's daughter in New York City? The one who works for the magazine?"

"I guess so," I said.

"Max said you're a real glamorous girl. Yessir. Real glamorous."

"Thanks," I said.

I went in the bathroom and washed my face. I looked tired. I looked too thin. I was growing a cowlick.

Very glamorous.

* * *

I called the number the motel man had given me for Guy Carpenter.

"Carpenter," he said.

"Guy Carpenter, the lawyer?"

"Yes, ma'am."

"My name is Libby Kincaid. Max Kincaid's daughter. I've been trying to get in touch with him, but I don't know where he is."

"Where do you live?" he said.

"New York," I said. "It's not that I think anything's wrong, but he's not at the motel right now that he was checked into, and . . . "

"What's his middle name?" he said.

"What?"

"What's your father's middle name?"

"Virgil," I said. "Why?"

"Just checking," he said. "You can't be too careful. What if you were somebody pretending to be Kincaid's daughter and I talked to you? Then I'd be in a pile of trouble, wouldn't I?"

"It hadn't occurred to me," I said.

"So you think old Max has skipped town?" he said.

Here we go again, I thought.

"No," I lied. "It's just that he seems to be out right now, and I know he was with you yesterday, and I thought that maybe he'd said something to you about where he would be today. I've got a message for him."

"No, ma'am," he said. "Your father never has much to say to me, even about his legal matters. Tight-lipped, I'd say he is. Kind of difficult to talk to, to tell you the truth. No, he didn't tell me anything about his travel plans."

"Mr. Carpenter," I said, "I'm kind of worried about Max and this divorce business. You know, that money he got in the lottery—it's not a tremendous amount to live on when it's parceled out over a long period, the way they do it. But it would mean some security for Max. Maybe he wouldn't be broke all the time. Maybe he could get a decent place to live. Maybe . . . "

My throat seized up.

Maybe he wouldn't drink himself to death in some fleabag motel, I thought. Maybe I wouldn't have to worry about him starving in some bus terminal somewhere. Maybe I could stop being afraid every time some homeless man with shaking hands and oozing eyes asked me for money—afraid that it might be Max.

"Ma'am," he said. "Are you okay?"

"In a minute," I said. "In a minute I will be."

I heard him clear his throat, then maybe run a pencil through an electric sharpener.

"Mr. Carpenter," I said. "Could Iris—Max's wife, that is—really get any of that lottery money in a divorce settlement? I mean, they weren't even married when he won it. They were seeing each other, I guess, but they weren't married at the time. And then they were married for less than two weeks when she filed for divorce! How can she get anything? It seems crazy to me."

"To be honest with you," he said, "it seems crazy to me, too. But the law around here has it that the marital property includes all the property that either party brings into the marriage at the time of the marriage. Of course, then it gets divvied up based on a bunch of factors in our equitable distribution statute. Behavior of the parties, and, you're right, source of the property and length of the marriage, and some other things. So it would seem that she wouldn't have much of a chance of getting very much of the money. But we've got some old-timer judges around here who might not like the looks of your father too much, might know a little about his dealings in the past, which I understand weren't exactly wholesome, and might not be too inclined to look very favorably on him. He might have some trouble at a trial."

I sighed. Poor Max, I thought. He wasn't exactly the picture of integrity, but he didn't deserve to have his lucky break sabotaged like this.

"But that's not really what I'm concerned about," he said.

"No? What then?"

"Her lawyer tells me that Iris claims that she paid for the ticket and picked the winning number with Max, while they were out on a date. And then when the winning number was announced, Iris was out of town, so Max collected it himself.

"Now if that's so," he said, "it sort of takes all this out of the realm of divorce law and into the world of—who knows?—fraud, breach of contract—that kind of thing. I mean, if she could prove that she did pick the number, it would make things entirely different. She could end up with some money. Quite a bit, maybe."

Good grief, I thought. I thought these things only happened on "L.A. Law."

"But that's only if she could prove she picked the number, right?" I asked.

"Right."

"So what does Max have to say about this? How does he say he came up with the number? I never thought to ask him when he was here. What do people usually use? Birthdays? Addresses?"

Suddenly I remembered Iris pumping Max and me for birthdates while we were eating at Windsor's Castle and when I was alone with her in Rockefeller Center. My birthday. Avery's. My mother's. For her astrology hobby, she'd said. No, for the family tree she said she was going to embroider—excuse me—that her friend was going to *liquid* embroider. Cripes, I thought. She was fishing for a way to figure out the number.

"I asked him," he said. "And he was kind of evasive. At first I thought he was going to tell me something like you just said—a birthdate or a telephone number—but then he said that it was random. That he'd picked the numbers at random. It was what I was thinking about when I told you he was tight-lipped."

"So what's the number?" I said. "Do you have it there?"

"Max brought me some copies of his lottery papers."

I heard a drawer open and close.

"Here," he said. "The registration form he filled out when he claimed the money; the newspaper clipping; and, oh yes, here's what I was looking for—a copy of the winning ticket. He said that they give you a duplicate when they take the original. For a souvenir or something.

"Here we go," he said. "111-333-5243-001."

I wrote it down on Max's postcard.

Thirty-three. November 13, 1933. Mom was born in 1928. Max was born in 1932. Fifty-two, maybe. Nope. Nobody born in 1952. The 524 combination looked a little familiar. Our telephone exchange in Darby? No, that began with a seven.

I tacked the postcard to my darkroom bulletin board.

"Are you there?" he said. "Anything familiar in the numbers?"

"Not right off," I said.

"Well, who knows," he said. "Maybe he did pick it at random."

"And if he did?"

"It would probably come down to Iris's word against his."

"I'm not sure who I would pick in the truth department," I said.

"I know what you mean," he said.

"Well," I said, "if Max calls would you let him know I was looking for him?"

"Will do," he said.

"And," he said, "don't worry. I'm giving this one all I've got. Don't worry. I'm trying to help your old man as much as I can."

"Are you getting paid? Did Max give you anything yet?"

"He did," he said. "Five hundred dollars retainer."

"Good," I said.

So he built in a little padding for himself, I thought.

I couldn't help smiling.

That's my Max.

18

DIVORCE. Max and Iris. Lacey and Silver. Hank and Delores. Probably half the married couples I knew.

Like my earring collection. Ten years they were all in pairs, each pair necking in its own little socket in my earring case. Now I only have one of the little jade fish because I lost the mate in a bed somewhere; only one of the turquoise balls because the other dropped down the drain; some of them just evaporated. I don't even try to keep them in the case anymore; I toss them into a Band-Aid box.

Good thing it's okay to just wear one these days, or poke the stray into the second hole in your ear.

Delores and Hank.

So how did he end up with all the money from the song they wrote together?

I called Martha Grant.

I waited on the line while she finished another call.

"Libby," she said. "You're psychic. I was just talking with a real estate lawyer here about your question. About the realty trust. What she said is that it's an extremely good device for concealing the ownership of property. The beneficiaries don't go on record."

"But the guy who's the trustee," I said, "doesn't he own the property?"

"That's not how it works," she said. "The trustee can be anybody—usually, Joanna says, the lawyer who set up the trust."

"So this Gardner Frye fellow—the trustee—would he be a lawyer?"

"Maybe," she said. "Just a minute."

I heard some bumping sounds.

"I'm looking in *Martindale-Hubbell*," she said. "It's got a list of everybody admitted to practice in the city."

I waited.

"James J. Frye," she said. "Diana Frye. Allen Fryer. Nope. No Gardner Frye lawyer around here. Unless he's dead of, course," she said. "What did you say the date on the deed was?"

"Two years ago."

More bumping.

"It's not in last year's directory either," she said. "Joanna also said that it would be possible—not legal, of course—if somebody were really going to lengths to conceal things—to put down a fictitious name for the trustee."

"They don't ask for verification that the person exists when you go to record the deed?"

"Apparently not."

"So what else can I do to find out who owns this property?"

"Just what you seem to be doing already. Snoop around."

"That's all?"

"That's all."

"One more thing," I said.

"What?"

"How can I find out the terms of somebody's divorce agreement?"

"You can't," she said. "Unless you just ask them and they tell you."

"You can't just look it up in the courthouse? I mean, could you, since you're a lawyer and all?"

"Not unless I'm the lawyer for one of the people who got divorced."

"Couldn't you just go and try?" I asked.

"Libby, for crying out loud. Think what you're asking me to do. I could get my license taken away."

"I was just wondering," I said.

"If you got divorced in New York, what courthouse would have your records?"

"I guess the Family Court," she said. "Libby, what in the world are you doing?"

"I'll let you know later," I said.

I hung yesterday's skirt in the bathroom while I showered, to steam the wrinkles out. Then I put on one of Claire's work blouses, her beige linen jacket, panty hose, and the pair of black pumps from hell that a sales clerk once tried to convince me would solve all my fashion problems.

I hunted through the blue pages and found the courthouse address. Then I walked to an office supply place on Broadway and bought myself a long yellow pad of lined paper—the kind Martha Grant was always writing on.

I looked at my reflection in the store window. Maybe I look like a lawyer, I thought.

I tugged at my hair. Maybe not.

The courthouse was on Lafayette Street. Funny how until Tuesday I'd been practically living in the courthouse district but I'd barely noticed it was there. Just a bunch of buildings I figured I'd never have any connection with, like the buildings on Wall Street.

I walked up the courthouse steps and continued, confidently, I hoped, down a wing to the left. No good. Just courtrooms, two of them with judges and people in them, one of them empty. I turned around and walked down the wing to the right, past a bank of pay phones, past a padlocked ladies room, past a security guard holding a crying baby.

Dead ahead there was a set of double doors with frosted glass windows and the words *Probate Records* painted in a black arc across them.

I went through the doors, walked up to a massive wooden counter, and stood next to a thin black man in a beige suit. He was talking across the counter to a woman who couldn't have been more than eighteen. She had her hair pulled on top of her head in a pink plastic clip that looked like it was meant for holding potato chip bags closed.

"I told you," she said to him. "I just can't help you. I don't know where anything is that's over ten years old. Mrs. Mayhew is at the dentist. Ron called in sick. Tully could help you but he just went out for coffee. If you come back in an hour somebody can help you then."

"Look," he said to her, "I know exactly where they are. I can't come back in an hour because I have to be in court in twenty minutes. I will put them back exactly where I found them. I won't let anybody know that you let me in."

He leaned over the counter toward her.

"And," he said, "I sure won't let anybody know how pretty you are when you're mad."

She lowered her lashes, smiled, and swung open a half door that was built into the counter. The man walked through.

I resisted an impulse to gag, smiled, and followed behind him.

"Paralegal," I said. "I'm with him."

I didn't look for her response.

I followed the guy through a door, down a flight of metal stairs, and through another door into a dim room filled with utility shelving packed with files.

"You were pretty smooth back there," I said.

He started flipping through a box of index cards.

"You didn't do so bad yourself," he said.

One bank of card files said "Plaintiff." One said "Defendant." They were all in alphabetical order.

I found the "M's."

I found Monsell. "Monsell, Harriet v. Monsell, Arnold G."; "Monsell, Hector Q. v. Monsell, Ruby Faye"; "Monsell, Roger W. v. Monsell, Roxanne." Then "Monsell, Harold J. v. Monsell, Delores."

Why am I always so surprised when I find what I want?

"No. 309-61H," it said.

I wrote down the number on my pad.

I wandered the maze of stacks and found the 300s. The guy in the tan suit was pulling something off the shelf.

"Doing okay?" he said.

"Almost," I said.

"You'll be lucky," he said. "They say they're going to transfer most of this stuff into dead storage before the end of the year. If they can find any place for dead storage."

I found the 309s, then 309-58, then 309-59, then 309-60, then a dusty accordion file with "Monsell v. Monsell" typed on a label in the corner.

I pulled it off the shelf and blew off the dust.

The court papers were bound into one file. Complaint, some forms, a marriage certificate. Then a three-page document called simply "Agreement."

Lots of "Whereases," lots of "therefores." She would get the car, but no alimony. They would split some money in a savings account. Neither would be responsible for the debts of the other.

Then,

> In exchange for the lump sum of $500, the wife relinquishes all rights to any songs jointly conceived and or copyrighted by Wife and Husband during the duration of the marriage.

Nice deal, Delores, I thought. That's how you lost all the money from "Empty Plate Blues."

But then you weren't exactly in a terrific bargaining position either, seeing as how you'd gotten pregnant by a man who wasn't your husband.

There was one more piece of paper. Something called "Motion for Modification," dated 1968 and submitted by an attorney for Delores.

I plugged through the exotic language and figured out that Delores was asking the judge to change the earlier agreement because Hank was suddenly making a lot of money from "Empty Plate Blues": "$30,000 in the current year to date," it said.

Then, at the bottom of the page written in ballpoint pen:

> Motion denied. Owens, J.
> Oct. 5, 1968.

Then another sheet of paper, also submitted by Delores, titled "Motion for Reconsideration," with a repeat of her earlier request.

And again, at the bottom:

> Motion denied. Owens, J.
> October 31, 1968.

Nice try, Delores, I thought. She must have been hopping mad. It takes money to do things like this.

But to stay mad for over twenty years?

To kill him?

And what did she have against Silver?

I replaced the file and walked back up the stairs.

The clerk was combing her hair.

"Thanks," I said. "Back to court."

19

I PRINTED the picture of Lacey's hands over and over, convinced that somehow perfection was attainable, and was finally satisfied with a print only a shadow lighter than the first I'd made, but somehow light-years softer-looking. The picture of Hank pretending to skate, suddenly my favorite image, I played with until the edge of the black met the edge of the white crisply, cleanly——the way Hank had danced. I thought about printing it big, maybe sixteen by twenty, a size of paper I didn't have.

I made some contact sheets of the pictures I'd taken at the zoo. The close-ups of the snake that Silver had held in his arms in the reptile house looked faintly interesting, but they gave me the creeps and I didn't print them. And score zero for Martha Grant's idea that one of the apartment pictures might reveal a potential witness—someone on the staircase, as she said, or on the balcony. Anything I'd shot that evening was dead, sterile, unpeopled.

The only one that looked faintly interesting was a picture of Silver's kitchen stove.

I slid the film into the enlarger and centered the image.

Beyond the darkroom door I heard the loft door locks click open and Lucas's toenails scuttling around on the floor.

"Claire? Is that you?"

Her work bag thudded on the floor.

"Yeah, hon—I'm here for the night. I've got a meeting at eight tomorrow morning. Saturday—can you stand it? Did you see the flowers I brought you?"

"Uh-hmmmm," I said.

For some reason I'm generally incapable of carrying on a conversation while I'm printing.

I sunk the paper into the tray of developer and waited for the shapes to arrange themselves on the surface.

Sometimes the process reminds me of a toy my brother and I had as kids: a coloring book with pages that were blank until you painted the surface with water; then a picture of a clown holding a bunch of balloons, or a big-eyed dog, or something like that would appear.

It used to drive me crazy with excitement.

Now the darkest shapes cropped up: the oven-door handle, some elliptical shapes that were the burners, the oblong that was the window in the oven door. A long pause while the chemicals caught their breath, and the middle ranges began to surface: the dashboard of the stove—the burner knobs, the light switch, the tapered hands of the clock. Then an even longer pause, and finally the white canister resting on the enamel stove top—very translucent-looking, very nice—floated into view.

Very nice, I thought. Kind of a Robert Frank rip-off, though. The same idea as his picture of the jukebox and the rose. Still, I thought, it's something I just might want to pin on the wall for myself.

I printed it a second time, hoping to make the canister look what—celestial?

The hands on Silver's stove clock drifted into view again. Two-fifteen. No kidding. They said two-fifteen.

What is this? I thought. Am I going crazy? We were there in the evening. We saw the sun go down.

Two-fifteen.

My forehead went damp.

But of course, I thought. Stove clocks are always broken. This one probably broke in 1952, or whenever the lousy thing was made.

Still, what if somebody like Harrell got his hands on this? I wadded up both prints and jammed them into the bottom of my trash can.

I did the same with the contact sheet.

It's not evidence, I said to myself. If it's all wrong it can't be evidence.

The negative I buried deep in my negative file. After all, it was a good picture. And it would take a Ph.D. in library science to decode my filing system.

I made a contact sheet of the pictures on the roll I'd shot when I'd been out to lunch with Iris—the ones of Iris standing on the sidewalk in front of Saks in her giant hat, looking like a cross between Charo's mother and Holly Hobby.

Lunatic, I thought. Astrology. Collecting birthdates for a family tree. Well, at least I didn't give her anything—or did I?

What? My birthday? Mom's? I couldn't remember.

I pulled the scrap of paper with the lottery number on it from the bulletin board and squinted at it in my amber darkroom light.

111-333-5243-001.

No. Nothing.

35-24-30.

Probably Max's weird idea of the perfect female figure.

His social security number?

Nah. Max would never be that boring.

Still, why did the numbers seem familiar to me?

Just from me staring at them?

Somebody was pounding on the darkroom door.

"Libby, listen to me!"

"Huh?"

"I said how long has it been since this poor dog's been out?"

Claire was hollering.

"I'm not sure, Claire. Maybe not since morning. I'll get him out now."

I had taken him for a walk when?—before I went up to the courthouse? After? I really couldn't remember.

"No. Keep working," she said. "I need to stretch my legs. And I need to get some groceries. Can I take your umbrella?"

"Okay. Thanks."

Lucas yipped; I heard them get into the elevator.

Good old Claire, I thought. She's a pretty good connection to reality. I've been starting to live like Max lately. Pie for lunch. Pop for supper. I'd probably start going to bed with my shoes on pretty soon.

I decided I didn't need any full-size pictures to remember Iris by, opened the darkroom door, and began to clean up. Trays rinsed and dried. Tongs rinsed and dried. Lids tight on the boxes of paper.

I wiped down the counters.

At least there's order someplace in my life, I thought.

I felt a little relaxed for the first time since I'd found Hank's body.

I put some Alberta Hunter music on.

I'll take a shower, I thought. Get the chemical smell off my skin. Pour a glass of wine. Then I'll lay on the sofa with Lucas and a picture book. Then maybe take a nap.

Then came the scream.

No, it was the sound of squealing brakes first and then the scream. A scream as loud and as sharp as a blast from a police car siren at close range.

And, superimposed over the scream, the sound of Lucas barking.

I hit the button for the elevator, then ran to the front windows.

The casements of our building's windows extend so far forward that it's impossible to see outside the perimeters of a narrow cone-shaped field. I could see the sidewalk across the street, but not on our side.

I couldn't see Claire or Lucas.

I could only see people running across the street.

The elevator coughed, ground to the second or third floor, and stopped dead. Something it does every six months or so.

Why now?

I unlocked the door to the stairwell and tore down the steps, tripping over a paint tray at the bottom, bursting out at the loading dock. As the door clanged shut behind me I realized that I didn't have a key to get back in.

Halfway down the block a small crowd of people stood around a shape on the sidewalk.

The shape was Claire.

She was lying on her side.

Somebody was holding her hand. Somebody was bent over her face. Somebody held Lucas by the leash.

"She's breathing," somebody said.

"It didn't hit her," somebody else said. "It was going to—it came right at her—but she threw herself behind the trash container. I think she just hit the pavement when she fell."

"The guy's over there calling 911," one of them said.

I bent over her. Her eyes were closed.

"I used to work in a hospital," somebody said. "Any blood coming out of her ears? Out of her nose?"

"No," somebody said.

I put my face near hers.

"Claire," I said. "Can you hear me? It's Libby. Do you hear me? It's okay. We're going to get you to a doctor. It's okay."

She just lay there.

"She's breathing," somebody said.

A guy in a red windbreaker took it off and started to lay it over her.

"We can't let her get chilled," he said. "She'll go into shock."

I started to lift her head off the wet sidewalk.

"Don't," somebody said. "What if her neck is broken?"

"Dammit," I said. "Where's the ambulance? Didn't somebody call an ambulance?"

Lucas was whining and pulling on the leash.

"Did anybody see what happened?" I said.

The guy who put the windbreaker on Claire was walking away.

I was crying.

I could hear sirens.

Claire opened her eyes and raised an arm.

"Where's Lucas?" she said. "I had to let him go. So he wouldn't get hurt."

She winced.

"It came right at me," she said. "It must have been drunk, or crazy. It was trying to run me over."

A couple of medics leapt out of an ambulance.

A police car pulled to the curb behind it.

"I can't really see right," she said.

The crowd started to disperse.

Somebody handed me Lucas. Somebody else handed me my umbrella—the one Claire had been carrying. It looked like a turkey carcass: The shaft was bent at a forty-five-degree angle and most of the spokes had ripped away from the cloth.

I gave my name and Claire's to the cops.

"Anybody see a license plate?" I said.

"It was too fast," somebody said.

"Too dark," somebody else said.

People walked away.

Claire raised herself on one elbow.

"It was brown, Libby," she said. "That was all I could tell. I guess it was just some kind of crazy person."

The ambulance took her to St. Vincent's.

I took Lucas to the deli, told the guy behind the counter the story about Claire and how I was locked out of the building, and begged him to watch Lucas until I came back.

"Okay," he said, "but I'm not going to be held responsible if he bites anybody."

I called Duncan's office on the pay phone.

Dee answered.

"I need Duncan," I said. "I need him right now. Claire's been hurt. She's in the hospital."

My teeth were chattering.

"Hold on," Dee said. "He's behind closed doors. I'll get him."

"Lady," the guy behind the counter said. "Calm down. You look like you got the D.T.'s."

I turned the other way.

Duncan came on the line.

"Libby, what's the matter? What's the matter with Claire?"

"A car tried to run her over," I said. "I think they thought she was me. She had Lucas and my umbrella, and some car was following me this morning. She's at St. Vincent's."

I tried to calm down.

"She's conscious, though," I said.

He hung up.

When I got to St. Vincent's, Claire was lying on a rolling bed in the hallway, talking animatedly to a nurse or a technician or somebody.

I hate hospitals. Just the smell of rubbing alcohol makes me feel like I'm going to faint.

"Get a load of this," she said to me. "They gave me the bill for the ambulance ride while I was still in the ambulance!"

I leaned against the side of her bed so my knees wouldn't wobble so much.

"This is ridiculous, you know," she said. "I've just got a lump on my head."

She prodded the hair at the back of her head with her fingers.

"Feel it," she said. "It's just spongy. No broken skin even."

The lady at the admitting desk gave me the hairy eyeball while I took a chair from the reception area, dragged it into the hall beside Claire, and sat down. I was seeing little prickles of light out the corners of my eyes.

"Put your head between your knees," Claire said. "Your lips are paler than your face."

I obeyed for a moment, felt a welcome rush of blood to my head, and pulled the chair up a little closer.

"Your eyes are okay?" I asked. "You said you couldn't see right."

"They're okay now," she said. "That was just when I was coming to."

A guy—a kid, really, maybe seventeen—with his hand wrapped in a dish towel, staggered through the door, moaning. A woman helped him into a chair.

I lowered my head again.

"Listen, Claire," I said. "I feel terrible. I feel really, really terrible. I know whoever was in that car thought you were me. He was trying to hit me, not you."

"Oh, come on, Libby," she said. "That's ridiculous."

"Wednesday night I got a phone call from somebody," I said. "He told me to stay out of Silver Gaines's business or he'd make sure I went 'bye-bye'. With Lucas, he said. And some guy in a brown car was following me in the Bronx this morning. I didn't tell you about it because I thought—well, I hoped, really—that maybe the call was a crank, because my name's been in the papers. And that maybe I imagined the car. You know—I'm feeling extra paranoid lately. But— you know—why would somebody who was just reading the paper know that I had a dog?"

She still looked skeptical.

"So why did he chase after me—not you?"

"Think about it, Claire. You walked out of the building with Lucas. Your face was hidden behind my umbrella. He probably saw me with it this morning. And it was raining. Who can see anything in the rain? Of course the guy thought you were me."

"Libby," she said, "stop it. It was probably some nut who didn't like the way I walked or something."

A woman in a green outfit came over and wheeled her into x-ray.

I sat in the chair for a while, trying not to look at the red stain spreading across the towel that bound up the kid's hand.

There was a commotion at the admissions desk.

It was Duncan, trying to convince them to let him go into the x-ray room with Claire. He had no jacket on, and his shirt was soaking wet.

He squeezed me by the arm—hard.

"Claire," he said. "Did you see her? Where's her doctor? How is she? I couldn't get a cab. I thought I was going to lose my mind."

"She's okay," I said. "At least she looks okay. She's talking and trying to sit up and everything. They're just x-raying her head to make sure."

He started breathing a little slower.

"I think I was a little overdramatic on the phone," I said. "It had just happened. I was really upset."

I told him about the car. About how it was the same car that had chased me in the morning.

He couldn't focus on anything I said.

"She's got to be alright," he kept saying. "She's just got to be alright."

He sat with his head in his hands. I pretended to look through magazines.

"The police," he said. "Did anybody call them? Did they talk to any witnesses? Did anybody get a license plate?"

"Nobody seemed to be able to see much. It was raining. It happened real fast."

The door opened. It was Claire, smiling and standing next to a doctor.

The doctor motioned us over.

Duncan hugged Claire. There were tears in his eyes.

"Good news," the doctor said. "It's just a concussion—nothing broken. This is one very lucky lady."

"What did I tell you?" said Claire, still smiling. "Just a bump on the head."

She was supposed to take it easy for a couple of days, take aspirin, not drink alcohol, and call a number that the doctor wrote down if she felt dizzy or had any problems.

We found a cab and brought Claire back to the loft.

Duncan brought her soup, played her favorite CDs, fluffed her pillow, and made her tea in a teapot.

They started talking about a trip they wanted to take in the spring. To Italy. And France, maybe.

I picked up Lucas at the deli and bought him a new bag of Purina.

I asked the guy at the counter what had happened to the blond kid who used to work the counter weeknights—the guy who I'd bought the chicken salad and beer from that I'd brought to Silver's.

"Who the hell knows," he said. "Down south somewhere. Carolina maybe. Maybe Alabama. Where his folks are."

He leaned over the counter, his chin on his knuckles.

"So you like 'em young, huh?"

I dragged Lucas out of the store.

Duncan slept over and left early. Like six-thirty. Cheerful, braced, very Duncan-like.

I heard them making plans before he left. He'd go to the office for a while, meet some people he had to meet uptown at four or so, get some fresh mozzarella—what were they going to do with all this fresh mozzarella, anyway? Fill an underground storage tank for the winter?—rent a couple movies, and drive out to the Island. She would cancel her meeting—he insisted—spend the day resting, and take the train out—no driving with that bump on her head—at suppertime.

Very lovey-dovey.

Claire was aglow.

I took over when he left.

No, the bump wasn't hurting so much this morning. Just a little tender when she bent over. She'd slept fine. Really.

"Claire," I said. "The trip that you and Duncan were talking about last night. The trip to France. Is it going to be a honeymoon?"

She laughed.

"I guess so," she said.

I knew I was supposed to be smiling. Hugging her. Congratulating her like in a Debbie Reynolds movie or something, but I couldn't. I mean I was happy for them and all, and I knew it was coming, but—I don't know.

Where did it leave me?

Roommates with Jean Harris?

They'd move to the burbs—I knew it. Then I'd really never see them again.

I squeezed out a smile.

"You'll have the cutest baby anybody ever saw," I said.

20

I NEEDED FILM. Tons of it. Also paper. Big stuff for printing that picture of Hank.

How could I have let my supplies run so low?

I walked to the train, hyperaware of brown cars, but nobody seemed interested in running me over.

I took the train to Times Square and the store where I'd bought my Leica—where I usually get a good deal on film. I must have kept looking over my shoulder while I was at the counter.

"Waiting for somebody?" the clerk said. "Meeting somebody here? What are you so jumpy for?"

I bought forty rolls of Cibachrome and eight boxes of paper.

Not that I needed that much. It's more of a security thing. When the going gets scary, I buy film. Fortifications, just in case. Like the way my mother stockpiled canned vegetables during the Cuban missile crisis.

I ate lunch at Chock Full O'Nuts, telling myself I'd chosen the place for the grilled cheese sandwich—burnt and wafer thin, just the way I like it—and not for the mirror that ran behind the counter so I could see anybody who came in the door.

Americans was just four blocks away. I decided to stop by. Just in and out, I thought. Just to see if I was still alive over there. It was Saturday. Octavia would be at her so-called farm in Connecticut, and I wouldn't have to stumble through any humiliating conversations with her.

Harry Medak was sitting on his stool next to the security check-in stand by the elevators. I winced when I saw him. He read the papers all day long, cover to cover. He had to have read about Hank and Silver and me. What must the guy be thinking?

"Hello, dear," he said. "How's your holiday coming along? Enjoy every bit of it; you'll be back soon enough."

He sounded very jocular, but his eyes looked troubled.

He walked me to the elevator.

"If there's anything I can do to help," he said, "tell me. I'm here every day."

My eyes misted over. I usually do okay until somebody is nice to me.

"That's a brave girl," he said, and the doors slid shut.

The place was at half staff for the weekend, but some of the crowd was there. The guys who usually wear jackets and ties were looking half nude in shorts and tee-shirts; the women were wearing cardigans swiped from secretarial stations and borrowed men's sportsjackets over their tank tops to keep off the chill of the air-conditioning.

It might have been me; it might have been my imagination; but the place seemed tense for a Saturday. The magazine goes to bed on Thursday; people don't usually get wound up again very tightly until Monday afternoon or Tuesday morning.

There was a meeting going on in the glass-walled conference room to the left behind the lobby. The windows were tinted, but I could make out Octavia's queen-sized Gucci bag on the floor near the head of the table and her blonde head bobbing as she spoke—why did I assume it was angrily?—to someone at the end of the table.

What happened to my timing?

I stood at what I hoped was an oblique angle from the wall, hoping nobody at the table could see me, but trying to figure out what was going on.

I could make out Dorothy Finney, from production, and Warren McKee from editorial. And I could make out Salem Frenett, the co-owner who had the brains, at the end of the table opposite Octavia. The guy from advertising with the ponytail, Jake somebody, was slumped forward on the table, his head in his hands.

From the looks of the soda cans and coffee cups heaped in the center of the table, they'd been there a long time.

I walked down to the research department. Everybody was gone.

I dumped my camera and shopping bag on LaDonna Knoblock's desk, and looked in my mail tray.

Wonderful. A form letter from Human Resources hollering at me for not filling out some form that I hadn't filled out because they never sent it to me in the first place. And a letter from somebody I'd taken a picture of two years ago for an article about children's beauty pageants complaining that I'd made her and her little girl look too fat. That was all.

"What are you doing?"

It was LaDonna, back at her desk.

"I'll move that stuff," I said.

"Don't worry," she said. "I'll just push it over here."

She shoved the shopping bag to one side, and my camera fell to the floor, lens side down.

I gasped. It's like watching somebody drop your baby on its soft spot.

The case lid sprang open and all the stuff I keep in the inner pocket spilled out. Chapstick, a five-dollar bill, travel aspirin, my wide-angle lens, and the now-mangled scrap of paper that I'd written on at Nicole's.

We both rushed to pick everything up.

"I've got it," I said.

"No, I do," she said. "Honest."

She fumbled it all back onto the desk and started poking the things back inside the camera case.

"What's this?" she said, smoothing out the piece of paper. "What's this bible stuff?"

"What are you talking about?"

"Ubednego," she said. "Except it's spelled wrong, you dummy. It's not a U; it's an A."

I took the paper from her.

"What do you mean, bible stuff?"

"You know. Or I guess maybe you don't. Where do you come from, anyway? Shadrach, Meshach, and Abednego. Daniel's three companions. Incinerated in the fiery furnace of Nebuchadnezzar. Daniel 1:7, I believe."

She smiled with intense satisfaction, having just relieved her brain of a bit of the obsessive knowledge built up inside it.

Sometimes she reminded me of a guy I'd seen on TV who couldn't feed himself or talk but could play all of the Chopin preludes.

"You know a lot, LaDonna," I said. "But that's not what I'm looking for. I'm trying to figure out who owns this damn building. Can you help me with that?"

She looked at the paper again.

"Obviously, Libby, the realty trust," she said.

"Thanks."

I put the camera in the shopping bag.

"So what's the meeting in the conference room about?" I said. "They look like they're really going at it."

"The memo called it 'New Directions,'" she said. "It seems a couple of advertisers skipped to *Vanity Fair* in a pretty big way."

"What memo?"

She started to fool around with her computer disk box. She looked uncomfortable.

"I told you," she said. "Octavia said not to send you any of that stuff anymore. She said you had enough on your mind. Besides, it just went to the brass."

"Layoffs?"

"Not that I know of," she said. Then, "But you know what they say: Once they stop saying hello to you in the hall you know you're on the way out."

I walked back out to the elevators. Warren McKee passed by me, heading from the conference room down the hall.

"Hey, Warren," I said.

He kept on walking.

"Hey, Warren," I tried again.

I heard the thud of the men's room door.

So maybe he's preoccupied, I thought.

Harry Medak took me by the elbow as I signed out of the building.

"There was a guy here looking for you," he said. "A couple minutes after you went up."

"Who?" I said. "Where did he go?"

"Wouldn't give his name," he said. "Wouldn't show me any I.D. I told him I'd call up and tell you he was here, but he said he didn't have time and he left."

"What did he look like?"

"Black guy. Young. Good-looking. Medium height. Dressed nice. White pants. You know him?"

"It's hard to say, Harry. I know a million good-looking young black guys who dress nice."

He gestured toward the lobby's revolving doors.

"I looked out a couple times to see if he was hanging around," he said. "But I don't think he is. I didn't like it that he wouldn't give me his name."

"Thanks, Harry," I said.

"You want me to call you a cab?"

"No thanks."

"You can't be too careful," he said.

"Yeah, Harry," I said. "I know."

21

NOBODY FOLLOWED ME downtown. No brown car. No guy in white pants.

There was a note from Claire on the table, a ten-dollar bill, and a key on top of the note.

"Libby," it said. "I hate to do this after I promised I wouldn't, but with all the commotion last night Duncan forgot about the cats. He called from the road really worried. I'd go, but my head is aching and I just want to get on the train. Could you? Would you? Just one more time? The money is for a cab."

I sighed. Well of course I would. She'd been babysitting Lucas, hadn't she? But why did it provoke me so much to do favors for Duncan through Claire? Maybe I felt like I was being ganged up on.

The cab money was ridiculous. I always walked to Duncan's. And it was daylight.

I left Lucas home. The trip would be faster if I didn't have to stop every twenty feet so he could sniff at the garbage.

Funny, I was getting used to the sight of the sidewalks heaped with trash—as though it had always been there. The weird part now was seeing trash bags on people's rooftops. Did they really think that once the strike was over they'd get somebody to pick it up from there?

Garbage or not, now that the heat wave had broken, it felt good to be walking in the afternoon sun. The air smelled okay. People didn't look so unhappy.

I bought a box of something called "Cockroach Extermination Chalk" from a table vendor on Canal Street and a bag of nectarines from a Chinatown street stand.

The nectarines were sweet. Juicy and sweet.

For a few minutes I forgot about watching out for the brown car.

Then, while I was crossing Lafayette, I thought I heard someone call my name. I spun around in the direction of the sound, and saw nobody in the crowd I knew.

Cool it, I said to myself. It's a big city, full of a lot of people named Libby. Also Bobby.

Somebody was probably calling Bobby.

I didn't hear it again.

I bought a can of Coke and stood for a while in City Hall Park watching a little girl play chess with an old man, their moves timed by a homemade timer that looked like an incendiary device. A bunch of Wall Street types in suits and ties stood around a guy pitching three-card monte; a couple of resurrected hippies sat on a bench playing Bob Dylan songs on guitars; a woman wearing shoes covered with aluminum foil tried to sell me a phony gold Rolex.

I relaxed a little. This is the New York I like, I thought. This is alive. This is why I stay here.

A woman in a leopard-skin bodysuit held a huge circular reflective tanning shield around her neck, like some weird Elizabethan space ruff.

I took her picture, then walked a little closer and took another.

I've been penned in too long, I thought. This is doing me good.

I picked up the pace as I got closer to Fulton Street. Maybe I'd go to a movie tonight. Hang out in Little Italy for supper, then go to that new theater on Houston and see something weird.

For some reason I felt like I'd be safer on the move than if I stayed at home.

I could taste the Junior Mints as I entered Duncan's building. Junior Mints and one of those buckets of Coke.

I nudged the mail out of the way with my foot and headed for the kitchen.

Stinko. The windows were shut and the cat bowls hadn't been washed for a couple of days.

I cranked open the kitchen windows. Good grief, Duncan, I thought. Sure you're depressed or something, but do you have to inflict your moods on your cats?

"Meesh!" I yelled. "Meeshy, Meeshy, Meesh!"

Why do people talk like this to cats? I was glad Lucas was a dog. "Luke," I would say. "Here boy." Not "Lukey! Lukey, Lukey, Luke!"

"Shaddy," I yelled. "Shaddy, Shaddy, Shad!"

One of the cats slithered through the kitchen door and chowed down his food. The other one was hiding, I guessed.

I swiped some ice from the freezer and poured a glass of water. I figured I ought to stay a while. Give the cats some company and let the place air out a little bit. Enjoy the view. Listen to the bridge.

I picked up the pile of mail from the floor, added it to another pile that Duncan had dumped on the couch, and started to deal it onto the table.

Magazines, magazines, magazines.

Organic Gardening, no less. A magazine about wooden boat building.

Why did he get so many if he obviously didn't read them?

The other cat still hadn't come to the kitchen.

I peeled my sweaty legs from the leather sofa and stood up.

"Shaddy," I called. "Shaddy. Meesh!" Who could tell them apart?

Where did he get those names?

Shaddy, Meesh.

Shaddy, Meesh, Abednego.

What had LaDonna Knoblock said?

Into the fiery furnace.

Shadrach, Meshach, and Abednego Realty Trust.

My hands shook as I took another sip of water. I was starting to get a headache. Right behind my right eye.

This couldn't be a coincidence, could it?

Duncan couldn't have anything to do with that place on Harnett Avenue, could he?

But isn't that how people's minds work? When you've got to come up with an alias, or a cash machine password, or a lottery number, your subconscious gropes for something meaningful to you—even if it's only obliquely meaningful. To help you remember, or for superstition's sake, or just to help you invent something.

But Duncan involved with a crack house?

And Hank with Duncan's papers?

I walked down the hall to the staircase and climbed it to the master bedroom.

It was hotter than downstairs. Hot and close.

Why didn't this guy keep his air conditioning going? I walked through the bedroom and jumped at the sight of my disfigured reflection in the funhouse mirrors next to his dresser.

Cool it, I said to myself. You know no one else is here.

I walked past the bed and stepped through the door to Duncan's study. I knew he kept personal papers in here—papers he didn't keep in his outside office. I'd been at parties a couple of times when Claire and Duncan retreated to this room to look at auction catalogs or neck or whatever they did. And I'd used the phone in here myself a couple of times. For privacy.

The study was smaller than most of the other rooms in the apartment. A bank of wooden filing cabinets filled one wall. A leather loveseat filled another. An arched doorway led to a steep stairwell that rose to Duncan's roof garden.

Very cozy. Very romantic.

Also very hot.

I tried to open the window next to the filing cabinet, but it was too warped to open more than an inch.

Against one wall, underneath two framed Peter Max posters, there was an antique oak desk with a roll top big enough to sleep in.

I tugged at the handle, but the top wouldn't move.

I slid open the top drawer of one of the file cabinets. Inside were insurance appraisals, clippings from magazines and auction catalogs about posters, and lists of dealers and galleries.

In the next drawer there were publicity clippings and press releases about the clubs Duncan had opened before Eleuthera; publicity stills of himself receiving the big advertising award he'd won when he was in advertising; copies of advertisements that he'd apparently had a hand in; things like that.

The next drawer was devoted to Home Again, the homeless shelter. Copies of fund-raising letters and brochures; correspondence about construction and building codes.

I skimmed faster through the rest of the drawers. A file of ten-year-old resumes; a copy of a term paper he'd written in college about bird imagery in the poems of Gerard Manley Hopkins ("Outstanding," it said on the top); folders of stuff about life insurance and Blue Cross, then four drawers filled with art magazines filed in chronological order.

I heard a thudding sound downstairs.

I quietly closed the drawer.

What was he doing home?

He couldn't be. He left for the beach hours ago.

Or did somebody break in? I couldn't remember if I'd locked the door.

I stepped out of the office and into the bathroom.

If it's Duncan, I thought, I can pretend I'm looking for aspirin or something.

I opened the medicine cabinet.

If it's somebody else, I thought, I can lock myself in here.

I closed the bathroom door, leaving just a crack to listen through, and leaned against the crack.

No more thuds. No footsteps.

But then, the whir of traffic on the bridge obliterated most sounds pretty neatly.

You're imagining things, I said to myself. Relax. It was probably just somebody slamming a car door. Or a truck backfiring somewhere.

I walked back into the study and tried the handle on the rolltop desk again.

Nothing doing.

No keyhole, even.

There were drawers on either side of the leg space, and a long narrow one across the top. All of them had keyholes.

The big one at the bottom left was locked, but the others weren't.

I looked in the ones at the right.

Stationery. Fancy stuff, with a ribbon around it. Postage stamps. Filofax inserts. Christmas cards. A collection of maps: the London Underground; the San Francisco Bart; New Hampshire; Vermont; Nova Scotia; Prince Edward Island.

The long top drawer was empty except for a fancy fountain pen and a jar of ink.

My grandfather had a desk like this. Not so big. Not so fancy. But with a roll top. His "schoolteacher's desk," he called it.

There was a trick to unlocking the top.

Press on a panel somewhere?

No, that was in a Hardy Boys book.

I closed the top drawer and opened it again a half an inch.

There was a low, satisfying click. Not even a sound, really. More the vibration of wood as something released in a lock mechanism.

I tried the roll top again.

This time it slid open as freely as an eyelid.

Thank you, grandad, I thought.

There were slots for papers, slots for pens, wooden drawers the size of cassette tapes. There was a dagger-sized letter opener. There were a few bundles of envelopes held together by rubber bands. There was a cardboard-bound notebook with a pebbly surface and the word *Ledger* embossed in the center in gold. The kind you can get at Woolworth's in the office supply aisle.

I opened it. The double-page spread was set up with surnames in the left column—many of them Hispanic, some not—and months of the year running across the top. Amounts of money—apparently rental amounts—were entered in the squares. At the top of the page it said Southern Boulevard. The next page was set up the same way, except at the top it said Seneca Avenue. The third page said Hunts Point Avenue; the fourth said Harnett Avenue.

I took the bundle of envelopes from its slot. They were addressed to Box 365, Grand Central Station, New York, New York.

Box 365. The number that the woman on Harnett Avenue had given me.

Duncan, I thought, you son-of-a-bitch.

So what did Hank have to do with it? What was he doing with papers that had to do with Duncan's property?

A cat yowled. A strange, pained-sounding yowl, a sound even stranger than the one a Siamese usually makes.

My hand started shaking.

The yowling wouldn't stop.

It sounded near.

"Cool it," I said. "I gave you your food."

It kept yowling.

I stepped into the bedroom, where the sound seemed to be coming from. There was a dressing area in an alcove on the east side of the room. The sound was coming from there—from the closet.

I slid open the closet door and was struck full in the face by the smell of cat pee. The cat was still yowling—somewhere way in the back.

"Come on out," I said. "There's food out here. Water, too."

For a moment I saw its eyes.

How long had the poor thing been in there? Duncan hadn't been home last night or all day today. Who knew? The cat was probably dehydrated and sick.

I crawled into the closet.

"Here Shaddy. Here Meesh. Whoever you are. I'm not going to hurt you."

I tossed a pair of shoes out of the closet. Black tie, with shoe trees in them. Then a pair of brown ones. Then a pair of tap shoes.

Tap shoes? Duncan didn't tap.

I dragged them out into the light.

The cat shot past me and down the stairs.

The shoes were black, but not really. Brown leather streaks showed through the black polish, and black polish had dribbled and dried on the inside of the shoes.

But some of the drips weren't black.

They were brown. No—red-brown. The color of school shoes. Ox-blood color, they always called it.

People-blood color.

A streak and a smudge down the center of the inner sole.

It was the right shoe.

I slid my fingers inside and felt a rough spot a little past where the ball of the foot would hit.

I pulled on the inner sole and it came out of the shoe without resisting.

There were two small holes, separated by about a half an inch of space, in the part of the sole where the ball of the foot would hit it. Small holes. Like the holes left after you pull a staple out of something.

I didn't doubt for a second that the shoes were Hank's.

Had Duncan put snake venom on tacks that ripped through here?

The phone rang.

Rang, and rang, and rang again.

Duncan's voice came out of the answering machine, asking the caller to leave a message.

"Duncan," the caller said.

It was Claire. She sounded mildly panicked.

"Where are you?" she said. "I thought you said you'd be out here before I would. I'm just anxious, I guess. And a little worried. You know how I get."

I thought about grabbing the receiver. But what would I say? Claire—your fiance is a murderer?

"I've got the grill going," she said. "I think we should have made Libby come out here with us. I'm worried about her. I'm worried about everyone, I guess. And I asked her to stop over and feed the cats like you asked me to. It kind of bugs me, you know, that you don't take care of things like that yourself."

Then,

"Sorry, I guess I'm just kind of testy with my head and all."

I picked up the receiver just as she hung up.

Claire, I thought. Poor Claire. This will kill her.

So where did he get the snake venom? Was Silver really in on this somehow after all? Did they do it together? So how come Silver and I wind up taking the rap?

And if he wasn't out at the beach house, where was he?

I shuddered.

He knew I was here, feeding the cats.

He wanted me to be here, feeding the cats.

I tied the shoes to my belt, ready to run.

I went into the study and took the ledger.

I heard a noise. Really a noise, this time. The noise of the door opening downstairs.

I froze.

Maybe the cats, I told myself. Maybe the cats.

But I knew it wasn't.

I took the ledger and shoved it through the crack in the window, so it fell the four stories to the heap of trash at the back of the building.

No way the shoes would fit through.

I glanced back into the bedroom.

Something moved in the funhouse mirror.

It wasn't a cat.

It was a guy in white pants coming up the stairs with a gun in his hand.

It was Jerome Monsell.

Jesus, I thought. They're in this together. Duncan and Jerome.

I reached behind me, trying not to make a motion fast enough to be visible in the mirror, and lifted the letter opener from the desk.

If I could make it to the roof-garden stairwell, I thought, I could get down the fire escape.

But he'd notice me move in the mirror.

He noticed me anyway and walked across the room to the study doorway.

"Taking care of business, are you, Libby?" he said.

The gun didn't go with his baby face. Didn't go at all.

"I don't know what you mean."

"What do you do for him?" he said. "C-c-collect the rents? Pay off the h-h-h-health department?"

I stared at him.

"Jerome," I said. "Really. I don't know what you're talking about."

He stepped backward, still pointing the gun at me.

"Oh, come on," he said. "I saw you up on Harnett Avenue yesterday. What were you d-doing—looking for an apartment?"

He was talking in a forced hard-edged tough-guy way. Like somebody from a TV police show. But he couldn't subdue the stutter.

I thought about the guy I'd seen across the street when I'd left the building—the guy in the yellow poncho.

"Where's Casavant?" he said. "What are you two going to do here? C-c-count the checks? Have a nice cha-cha-champagne dinner in memory of Hank? Nicole has the copies of the deeds, you know. You forgot to take them with you when you m-m-made your consolation call."

"You think she's pretty stupid, don't you?" he said. "And you th-think Silver's pretty stupid, too. It was pretty smooth of you guys to realize the cops would do anything to see Silver locked up after he got those cops thrown off the force."

I opened my mouth, but no words would come out.

"Pretty stupid, Libby," he said. "And you thought nobody would find out, d-d-didn't you?"

Wasn't this what I was supposed to be saying to Duncan?

Jerome reached into his shirt pocket and pulled out a square brown thing. Cigarettes, I thought. No, a dictaphone. Like the one Octavia uses.

He pressed a button and threw it on the bed.

"Tell me everything," he said. "Nice and loud. I want to have something to give to the police."

I dropped the letter opener on the floor.

I still couldn't talk.

"Hank told me everything," he said. "Told me how he picked up the wrong line in Casavant's office and heard him talking about that building on Harnett Avenue."

"So was that it?" I asked. "Was Hank blackmailing Duncan? Was he making Duncan pay him not to go to the press and expose him?"

He looked at me the way New York bus drivers look at you when you ask them if they can change a dollar.

"Are you kidding?" he said. His voice was angry, but now more like the real Jerome's, not the character he'd been playing.

"Hank would never do anything like that. All he wanted was for D-D-Duncan to get rid of the buildings. Hank couldn't do business with a man who was ripping people off like that. He-he-he just told Duncan that if he didn't get rid of them before the Eleuthera opening, he was going to let the world know what he was up to. He gave him a chance to get out of it. A long chance, as far as I can tell."

"The copies of the deeds," I said. "What was Hank doing with them?"

He gave me a dull look.

"You're not going to quit, are you?" he said.

"Look," I said. "I was up at Harnett Avenue because I was trying to figure out who owned the building. I was trying to figure out who owned the building because I'd seen the deeds in Hank's papers and I was trying to figure out what he had to do with it. And I was trying to figure out what he had to do with it because if I don't, it looks like Silver and I are going to jail, because nobody else is trying to figure out who really killed Hank."

He was tapping on the gun with his index finger.

I wondered where he got it. I wondered if it was real. I couldn't believe that he knew how to use it.

"Jerome," I said. "You've got to believe me. You think I'm in some kind of cahoots with Duncan Casavant? Even if I were, do you really think I'd let myself be convicted and put in jail and watch Duncan go free? What kind of crazy thing would that be for me to do?"

I yanked Hank's shoes out of my belt and held them out to him.

"Look at those," I said. "I just found them in here. In the back of Duncan's closet. He painted them over, but he didn't take the insoles out. There's your snakebite for you."

He studied my face for a second, then put the gun in his other hand and took the shoes. He pulled the right insole out and studied the holes.

"What were you doing," he said. "Getting rid of the evidence?"

"If I were getting rid of evidence, don't you think I would have done it the day he died? Do you think I would have hung on to them?"

"So why didn't Duncan get r-rid of them?" he said.

"Why? I don't know. Maybe he thinks they're a trophy or something. Maybe he thought no one would ever find them."

This time I really did hear someone at the front door.

"Jesus," I hissed at Jerome. "It's him. He knew I was here. He set me up. He told Claire to tell me to come over and feed his damned cats."

Duncan was whistling downstairs.

I pointed at the stairwell in the study.

"It goes to the roof," I whispered. "I'll take the shoes."

I slung them through my belt again.

The whistling came closer.

Jerome shoved me ahead of him into the stairwell, then raced to the top. I followed and watched him try to open the handle on the door.

Who would have thought it would be locked from inside?

Then Jerome did something that I've only seen people do in the funny papers. He climbed the walls of the stairwell, which was narrow and tall, his hands pressed against one side, his feet pressed against the opposite wall, so he hung, suspended, over the steps.

Then he motioned for me to do the same thing. I shook my head no. I'm no tap dancer.

I heard Duncan clear his throat on the stairs.

With the kind of adrenaline surge that is usually reserved for women who lift pick-up trucks off their husbands I climbed up the same way Jerome had.

I held my breath and listened to the sound of Duncan's shoes on the hardwood floor.

I'd left the closet door open, shoes strewn on the rug in front of it. He'd know what I'd been doing.

Silence. Then the sound of the bathroom door clicking open, then closed again. Then the sound of a drawer sliding open.

We heard him rewind the dictaphone, then the sound of our own voices.

"*Look at those,*" I heard the tape of myself say. "*I just found them in here. In the back of Duncan's closet. He painted them over, but he didn't take the insoles out. There's your snakebite for you.*"

The thing kept running.

My legs felt dead, and an intense, electrical-feeling pain shot through my neck and shoulders.

Jerome's foot slipped, making a scuffling sound.

Duncan stepped into the stairwell.

We had the advantage; Duncan was staring into the dark from the light of the study, but our eyes had already adjusted to the dimness.

Jerome jumped.

I either jumped or fell, I don't know which. But we landed on Duncan.

Somebody's foot—it could have been Jerome's—kicked me under the chin. A squirt of warm salty liquid filled my mouth.

I held Duncan's legs against the floor. Jerome lay on Duncan's back, pinning his chest and arms against the floor.

I reached into Jerome's pants pocket and pulled out the gun.

It was little. Like Nancy Reagan's, I guess.

I pointed it at Duncan's head, walked backward into the study, and fumbled for the phone behind me on the desk.

Both cats walked into the room, sniffed at Duncan, and walked out.

I called 911 and told them that there was a man at this address who was trying to kill me.

Duncan lay underneath Jerome, his eyes closed, fully conscious, a yellow extension cord in his hand.

My gunless hand rose to my throat.

I kept it there until I heard the sirens pull up in front of the building, and while the cops peeled Jerome off Duncan, yanked the cord out of Duncan's hand, and put the cuffs on him.

I gave the shoes to the lady cop and asked her if she'd go outside with me to look for the rent ledger book.

It was more or less where I'd dropped it, sunk between a broken wooden crate and a torn trash bag in the heap behind the building, a little moist from a spilled can of grape soda.

Two sides of the wooden crate were wire mesh. A picture of a honeybee was branded into the wood.

"I think this is important, too," I said to her, and took it upstairs along with the ledger book.

Just a hunch, but hadn't there been something in Delores's album about Hank being wiped out from an allergy?

Of course Duncan had seen the album, too; we'd looked at it together when we were finding the art for the Eleuthera programs and posters.

While they were taking Jerome's statement, I found the bee-supply catalog on the coffee table downstairs——the one I'd laughed at as part of Duncan's gentleman farmer fantasy the week before—and called the number on the back.

"James Bees," a man answered.

"I'm calling about an order for Casavant in New York City," I said.

He paused for a moment. Then,

"One two-pound package of Three-Banded Italians with a young laying queen," he said. "We shipped it out three weeks ago, Mrs. Casavant. Let me check the address."

"Thanks," I said. " But don't bother. I'll wait a while longer."

I went back upstairs.

Jerome was sitting on the edge of the bed.

"Jerome," I said. "Do you know if Hank was allergic to bees?"

He looked at me blankly.

"No," he said. "No, I don't. But that doesn't mean he wasn't. He just wouldn't have let anybody know. Admission of weakness or something. He didn't even tell Miles and me the doctor had told him to slow down because of his heart."

I called Nicole.

She answered and breathed heavily into the phone.

"Nicole," I said. "Was Hank allergic to bees?"

"Oh baby, you better believe it," she said. "He was supposed to carry medicine for it with him, but he didn't. The doctor said he was crazy. He said he could die the next time he got stung."

Then she started yelling.

"Five minutes," she screamed. "Five minutes!"

"What's going on?"

"We're waiting for the cab," she said. "Five minutes between contractions."

"Good luck, Nicole," I said. "Good luck."

The police were taking Jerome's statement.

Waiting my turn, I walked to the wall of books in Duncan's living room, slid the ladder along the rail, and read every title until I came to what I was looking for——a little yellow paperback called *Beekeeping Basics.* "Duncan Casavant" was written in a fat, childlike hand on the flyleaf.

Boy naturalist, I thought. He was into everything even when he was a kid.

I scanned the index and turned to the section about stings. "Beekeeping is not for everyone," it said, and then:

> Somewhat less than 1 percent of sting victims will suffer anaphylactic shock, a reaction that can be fatal if appropriate medical help is not obtained immediately.

And on the next page:

> Bee venom contains formic acid, which causes the initial severe pain of the sting. Another component, Phospholipas A, a neurotoxin, is also present in Indian cobra venom.

I set the book aside to give to Martha Grant.

We went in front of a judge on Monday, who ordered another round of tests, this time from an independent lab, of Hank's blood samples. When we went back the results were just what we expected—it was bee venom, not cobra venom, that killed Hank.

We have no proof, of course, but it also seems that Jerome's theory—that the police were making it tough for Silver because of his part in exposing the police scandal so long ago—had some truth to it:

Martha found out that Childress's brother, Roger, a rookie at the time Childress was dismissed from the force, worked out of the Sixth Precinct now. We figure that once Silver got pulled in for Hank's murder, he was happy to make things as bad as possible for Silver, out of brotherly love. Hence the eternal delay in getting Silver's prints back from Albany and the warnings to me not to get involved.

After the hearing, Claire, Martha, and I wandered through the Sixth Precinct parking lot looking for a brown car, but we didn't find one. I wonder, though, if it wasn't Childress himself who was following me around and tried to hit Claire. He's got plenty of time on his hands.

We also walked down 13th Street for a last look at Eleuthera.

There's a big orange sign on the front door, right between the etched glass seashells, that says, "Seized by the order of the IRS."

Claire says that she knew things were dicey financially for Duncan all summer—she was pretty sure that there was no air-conditioning at the club on opening night not because it was broken but because Duncan couldn't make the payment—but she didn't know just how dicey until we read it in the paper. At the time he was arrested, the feds were after him for close to a million dollars in back taxes on the other two clubs. He was siphoning from them to fund Eleuthera and in no position—he thought—to staunch the flow of rental income the way Hank wanted.

We've already shipped the cats to Duncan's mother in Tennessee.

22

TODAY, exactly one month after the scene at Duncan's, I'm sitting with Claire in a theater on West 124th Street, waiting for the curtain to rise on the first act of a show called "A Tribute to Hank Monsell"— proceeds to go to the future Monsell Theater.

Nicole, who borrowed the building from her tenants for the night, plans to have the theater off the ground a year from now— Lacey and she as co-owners and directors. Motherhood has been good to her; I've been watching, and she can't bear to put the baby in her sister Lorraine's arms, the way Lorraine keeps telling her to. I sneaked a peek into the receiving blanket on the way to my seat, and the little fellow looks exactly like a pint-size version of Hank.

According to the program, Lacey, Miles, and Jerome will be dancing, Apollo Monroe will read a tribute to Hank, and Nicole will sing "Empty Plate Blues" while Delores Monsell accompanies her on the piano. I wish I knew what was going on there, but I guess I never will.

They say that now Hank's dead Silver won't dance with the group. I've tried to call him a few times since the charges against us were dropped, but he doesn't answer and he doesn't call back.

Claire's doing okay so far. She talks about Duncan, whom she refers to as the "Yo-Yo," which is kind of funny, as though he's dead, which is kind of weird, but if it works for her then fine. She's also started going to the "Thinking About Single Motherhood?" seminars that she was going to before she met Duncan. I'm worried, though, that she's going to crash after the distraction of the big show at the museum is over.

As for me, I'm still trying to get in touch with Max, because I have something important to tell him.

This afternoon I was fishing through my dresser for the globe necklace he gave me because I wanted to wear it to the show.

Along with the necklace, I pulled out the wad of letters he wrote me when I was in junior high and he was in the pen. They'd gone yellow and chewed-looking, and needed a new rubber band to hold them together. While I was winding a new one around them, the prisoner identification number on the return address—1113335243001—caught my attention. It looked mighty familiar.

I called up Guy Carpenter and told him what I'd found.

He cracked up laughing. Then he said that Max was probably nervous that the state would take his money back if they knew he was a convicted felon.

I figure he's right.

He said he's ready to fight that one tooth and nail. He also said that there's no way Iris would end up with the money when Max can prove in court that he picked the number himself.

At least she wouldn't get all of the money.

Maybe Guy Carpenter would.

So anyway, Max, if you're reading this, call me.

I've got plenty to tell you.

Okay?